Difficult Choices

By

Wanda Arrington Akorede

Difficult Choices

PUBLISHED BY

BOOKSURGE PUBLISHING LLC

An Amazon.com Company

ISBN 0-9709247-2-0

Library of Congress Number: 2005908409

BOOKSURGE PUBLISHING LLC

An Amazon.com Company

5341 Dorchester Rd., Suite 16
North Charleston, SC 29418
Web: www.booksurgepublishing.com
customerservice@booksurge.com
(843) 579.0000 ext. 138
AUTHORS WEBSITE: wandaakorede.com

To my mother,sisters, husband, children, granchildren, family,and friends thank you for your love, encouragement, and complete support.

A special thanks to my brother in law, Dr. Clement Rose and his wife, my sister Laura Rose. With your support, you helped to make this book possible.

1

*L*ola Adegoke's mind was in a daze. The trip home from the Lagos International Airport was a long one. She felt drained and tired, as if she had been fighting a war and lost. At first, there had been a feeling of renewed hope — the release that came with the words Janice spoke before boarding her flight to Amsterdam, "Tell Femi I forgive him and be happy, girl."

Now she just kept turning the words through her mind. *I know that Olu will never be happy without her! I am such a fool to think that I can ever be woman enough to erase her memory from our husband's heart.* Lola sighed. With a feeling of defeat, she drove into the driveway and entered the house. Her husband, Olufemi, and her brother, Segun, were waiting for her, wondering where she had been.

"*E'kabo* (Welcome), Lola. Where did you go?" Olufemi spoke first.

"I went to the airport to see Janice," she admitted.

The two men stared at her as if she were insane.

"Lola, are you crazy? Why did you do that?" her husband asked, incensed.

"I wanted to see if I could change her mind about leaving, but I failed, Olu." The beautiful woman sighs as tears began to fall down her copper-toned cheeks.

Her brother rushed to her, trying to be of comfort.

"*O-ti-toe*, sister *mi,* it will be all right. The *Oyinbo* did not wish to stay. You cannot be blamed for that."

Olufemi walked to the window and looked out into the quiet street as he thought of the last conversation he had with his other wife, Janice. She had asked him to give her time … just give her some time. It had hurt him deeply that she was unable to accept his culture. Bringing an American woman into a Nigerian way of life was more of a difficult task than he had expected.

"Lola, it's all right. What did she say to you?" Olufemi asked.

She sat upright, surprised at her husband's calm attitude, then she blew her nose and delicately dabbed at her eyes. "Janice told me to take good care of you and be happy."

Olufemi looked at his first wife with sadness, struggling to hold back his own tears. Silently, he left the room.

*****

The flight arrived in Amsterdam on time, allowing Janice to make her connection to Chicago with ease. During the flight, she met some vacationers coming back from an extended European stay. They sat in the same row with Janice and drew her into conversation with them.

She told them about her life in Nigeria, and about her honeymoon spent in Europe. They were fascinated that she had lived in Nigeria and wanted to know all about it. So she told them more about Nigeria and her family, leaving out the part about Lola. They pressed her for more details, but Janice told them she was tired and did not feel like talking anymore. The woman understood and told Janice to try to get some rest before dinner. Janice was five months pregnant.

After dinner, she turned and looked out the window of the jet. She could not see anything but the clouds. It gave her the chance to think about what she had left behind in Lagos. Janice touched her round stomach, feeling the child moving, and sighed.

"Femi, my husband, our child is restless," she whispered sadly. She wanted to sleep and forget some of the pain she felt inside. She turned in the seat, adjusting her pillow and tried to get more comfortable. A picture of Lola kept coming into her mind every time she tried to sleep. The final meeting at the airport was just as tense for her as it was for Lola. She knew that her present situation was hopeless; that there was no way she could continue living with Femi in that way. It had never been her plan to be a second wife. With that, Janice convinced herself that she made the right decision, and within moments finally fell asleep.

The plane touched down at the International Airport in New Orleans, Louisiana. Janice had telephoned her mother from Amsterdam, giving her the time she would be arriving. What she didn't tell her mother was the whole story. Janice let her mother think that she and Femi had decided to have the baby in America, using the excuse that America had the best medical care and they wanted only the best for their first child. She felt badly, knowing she had not been honest with her.

"Janice, baby," Edna called from the gate, rushing towards her daughter.

She was so glad to see her mother's familiar face. "Mom," she cried, hugging her tightly. Edna had a hard time getting her arms around her daughter, because Janice had gained some weight during the pregnancy.

"Let me look at you," she said, beaming happily at the sight of her only child. Edna had been worried about Janice. She was not a woman to let too much escape her, and she knew that there was more to her daughter's story than she let on. Instead of pushing her, she decided to let Janice tell her in her own time.

"How is the family in Nigeria? I hope your in-laws were not upset with your decision to return home."

"No, Mom, they only want me to be happy," she lied.

"Come on then, Janice," she said, pulling her towards the baggage area to collect her luggage. "Let's get you home so you can rest. You look tired, child."

The trip from the airport took longer than usual due to the heavy traffic on the bridge. Edna had a small ranch home in the eastern part of New Orleans. Janice looked out the car window as her mother drove through the heavy traffic. *New Orleans is very similar to Lagos,* she thought to herself, already missing Lagos.

"You're awfully quiet, Janice. How was your flight?"

"It was fine, Mom. I met a couple from America on the flight from Amsterdam. I told them so much about Nigeria that they decided to include Africa in their next vacation."

"It's still hard to believe that Bordeaux went to Africa. I have always wanted to visit someday. Maybe I can go back with you after the baby is born," Edna said thoughtfully.

Janice looked at her mother's loving face, feeling guilty. She wished that she had been honest with her. *No, now is not the time*, she thought.

Edna pulled into the driveway and parked the car. The two women struggled to carry the luggage. They took it into Janice's old room.

"Everything is just as you left it, Jan, before you went to Chicago to live with your cousin, Melinda."

Janice walked around the familiar room touching some of her memorabilia still sitting on her dressing table.

"Thanks, Mom," she said hugging her. "Thanks for keeping my things for me." Her mother left the room, closing the door. Janice walked to the bed to lie down, too tired to cry.

After a nap, she awoke to the smell of chicken frying in the kitchen. She got up slowly, smiling to herself, took a shower, and changed into some clean clothes.

Edna knocked on the door.

"Jan, I cooked some dinner for you."

"Okay, Mom. It smells delicious. I'm coming right now."

The phone rang and Edna answered. Janice heard her name mentioned as she followed the delicious aroma to the kitchen.

The back door was open, and she could hear their neighbor and good friend, Karen, calling her kids to dinner. Karen saw Janice looking through the screen door and waved.

"Janice, when did you arrive?"

"I arrived this morning," Janice shouted. "Karen, how are the boys?"

"They are all fine, Janice. Where is Edna? Tell her I saved her a piece of that lemon pound cake she likes so much."

"Mom is on the phone. I'll tell her."

Karen waved good-bye, and then ran off to look for her children before it got dark. She was a divorced mother with three strapping boys ranging in age from seven to fifteen. She was always either hanging laundry or cooking meals. Her husband of twelve years just up and left her one-day to raise the boys alone. He never came back. She was a bright and cheerful woman of forty. While Janice was growing up, always let her baby-sit her boys.

Karen and Edna worked for the same company. The two women always looked out for each other, because being a single parent is not easy.

"Janice," Edna called. "Telephone!"

Janice picked up the phone in the kitchen, and to her surprise, it was her cousin, Melinda. "Mindy, hi," she said excitedly. "How are you and Bill?"

"We're both fine, Jan. What are you doing back here? Is everything all right?"

Janice was tempted to tell her the real reason why she was back, but her mother came into the kitchen at that particular moment.

"Mindy, I came back to have the baby," she said instead. "Femi and I decided that it would be better for me here because of the medical care."

There was silence on the line as Melinda took time to digest what Janice just told her. Janice was not sure if she bought the story or not.

"Janice, if you say so, but girl, I don't know how you will be able to be separated from that gorgeous man for so long."

"Mindy, you seem to forget, this is not by choice," she retorted. "I came to have my baby safely. We decided to make this sacrifice for our child."

"That's great, Jan," she said carefully, not quite understanding Janice's tone. "I really missed you. I hope that I will see you before you have the baby."

"Mindy, I wish you were here now," Janice said, her voice shaking with emotion.

"Janice, are you sure you're all right?" Mindy asked with concern. "Let me speak to Aunt Edna." Janice gave the phone to her mother.

Melinda expressed her feelings of concern about Janice to her aunt. Edna promised that she would find out what was really the problem and call Melinda back. After she hung up, she took her daughter by her shoulders and looked seriously into her eyes. It was obvious to her that something was wrong and Janice was hiding the truth.

"Janice Marie Bordeaux-Adegoke," Edna stated, calling her by her full name. She always did that when she was going to have a serious talk with her daughter.

"I demand that you tell me what happened in Nigeria! Why did you return without your husband?"

Janice lowered her eyes as the tears began to roll down her face. She covered her face with both hands, and leaned into the safety of her mother's breast. She cried until she could cry no more, with heavy, gulping sobs shaking her body. Edna was so moved by her daughter's display of emotion that she began to cry with her.

"Janice, please child, tell me."

Janice took a deep breath, attempting to compose herself, and then she said softly," Mom, for you to be able to understand, let me start at the beginning. It begins with Lola."

Edna looked into her daughter's eyes and asked, "Who is Lola?"

Janice closed her eyes and sighed before speaking further. "Mom, Femi was not honest with me. He married me under false pretenses."

"What do you mean, Janice?" her mother asked, confused. Not understanding, she laughed at her daughter.

"Janice, we all know that he is married to you."

Janice looked at her mother, seeing that she still did not understand what she meant. "Mom, he is married to another woman, a Nigerian. Her name is Omolola!"

She watched the color drain from her mother's face as she gripped the arms on the kitchen chair for support.

"Janice, I am trying to understand what you are telling me, but I still don't get it," she said with dismay.

Janice took a deep breath and started again. "What I am trying to tell you, Mom, is that Femi had another wife before I married him, and he did not tell me about her. I found out after we were in Nigeria!"

Edna Bordeaux was normally a gentle woman. It would take a lot to upset her. But when it came to Janice, she was like a mother lion trying to protect her cubs from danger.

"Janice, let me get this straight. Femi had a wife in Nigeria before the two of you got married, and he never told you?"

Janice nodded her head, afraid to say anymore. She had never seen her mother so angry.

"My Lord have mercy! Janice! I am so sorry, my child. What happened to the nice man I met. I cannot believe that he would do something like this to you. I trusted him with your life!"

Edna would have never let her daughter go halfway across the world otherwise.

"I want you to tell me everything, right now!"

Her mother was furious as Janice told her everything that occurred after she found out about Femi's other wife.

"Lola did not know what was going on either. She is a good woman at heart, Mom. She was just as surprised as I was. Femi wrote her a letter to tell her about me while we were on our honeymoon."

Janice stood, feeling the baby kick.

"I will never understand how he could do this to me. I know it is part of their culture, but he took all my choices. He never gave me the chance to say *No* to having a polygamous relationship with him."

Edna stood behind her daughter, her hand on her shoulders in support. "Janice, what about his family? Why couldn't they do something?"

She turned and looked into her mother's eyes and spoke gently. "It is a part of their culture, Mom. Either I accept Lola, or I leave. I chose to leave. I refused to share my husband with another woman. Femi even had us on a schedule, with me on alternating weeks!"

That revelation was too much for Edna. She was very angry. And not just with Femi.

"Janice, why didn't you tell me when you called? I asked you if everything was all right. Why did you lie to me?"

Janice turned away, looking out the window at the yard. "Mom, I still love him ... that's why," she said softly, biting her lower lip, her arms hugging her body.

Edna took her daughter into her arms, holding her, trying to comfort her. She knew that there were no words she could say to make the pain go away. This situation was out of her hands, and she decided for the moment to leave it with God.

Later, they sat in the kitchen, trying to eat the delicious dinner Edna had prepared. But it was no use; they'd both lost their appetites. Janice went into her bedroom to try to sleep. Her mother followed her into the room.

"I just came in to see if you were comfortable."

"Thanks, Mom, I am fine."

Edna tucked the covers under Janice's chin, just like when she was a child.

"Janice," she whispered, "sometimes a woman has to bear a whole lot more than the pains of childbirth. No parent wants to see their child hurt for any reason, but try as we may, sometimes we cannot protect our children once they leave the nest ... Just remember, I love you and you will always have a home with me."

She gently touched her daughter's stomach. "You will not bear this pain alone. I will be with you every step of the way." Then she kissed her daughter on the cheek and slipped out of the room.

2

*J*anice awoke the next morning to the smell of sausage frying in the skillet. *My mom is taking good care of me,* she thought to herself, feeling happy and content in her own room.

"Janice," Edna called, "come and eat breakfast with me before I leave for work."

"Okay," Janice shouted to her mother as she got up to shower.

Edna had made an appointment with her gynecologist for Janice later in the day. Janice needed to see one due to the situations that almost caused her to lose the baby in Nigeria. She sat across from her mother and ate; Edna did not mention anything about their conversation last night.

"Janice, I am so glad you are home," Edna said, touching her daughter's cheek thoughtfully.

Janice smiled and asked her mother if she had a man in her life. To her surprise, she blushed.

"Okay, Mom, who is he?" Janice teased.

"Remember Professor McKinnon, the man I met at your wedding?"

"Yes, Mom, I do."

"Well, he and I have stayed in touch with each other and he invited me to come to Chicago for a weekend," she said, her eyes glowing, making her look younger than her 45 years.

"But now, I'm going to ask him for a rain check, so you won't have to stay here alone."

"Oh, no, you won't," Janice said. "I can travel with you. After all, Mom, I am only five months pregnant, and if I can travel all the way home from Africa, surely I can fly two hours to Chicago."

"Well, we will see what the doctor has to say about you today," Edna responded.

She kissed me on the cheek and gave me the key to her spare car.

"Have a good day, Mom," Janice yelled from the door.

Janice left a few hours later for her appointment. She entered the doctor's office and sat down among the other women, each in a different stage of pregnancy. A woman who looked to be middle aged started a conversation with Janice, but she was content to read a magazine instead.

"When is your baby due?" she asked, wrinkling her nose in a friendly fashion.

"I'm due in a few months," Janice replied, not taking her eyes off the magazine.

She said, "how nice," just as they called Janice's name to come into the examination room.

"Hello, Miss Bordeaux," Dr. Mason said. He was Edna's gynecologist and did not know Janice was married.

"I am now Mrs. Janice Adegoke," she replied, correcting him.

"Well, I'll be — li'l Jan is married. My, how time flies. I remember when I delivered you."

Janice laughed at his revelation and was happy that someone with so much experience was handling her delivery.

Dr. Mason took a complete medical history, did a physical, and ordered lots of tests. Janice told him that she had almost lost the baby in Nigeria. He said she appeared healthy and so did the fetus, but he should know more when the tests come back. She asked him about flying to Chicago with her mother for a few weeks, but he advised her to wait for the test results first.

Janice got home around 2 p.m. and fixed a late lunch. She was going to lie down when the phone rang.

"Janice, hello, this is Aduke."

"Hi, Aduke," Janice greeted her happily.

"I'm in Chicago, back at school. Girl, I stop by and bother your cousin every day like I used to do you."

She laughed, remembering how every day; Aduke would come into her office and sit on the desk, pestering her.

"How are you, Janice, and where is Femi?" she asked, puzzled by her sudden appearance in America.

"How did you find out I was back?"

"Oh, Melinda told me; you know she cannot keep a secret." They both laughed at that.

Janice told her about the events leading up to her departure from Nigeria.

"Janice, I am so sorry that things did not work out. I warned that husband of yours to be honest with you."

"I know you did, Aduke, but when I caught them in bed together, that was the last straw," she said, remembering the scene as if it just occurred. It always causes me pain to think about the man I love sleeping with another woman, even if she is his other wife."

"Janice, how is the baby coming along?" she asked, changing the subject. "I can't wait to be a godmother."

"The baby is fine, so far, and who said you would be the godmother?"

Aduke laughed, her voice sounding like water tinkling in a glass. "I did; you know that no one else can have that honor."

"Mom and I will be coming to Chicago, that is, if the doctor says that I can travel. I'm getting pretty big now, girl; you will hardly recognize me."

"Don't worry, Janice," she consoled me. "Your figure will return in no time."

"I hope so," Janice returned, bidding her friend good-bye, and promising to meet with her when in Chicago.

Later that evening, Janice and her mother sat down for a quiet dinner and she told her what the doctor said.

"Then you may be coming with me? That would be great. I know Melinda will be ecstatic!"

During the next few days, Janice took it easy, following the doctor's advice. All the lab results came back negative, so she was given the all clear for the trip.

Janice and her mother left for Chicago. The weather there was cold and windy, a big change from the mild temperatures in New Orleans. Janice tied a scarf around her neck as they walked out of the terminal looking for Professor McKinnon.

James McKinnon was professor of English at the University of Chicago. He and Edna met at Janice and Femi's wedding. Edna looked radiant as she caught sight of James waving in the crowd.

"Edna, I'm over here," he called over the crowd.

She waved and ran towards him, the skycap following quickly with the luggage, rushing trying to keep up. The two of them embraced and kissed unaffected by the crowd around them. Janice felt a twinge of envy as she thought about Femi. Realizing where they were, they pulled apart, laughing at their actions.

"Janice," he said happily, "my, how you have changed."

She smiled and touched her protruding belly and replied, "Yes, I have Professor McKinnon."

"Please, Janice, call me James."

"I would be honored to James."

My mother beamed at us, glad that we hit it off well.

"Come on, my two women. Let's go to my place."

He hooked arms with both of us and we walked to the car. Then he drove down the expressway with ease, taking us to his house near the university. He opened the door to the house, and my mother remarked,

"James, this is lovely."

Janice also appreciated the traditional decor of his home. He led them into his living room. It smelled like mellow pipe tobacco and tweed. He had a large Persian cat name Jinx that jumped off the sofa as Janice went to sit down.

"Can I get you a drink, Janice, or would you like to lie down before dinner?"

"To lie down, please," she decided. "I guess I'm tired from the airplane ride."

He showed her to a comfortable room on the second floor. It was as if the room was made for Janice. It had a beautiful satin coverlet in her favorite colors. She smiled, thanking him for carrying her heavy suitcase up the stairs.

"This used to be my daughter's room," remarked James, noticing Janice's look of admiration.

"If there is anything I can get you, please don't hesitate to ask."

Professor James McKinnon was in his 50s. He was divorced from his first wife, who lived in Florida with her latest boyfriend. He also had one grown daughter, who lived in Minneapolis with her husband and family.

Janice was undressing when her mother came into the room.

"Janice, will you be alright here?"

"Yes, Mom, the room is very comfortable, and James is a perfect host."

"I'm so glad that you two hit it off," she said, looking upwards at the ceiling and shaking her head with joy. Then she walked over to the bed and sat down. "Baby, I think I am in love with him. I didn't tell you earlier because I wanted it to be a surprise, but James has asked me to marry him."

Janice's heart skipped a beat at the sheer happiness and beauty that gleamed in her mother's eyes at that moment. She rushed to the bed and hugged her, crying, "Oh, Mom, I am so happy for you! You really deserve it!"

They were both crying and wiped each other's face.

"I just wanted to make sure, Janice that you were all right, before I told you. I know how hard things are for you at this time."

Janice took her by the shoulders and looked straight into her mother's eyes.

"Mom, nothing could make me happier than to see you married to a good, sweet, and gentle man like James."

After her mother left, Janice lay alone in the strange room, looking at the ceiling and thinking about her own troubles. The baby kept kicking, not allowing her to rest, so she got up and sat by the window and looked out on the tree-lined street, thinking about Femi and Lola, wondering what they are doing right now...

*****

Olufemi entered the gate of his sister, Bisola's home in Ikoyi. She and her husband had just finished dinner and were in the den with their children, Ajoke and Taju Jr. The steward Joseph showed Olufemi into the room.

"Welcome, Brother. What brings you out so late?" his sister asked with concern.

"I was just out driving and decided to pay you and your family a visit."

Taju got up and walked to the bar to fix himself a drink. Then he offered his wife and her brother one.

"You see me every day, Olu," Taju remarked. "I hope there is no problem at home."

Olufemi took the drink from Taju. "No, brother-in-law, all is quiet there since Janice is gone." His face took on a somber look at the mention of his second wife. Bisola sensed that he wanted to talk to them.

"Olu, it has been a month now. Have you had any word from her?"

"No, I have not, Bisi; that's what bothers me. I thought that a little time away would be sufficient for her to get over this, but I guess I was wrong."

Bisola went to her brother and stood behind him. She placed her hand on his muscular shoulder and began patting to comfort him.

"How is Lola?"

"Lola is fine, Bisi. She is at home, as usual."

"Why do you say it like that, Olu?" Taju asked.

"Lola doesn't like to go to the club with my friends. All she wants to do is stay at home and make love all the time."

Taju and Bisi looked at each other and laughed at the helpless look on Olufemi's face.

"She is trying to make up for the past two years that you were away, old man," Taju teased.

"Yes," his wife cut in, "you know she is trying to have a baby, Olu, and that takes a lot of bed time," she said, giggling at her brother's discomfort.

Olufemi looked at the two of them and realized that what he said was very funny. The laugh that came out of his large frame filled the room with mirth. Olufemi continued laughing, until tears rolled down his cheeks.

"I'd better get going," he said, still laughing. "Don't want the bed to get too cold."

With that remark, they all were filled with spasms of laughter again. Olufemi left them a few minutes later, driving home like a man on a mission.

He reached the home in Surulere that he shared with Lola. Whistling gaily, he strolled into the parlor, looking for his beautiful wife. He knew that he had been neglecting her lately, pretending to be preoccupied with work. Olu thought, *I will make it up to her. I must begin to get over Janice sometime.*

Lola was in the kitchen preparing his dinner.

"Lola, where is Grace. I don't want my wife tired from all this cooking."

She turned to see Olu standing in the doorway. She was surprised at her husband's good mood. Lately, he was always cross when he returned from work, but tonight, she was glad that he was happy. She smiled and said,

"I gave her the night off. I was not sure you were coming home."

He embraced her, rubbing gently against her body and smelling her familiar scent.

"I am not really hungry for food, darling. Let's go upstairs and make love."

Lola was really surprised now, because lately she had been the one to start their romancing.

"Ummmm, that sounds like a fabulous idea, darling."

Olufemi lifted her off the floor and carried her upstairs. He laid her gently on their bed and began slowly to undress her, taking his time removing each piece of her clothing, followed by a sexy kiss. Lola squirmed with pleasure with the loss of each piece of her outfit. He stopped only briefly to quickly remove his own clothes. The beautiful simplicity of the next few moments defined all the emotional power in Olufemi's heart. *He was sure he was able to love two women at the same time,* he thought as he entered his wife's body. Lola was moist and ready to receive her husband and return the pleasure equal to his adoration. Their bodies were locked in a struggle in which each would come out a victor. There could be no losers. Olufemi cupped her firm, ripe breast and kissed its tender spots. Lola shivered with delight as his thrusts became deeper and more determined.

"*Olo-u-fe-mi*, I love you, Olu, with such a deep passion that I would die if you ever leave me."

He looked into her eyes, searching into the depths of her soul as he imprisoned her body with his for the final ride to glory. His body began to shudder as their sweat mingled together and ran onto the bed. Lola braced herself by holding onto his back and crying out boldly,

"Olu!"

As they climaxed together, his eyes were filled with agony instead of love as he remembered again, his other wife's love for him and his for her. Lola felt him pull away even as he lay still inside her. She sought to bring him back to her.

"Olu, I love you so much. I hope that this time we made a baby!"

He looked away from her as he got up and walked into the bathroom to shower. She reached out to him, grabbing at the air. In the past, their lovemaking kept them in bed all night, sometimes until the next day. Lola sighed, and turned into the pillow, unable to stop the tears that were falling. She hurt from the depths of her being, for she knew that a part of the man she married was lost forever...

*****

Jide and Kemi's marriage was happy. Every morning Kemi dutifully prepared her husband breakfast before he went to pick Lola up and take her to work. He and Olufemi were childhood friends. Jide had taken good care of Lola while Olufemi was in America. Even after his friend returned, he continued daily taking Lola to work. Jide loved both of his friends and would do anything he could to help them. He arrived at the Adegoke residence at seven in the morning. Grace, the housemaid, opened the door and let him inside.

"*E'kabo,* Grace. Is Lola ready yet?"

"Yes, sir," Grace answered. "She will be down shortly."

Jide sat on the couch just as Olu came running down the stairs to the parlor.

"*E'kabo*, Jide. How is life treating you today?"

"About as good as yours is treating you, my friend. Is Lola ready yet?"

"Yes, she is," Olu, said, straightening his tie in the mirror that hung over the fireplace in the parlor. "I have to leave now; I will talk to you later," Olu said, rushing to the door. "Maybe we can meet for lunch this week?"

Jide did not answer as his friend closed the door. He sensed that there was trouble in the Adegoke house and was anxious to ask Lola about it. She walked into the parlor, looking very tired for the early morning hour. She greeted Jide, and then they got into the car, neither saying anything.

"Jide," Lola began as they entered the early morning rush hour traffic, "I don't know what to do anymore. Olu is not the same. I know that he tries to act as though nothing has happened, but I feel that he is not happy; he tries too hard to please me," Lola said sadly as her friend watched the road, trying to choose his words carefully.

"Lola, my friend, I have known Olu for many years. Since Janice left, I have been observing the two of you. I can see that things are not going well. I intend to speak to Olu when I get a chance. He is always busy these days. He seems to be lost inside himself."

"I know, Jide, and I have done everything in my power to bring him back to me. I have failed miserably." Lola's pretty face changed into a tearful one as they reached her office.

"I don't know how much longer I can take this, Jide." Her friend patted her on the back, trying to console her.

"Cheer up, Lola. All is not lost yet. Olu is here in Nigeria with you, and that shows that he loves you."

Lola blew her nose delicately on her handkerchief and wiped her eyes. "I hope that is enough Jide, but lately I don't think it is."

She got out of the car, adjusted her cotton wrapper, and walked into the office. She had returned to work after Janice left. Olu was seldom at home, and when he was, he was often lost in his own thoughts. She needed something to keep her busy, so she decided to return to her job at the Ministry of External Affairs as a secretary to Alhaji Mohammed Yaro. The situation between Lola and her boss was better now, but Lola knew he would still jump at the chance to have an affair with her if he could. She entered her office and prepared tea for him as he joined her at her desk.

"Sannu, Lola; how are you today?"

"I am as well as can be expected, sir."

She served him the tea in his office and went back to sort out his messages and mail. Sitting back, she remembered the day that she opened the letter from her husband, telling her that he had married another woman. Her eyes took on a whimsical air as she tried to remove the horror of that moment from memory.

The day went slowly as she tried to concentrate on one task after another. Alhaji noticed her distraction and asked her to come into his office for a chat. He looked at his secretary with concern.

"Lola, is everything alright between you and your husband? You know that I care about you and want to help in any way."

She looked down at her hands and spoke softly, "Sir, my husband is not yet over the fact that his other wife returned to America."

Alhaji Mohammed Yaro listened intently as his secretary explained all the troubles she had convincing her husband that she was woman enough for him.

"Lola, you can never erase that woman from your husband's mind. It's like poison without any antidote."

"Sir, I have to try," she said passionately. "I cannot lose him again."

Alhaji reached out for her hand. "Lola, do not go on blaming yourself for this situation; you need to try to find happiness any way you can. Remember, you only live once, so don't waste your youth and beauty trying to change a situation that you cannot."

Lola stood up, thanking her boss for his advice. She knew that she loved Olu and nothing and no one could ever change that.

When the workday was over, Jide picked her up and took her to the house in Surulere. Lola was quiet, thinking about her conversation with Alhaji and what she could do to try to make Olu happy. When they arrived at the house, Bisola, Olufemi's sister, was waiting for her.

"E'kabo, Lola; how are you? Long time, Sister *mi,* (my sister)*"* Bisola, her sister in-law, greeted her effusively. The two women stood in the doorway, hugging, until Grace came and opened the door. Then they walked into the cool parlor, taking seats opposite one another.

"Grace," Lola said, "bring soft drinks for my guest."

Jide bid them good evening and left as the two women sat in the parlor, talking about Lola's problems.

"Bisi, I don't know what else I can do," Lola began sadly. "I have done everything to make your brother love me again."

"I know, Lola. It's not easy to live in a situation like this, especially with Janice being overseas. It would be easier if she were here in Nigeria. It's difficult to fight a memory."

"Then what can I do? Should I ask her to return?"

Bisola looked with pity at Lola. "No, she would refuse to come, anyway."

"She will be having the baby soon. Oh, Bisi, I am so afraid that Olu will leave me then." Lola's eyes brimmed with tears; she stood up and walked to the window, looking into the garden. Bisi came over and put her arm on her shoulder, trying to console her.

"There, there, Lola, don't cry anymore. God will provide the answer; just leave everything in His hands."

*****

Olufemi Adegoke was not in a hurry to get home tonight. He took the long way home sighing deeply thinking, *Janice I miss you.*

I wonder what you are doing now. He maneuvered the car along the expressway. The traffic was light this time in the evening. When he got near his house, he saw a man selling bananas and oranges along the road. He thought Lola would probably like some and bought a dozen of each to take home to her.

He arrived at home just as his sister was leaving. They exchanged greetings and she told him she could not stay, that Lola was waiting for him. Bisola saw the melancholy look on her brother's face and thought; *I have never seen him so blue. Maybe Lola does have something to worry about.* She drove home, thinking about the two unhappy people.

Olu went inside and changed his clothes for dinner. Lola always had it ready for him. Grace set the table and served the meal as the two of them ate in silence until Olu remembered the fruit he brought for her. "I bought some oranges and bananas for you, Lola; they are in the car."

"Thank you, dear. I'll send Grace to get them. How was your day, Olu?"

"It was very busy; in fact, we have a new government contract to fill. I may have to go overseas for some of the products."

Lola's face perked up at the mention of going overseas. "Where overseas, Olu?" she asked, her voice trembling. He promptly realized that he should not have mentioned what he and Taju had earlier discussed in the office. The two men knew that they could not fulfill the contract without the chemical order, and since Olu was the expert with chemicals, the logical choice would be for him to go.

"I am not sure Lola; we can probably get the products from London."

"That's nice, dear. Maybe I can come with you on the trip."

"I don't see why not, dear," he said blandly. "I would welcome the company."

They finished their meal in silence, and then Olu went outside for a walk. Lola came out to join him. When they returned they sat in the garden, looking up at the stars, "Olu, what has happened to us? We are like two old people."

He laughed. "What do you mean, Lola? Is it because we are sitting outside, looking at the stars?"

"No, silly; it is because we are young and should be spending our time trying to make a baby."

Olu took her in his strong arms and hugged her. "We have plenty of time for that, my darling," he whispered seductively into her ear.

She moaned with want and need because their lovemaking had not been like it used to be.

"Olu, come my love; let's go inside before the mosquitoes make us their dinner."

The couple walked slowly inside. Olu lifted Lola off the floor into his arms and carried her up the stairs to the bedroom.

"Darling," she said breathlessly, "I love you so."

He laid her gently on the bed as he removed her clothes, piece by piece, until she was nude and lying sexily on the cool sheets. He stood over her and undressed. She watched thrilled, because naked, Olufemi had a body that any male stripper would envy. He lay down on the bed beside her, gently caressing her firm breast with one hand. Lola looked seductively into his eyes, waiting for them to begin their lovemaking. Slowly and deliberately, Olu kissed each and every part of Lola's body, until she was shivering with delight. She returned his adoration with a zest that would rival their wedding night. Their souls were on fire with passion as they each took pleasure in pleasing one another. He took her to the sky and they both came, tumbling down together, holding on to one another and trying to catch their breath, exhausted. Their passion spent, Lola slept while Olufemi turned over on his side, thinking about Janice, his other wife.

3

The next day at the office, Taju had a meeting with Olufemi about the proposed trip to London.

"I feel, Olu that we cannot wait any longer. I need you to go and purchase the product for our contract. How long do you anticipate being gone?"

Olu sat back in his chair, looking over the file in his hand.

"Mr. Edmonds of Matthews Chemicals has arranged a meeting with me for next week. I don't think that I will be gone more than a few days."

"Will you be taking Lola?"

Olufemi looked away from his brother-in-law, clearing his throat before speaking. "She will not let me out of her sight, Taju, so the answer is yes."

"I thought so, Olu. Maybe it is for the best. At least this way, she can be sure you will return alone."

"I do owe her that much, Taju."

That evening after dinner, Olu told Lola about his plans to leave next week for London.

"Can you get time off from work, dear?"

Lola's eyes gleamed with joy. "Yes I can! I would love to go to London! It will be fun, Olu. You and I, together, enjoying each other away from Nigeria. I can't wait to leave!"

"Then it's settled. I will take your passport and get you a visa to England."

That night, Lola slept comfortably. She was happy that she would be accompanying her husband on his trip. She vowed she would never let him travel again without her.

On her way to work the next morning, she told Jide the good news. "It will be like a second honeymoon. Oh Jide, I am so excited!"

Jide maneuvered the car through the heavy Lagos traffic, taking care not to run over a man pushing a cart loaded with produce for the market.

"I am happy for you too, Lola. Wait until I tell Kemi. She will meet you with a list of things for you to bring back for her."

"I know, Jide. Think of it ... This will be my first trip abroad."

They ended the conversation as they reached their destination. He parked the car and walked Lola to her office building.

"See you this evening, Jide; *odabo.*" Lola called cheerfully.

Lola met her boss on the stairs. *"Sannu*, Alhaji," she said, the old glow returning to her face. He opened the door to their office for her, and they walked inside.

"Hello to you, Lola. What has happened to make you so cheerful today?"

"Well, sir, I need some time off. My husband has asked me to accompany him to London!"

"How wonderful, Lola. Does that mean that he has forgotten about his other wife?"

Alhaji could not resist throwing in that question. The smile left her lovely face and was replaced with anger.

"Alhaji, that was out of line. Why would you bring her up on such a happy occasion?"

"I did not mean anything by it, Lola. You know that you can take as much time off as you need. Your job will be waiting for you when you return."

Suddenly, Lola was filled with gratitude. She rushed to her boss and kissed him on his cheek. Alhaji was startled by her action, wishing that the kiss were on his lips. He sighed and was grateful for any attention, positive or negative, that she would bestow on him.

"Thank you, thank you, Alhaji. If you don't mind, sir, I would like to take the day off to shop for my trip."

"Anything you wish, Lola," Alhaji replied, his eyes glossy as he stared at his secretary.

"Lola," he said, touching her cheek, "I wish," he began, but could not finish. Instead, he continued touching her cheek gently. He wanted more from his secretary than she was willing to give. But Alhaji Yaro was a very patient man and willing to wait.

This move was not lost on Lola, who avoided his eyes as she grabbed her purse and ran down the stairs to get a taxi. Alhaji stood at the window, watching her leave, wishing that he had not made it so easy for her to go.

Lola's first stop was to Bisola's house to share the good news with her, and ask her to go shopping with her. After the taxi dropped her off in front of the house, Lola rang the doorbell. Joseph answered the door and led Lola to the living room.

"Hello, my sister," Lola cried as the two women hugged each other.

"How is my brother, Lola?"

"He is fine, Bisi. In fact, that is why I am here. He is taking me to London on his business trip, and I want to go shopping for a few things. Will you come with me?"

Bisola stood there looking at Lola, amazed. "That's wonderful, Lola! When are you going?"

"Next week!" she exclaimed, excited.

"Well, that doesn't give us much time. Come on, let's go shopping at *Falamo* market and buy you some traveling clothes."

Lola adjusted her colorful wrapper and head tie, and the two gaily dressed women got into the Mercedes.

"Where to, Madame?" the driver asked.

Bisola told him to take them to Falamo Shopping Center. They spent the entire afternoon buying Lola suitable clothing for her trip abroad.

It was late in the evening when Lola finally returned home. She rushed into the kitchen to see to dinner. Grace was there, washing the dinner dishes. She told Lola that she had already given Olufemi his dinner, and that he went out to his club with friends for a drink.

"I have already finished, Madame. Is there anything else you require tonight?"

"No, Grace," Lola answered. "But, I will need you to help me pack for my journey next week."

Grace turned happily to her mistress.

"Where are you going to travel, Madame?"

"Grace, my husband and I are going to London for a week!" Lola said happily, hardly able to contain herself.

"I am so happy for you. Then that must mean things are better between you and Mr. Olufemi."

Grace put the last of the plates in the cabinet. She then followed her mistress into her bedroom and admired all the beautiful clothes Lola had purchased.

"Madame, you will look like those *oyingbo's!*" she exclaimed, holding a dress up in front of her. Grace gently took the dress and the other purchases and hung them in the closet. She was pleased that her prayers for her mistress appeared to be working.

At the club, Olufemi was sitting with Taju, having a beer. The two men were discussing the travel arrangements.

"Olu, have you heard anything from Janice?"

A sad look came across the handsome man's face. It was a look that made him to appear older than his thirty-two years.

"No, Taju, I haven't. But she is always in my thoughts."

Taju shifted in his seat, frowning as he looked at the younger man.

"Olu, maybe when you return from London, your next trip will be to Houston. We need some chemicals that cannot be purchased elsewhere."

Olufemi's eyes began to shine. "Yes, Taju," he answered with glee. "And this trip, I will take alone. But for now, I owe Lola something for the rotten time I have given her. I hope that the trip to London will appease her for a while. My baby will be due soon, and I want to be there, even if Janice does not want to see me. I must impress on her that, no matter what, I am the father of the child and we are still married."

The two men paid their tab and walked to the parking lot. There was a cool, tropical breeze blowing in from the ocean. Olu looked up into the clear sky filled with stars before speaking again.

"Taju, you are the only one that understands me. My friend, Jide, does not. He always questions anything I do that affects Lola."

"Olu, you know Jide is very fond of Lola. Remember, my brother, he took good care of her for you while you were in America."

"I guess you're right, Taju. Maybe I should be a bit more tolerant. Well, good night. I will see you at the office in the morning."

*****

Kemi was preparing dinner for her husband Jide. The fragrant smell of the fish stew and rice wafted out into the yard of the flat. The couple lived in a government flat near Surulere. Since their marriage, Kemi strived to be the perfect African wife. She washed her husband's clothes, cooked his meals, and was always attentive when he spoke. She also would visit his mother often.

Kemi had a shop in the market, where she sold fabric for clothing. Every morning, she would take the bus to Balogun market on Lagos Island to sell her wares. Jide was a civil servant at the Ministry of Works. She sometimes wished he had gone abroad to London with Olu to get his degree. It seems that he could not get a better job without education.

She adjusted her wrapper that was coming loose from her waist. Jide wanted to start a family right away, but Kemi did not. She was still hoping that someday they, too, would travel to America to go to school. She had her own dreams of success and thought about her cousin, Yetunde, who was in Chicago, Illinois, studying medicine. For Kemi, who came from a poor family, just getting a primary education was a luxury. Education was still out of reach for many Nigerians, but she was lucky enough to be able to pay for her secondary education. Kemi was very enterprising and worked hard for a woman who owned a clothing shop in the market. Now she had her own store.

Jide walked in the door as she was frying the last plantain.

"Ekabo," she cried, welcoming her husband in the traditional African way.

He returned her greeting and went to wash before having his dinner. He came to the table, and they said a prayer before eating. Jide complimented his wife on the delicious meal. After dinner, he told Kemi the good news about Lola and Olu's trip to London.

"That's wonderful! I am so happy for my friend. I will have to visit her before she goes."

Jide noticed that his wife appeared preoccupied tonight. Usually Kemi was very jovial and filled with conversation. She would tell him all the funny stories and gossip that she heard at the market where she worked. But tonight, she was unusually quiet. He looked at her chubby brown face, motioning her to come to him and tell him what was on her mind.

As she got closer, he looked into her beautiful, large, brown eyes. They were very expressive, like a window to her heart. Jide could always tell when something was bothering her, because her eyes would become dull and listless. And whenever she was trying to hide something from him, Kemi would go to great lengths to avoid his eyes. She normally had an argumentative personality, yet tonight, she was very quiet.

"Kemi, *kilo-se?* What is wrong with you tonight?"

She looked passively at her husband and smiled. "Nothing, my husband. Why do you ask?"

"You look so solemn. Are you sure you don't want to talk about anything?"

Kemi put down her dishrag and walked into the parlor. Sitting on the arm of the sofa, she began to tell Jide what she felt about going to America to pursue their education. She also told him of the letter she had received from her cousin, asking them to come and live there.

"Yetunde told me it will be simple, and she will offer us a place to live in Chicago. She has a large flat with three bedrooms and we could have one bedroom until we get on our feet." Kemi paused a moment to catch her breath, while watching her husband's face for his reaction.

Jide rubbed his chin, thinking *Kemi has not been happy of late. I wonder if this is what has been on her mind.* "Well, my wife, you seem to have thought of everything."

Kemi breathed a sigh of relief.

"No, Jide, I have not. I just feel that we could get ahead so much faster if you had a better job."

"You may be right, Kemi. I know I have not been able to give you the things that Olu gives Lola, but I am doing the best that I can on my salary. I will think about it, Kemi. How will we pay for this adventure?"

Kemi's eyes glowed with delight. She could not wait to tell Jide about the money she had been saving for their house, but instead, she answered, "Do not worry, Jide. God will provide." Then she gave him a big hug and rushed back into the kitchen to finish the dishes.

*****

The driver sped through the heavy Lagos traffic towards the airport. Lola reached for Olu's hand, and he smiled at her. They were on their way to London, and Lola could hardly contain her excitement. Olu, sensing this, kept telling her of all the places they would go while there. They would also stop in to see his cousin, Bankole, and his English wife, Patty. They just had a baby girl.

"Lola, did you remember to pack the baby gifts for Bankole and Patty?"

"Yes, darling, I remembered everything."

Lola also remembered that Janice and Olu had spent part of their honeymoon with Bankole and Patty in London. This was one memory that she hoped to erase from her husband's heart.

The couple boarded the plane for England. The flight was five hours. Lola was a bit nervous, and she tightly held onto Olu's hand until the plane took off. Then she began to relax as the stewardess passed out refreshments. She just leaned back in her seat and sipped her coke, watching an in-flight movie. Olu began a conversation with one of the other passengers. Lola was fascinated and in awe that some people had the opportunity to travel frequently. She knew that this would not be her last flight. She was planning to take many more with Olu.

The plane touched down at London Heathrow International Airport. There was a slight drizzle and that famous London fog in the air. Olu retrieved their luggage, and they took a taxi to their hotel. They were staying in one of the better hotels near downtown.

After they checked in, Lola lay across the large bed, reveling in the luxury of their suite. She had a surprise for Olu after dinner, and she hoped that he would be pleased. She smiled seductively as he returned to the room. He chuckled, seeing his wife lying on the bed in the afternoon, waiting for him to make his move. He hesitated as she caught the look in his eyes.

"I've got to call Mr. Edmonds at the plant before I can relax. Business before pleasure, Lola."

Lola sighed and rolled over on her stomach, disappointed that he was not in the same mood as she was. She thought to herself, *that is all right, Olu. You cannot resist what I have planned for tonight, darling.*

Olufemi picked up the phone and called his contact, Mr. Edmonds, to let him know that he had arrived in London. The two men talked about the meeting and finished up the conversation with other company business. Not wanting to see Lola, Olufemi remained in the sitting room of their suite. Even in London, he could not escape his memories of Janice. He sat back in the chair, holding his head, trying to will the thoughts of his other wife from his memory. He sighed and a lonely tear rolled down his cheek. He clenched his fist and wiped the tear away, lest Lola would see him.

He knew Lola wanted to make love, but from the time that their plane touched down at the airport, all he could think about was his honeymoon and the week that he and Janice spent in London. He could still see her smiling face, wet from the London shower.

Her laughter rang in his ears. He imagined her touch, her kiss. He missed her immensely. He knew that he was being unfair to Lola, but he could not help it, especially since Janice was carrying his child. The more that he tried to put her away, the more vivid her memory became. It seemed like only yesterday that he was making love to her in the afternoon. If only she would talk to him!

4

*M*elinda picked up the phone and to her surprise it was Janice.

"Hey, cousin, how are you and that load you are carrying?" Melinda teased her as the two renewed their close relationship.

"I'm fine, Mindy. I'm in Chicago with Mom, and we will be here for several weeks."

"That's great, girl."

"Wait, Melinda, there is more news. Mom is getting married!"

"Girl, you lying! Aunt Edna, getting married!?" Melinda could hardly contain herself. "Who's the lucky guy, Jan?"

"Professor McKinnon. Remember my wedding. He was the one who would not let Mom out of his sight. They fell in love after I left for Nigeria. I expect them to get married sometime before the baby is born."

"How much longer will that be?"

"I'm due in a few months. I'd rather stay in Chicago to have the baby, but it all depends on Mom. I really don't have to ask about you and Bill. I know you two are ecstatically happy."

"You are right, Jan; marriage has been good to me."

I sighed with mixed emotions.

"Oh, Jan, I am so sorry about Femi. He seemed like a perfect catch. I should have figured it out, especially after Dele."

"Melinda there is no way that you could have known about his other wife. Aduke didn't even know."

"I know Jan, but it is still so unfair."

After the phone conversation, Janice was very depressed and the baby seemed to sense her mood and proceeded to kick her for the rest of the day. But, on a positive note, her mother was radiant. She spent every day with James. They went to the latest shows, the theater, and out to dinner almost every night. They constantly asked Janice to go with them, but she felt she would only be in the way. Instead, I'd stay at home alone, dreaming about happier times when I too, was in love.

"Oh, Femi, why? Why did you have to lie to me?" I constantly asked myself, touching my protruding belly, feeling the life within me moving.

"I live only for you, my child. Only for you," she declared fiercely.

Melinda invited Janice to lunch at the university. She was filled with nostalgia as she walked down the familiar corridors towards her former office. Janice peeped around the corner to find Melinda hard at work.

"Working you to death, I see," Janice said, laughing, as she walked into the office.

"Janice! Hi!" Melinda screamed, jumping up from the desk and giving her one of her smothering hugs.

"Mindy, how are you, dear?" she replied, wrapping her arms around her as much as she could, considering her large stomach that was in the way. We wiped tears of joy from one another's face.

"Come and sit down, Jan. God, I can't believe it, girl! You are really pregnant!"

"Thank a lot, Melinda. I envy your figure."

"Well, Janice, I envy yours. Motherhood appears to agree with you, child. You are simply stunning."

Janice had to agree because since she became pregnant, her hair had grown longer, her nails too, and she had only gained the weight of the baby. She was wearing the latest maternity dresses, and they flattered her figure.

"Come on, Melinda. I'm on a schedule for eating now. The baby is hungry," she laughed.

"Okay, let me tell Mr. Dotson that you are here, and then we can go."

Her former boss was so happy to see her that he offered to take them to lunch. They declined, telling him that they had a lot to catch up on and gave him a rain check.

On the way to the cafeteria, Janice met a lot of her former co-workers. Sitting in a corner, surrounded by a group of males was Aduke. She rushed over to Janice.

"Janice, *E'kabo* (welcome), my sister."

To Melinda's surprise, Janice answered her flawlessly in Yoruba. *"Se'da da ni?"*

Aduke smiled and answered, *"A-dupe."* Then she gracefully curtsied to me the traditional African way.

"Melinda," Janice said, "close your mouth."

Even Aduke was surprised at how easily the greeting flowed from my lips.

"Janice, you look good, girl, and you have not lost the Yoruba you learned in Lagos."

"No, I have not, Aduke. How is your family and your brother, Tunde, doing? Is he still in London?"

"Yes, my family is well, and Tunde is getting married soon. He told me to invite you to the wedding. I was so surprised when he telephoned to say that he was marrying a white British woman. He said they worked at the same place. My mother is happy, but my father is complaining. He never wanted his children to marry out of their culture." She continued, "Tunde heard about you leaving Olufemi. He said he was very sorry."

Janice lowered her eyes, trying not to show how upset she was at the mention of her husband's name. Melinda changed the subject.

"Come on, Aduke. Don't bother Janice with all those unnecessary memories. Let's eat lunch."

While they were eating, two of the men who had been sitting with Aduke came over to the table. One had a familiar face; the other Janice did not know. Both men were African. One of them seemed to know Janice because he said,

"Janice, you look well. How are you?"

She looked at the gentleman, inquiringly. "Do I know you?"

"Yes, Janice, I'm Dominique. Don't you remember me?" he asked with a French accent.

Just then, their eyes met and she remembered that he asked her to dance the same night she met Femi. Her hand flew to her mouth.

"Yes, yes, I remember you!"

"May we join you, ladies?" Dominique asked, never taking his eyes off me. His look was not lost on Melinda or Aduke. No answer was needed, just the smile on my face. After Dominique joined us, the rest of the lunch went great.

By the time it was over, Melinda had invited Janice over for dinner the next day. She was walking back to the car when Dominique caught up with her.

"Wait, Janice. I want to talk to you."

His French accent was lilting and sounded quite appealing. Dominique was from Senegal. He was a tall, slender man and was impeccably dressed. He had very pronounced features and his complexion was medium brown. He held a permanent position as a lecturer at the university. He was also a friend of Aduke's. Janice always thought that he and Aduke would get together after she broke up with Nelson, but somehow that never happened. No one knew what went on behind those dreamy eyes and his haughty facade. All I knew was that I was lonely, and he offered me the companionship that I needed as my pregnancy progressed.

We became good friends, almost too good in such a short amount of time. No one could understand his chivalry, especially Edna, who thought it unnatural for a single man to volunteer to be with a pregnant, married woman. She was all too anxious to get me back to New Orleans and out of his reach.

She would say, "Janice, have some class. I know you miss Femi, but not another African."

Janice would only answer in Creole. "What's wrong with another African, especially one who speaks French?"

I was having all the fun that I could before the baby was born, but soon our visit came to an end and we returned to New Orleans.

James promised to come to visit next. I knew I would not be traveling again until after the baby was born, so I settled into life at home in New Orleans.

Time moved slowly for me. Every other day I would receive a call from Dominique; sometimes he sent a card or flowers. I knew that Mom did not like it, but I was bored and needed someone to talk to. Besides, I was too large now to go many places, and the heat in New Orleans was unbearable at times, so waiting patiently for the birth of my child was pretty much the only option I had left.

James flew down to see Edna, and while he was in town, I was no longer bored. They took me to the theater and afterwards to dinner. Although I felt like a third wheel, they never made me feel that way.

That was, until the phone rang one afternoon. Janice answered and the voice on the other end sounded like it was in the room with her.

"Janice, it's me. Femi."

I held my breath before speaking. "Femi, how are you?" I asked calmly.

"I'm fine," he said, his voice sounding shaky. "How is the baby?"

"Kicking daily," I laughed.

"I miss you," they both spoke at the same time.

"I am so sorry, Janice. I never meant for things to go this way."

Janice let out a sigh and felt all the emotions that she had held pent up inside her flow to the surface.

"Oh, darling, it has been so lonely here. How are your family and especially Bisola?"

"Everyone was fine the last time I saw them. I am not in Nigeria. I'm in London."

"London? Did you go there on business?" I asked, relaxing.

"Yes, I did," he answered casually.

Then Janice decided to dive in and ask, "Femi how is Lola?"

The silence on the line was deafening. He cleared his throat before speaking, trying to decide whether to lie and say that Lola was not with him. He decided against it, thinking that there had already been too many lies in the relationship.

"Lola is fine, Janice. She is here with me in London."

Janice felt her heart begin to beat fast. She wanted to jump inside the phone and rip his heart out.

Feeling the hot tears scalding my cheeks, I held my stomach and screamed, "Then what do you want with me? You have your other wife with you!"

"No, Janice! Please understand! I love you!"

Seeing that he had gotten Janice upset, Femi tried everything he could to calm her down, but her anger came back. It was as if she could see them making love, the way she had caught them in Lola's house at Surulere.

Janice closed her tear-flooded eyes and cursed. "Shit, Femi! Why can't you leave me alone?"

From the sound of his voice, Janice could tell he was crying. "Janice, please, I am sorry! I love you! I can't help myself!"

I slammed down the receiver, not wanting to hear his pleas any longer. Mother heard me shouting and rushed into the room, only to find me sobbing into the pillow.

"Janice, what has happened to you? Whom were you talking to on the phone?"

"Oh, Mom, it was Femi," Janice said through her tears. "He called me from London, and Lola was with him," I continued sobbing.

"Why would he do that to you?" Edna shouted. "He has no right to call you and upset you in your condition!"

Edna took me into her arms like I was a baby and rocked me gently, trying to console me.

*****

Femi was aghast to think that he had upset Janice so much. He replaced the receiver and sat down on the chair. Lola had been in the bathroom and came out to see her husband deep into his own thoughts. She did not know that he had been on the phone. Olufemi was confused and devastated at Janice's reaction to him being with Lola. *After all*, he thought, *she left me.*

He turned to his wife, who was looking at him, waiting for him to say something. He took a deep breath to calm himself and told Lola to get dressed to go sightseeing.

Being in London was like a dream come true to Lola. All the places she heard about from some of her friends who traveled frequently were true. Nigeria was very much like London. Olu and Lola stopped at a restaurant to have lunch. "Oh, Olu, it is so much fun to be here with you. Thank you for bringing me."

Olufemi looked at this beautiful wife and smiled. He felt guilty not telling Lola that he spoke to Janice. He went out of his way to show her a good time, while feeling like dirt. Lola sensed his mood and did everything to appear cheerful, when inside she felt like crying. She knew that Olu and Janice had their honeymoon in London.

"Lola, Bankole is having us over for dinner tomorrow."

"That's fine, Olu. I look forward to meeting your cousin."

They spent the rest of the day sightseeing and doing light shopping. They were spending a week there, and Lola was going to have fun whether Olu did or did not.

5

*K*emi had been making inquiries. Recently she received a letter from Yetunde saying it was okay for her and her husband to come to America to visit. If they liked it, they could file papers to become residents and stay. Kemi was so happy she jumped up and down.

"Thank you, God!" she shouted. Now she had all the ammunition she needed to further convince Jide that this was the right thing for them to do. Kemi went to see Bisola to tell her the good news.

"Just think, Bisi ... America ... Jide and I will be able to go to the university."

But Bisi was not so sure, thinking back to what happened to her brother meeting Janice and all.

"Kemi, *kilo-se'*. What is wrong with Nigeria that everyone wants to leave?"

Kemi sat back in her chair, her mouth open to protest, but then she decided against it. Instead she said softly, "It is easy for you to say that, Bisi. You are married to a rich husband. Jide will be a civil servant all his life. All he wants now is for me to have children, and once I do that, all our chances for leaving Nigeria will be gone."

Bisola knew she was being insensitive to her friend, but she really did wish her well and told her so.

Kemi went home and prepared Jide's favorite foods for dinner. She planned to tell him tonight that she had heard from Yetunde, and he should let her know his decision.

Jide arrived to the delicious smell of *moyin-moyin*, *jollof rice*, and goat meat stew. He knew Kemi had gone to a great deal of trouble to make this meal.

"Kemi, you must have cooked all day to prepare the food. It smells delicious. Now, what do you have to tell me?" Jide knew his wife would not have gone to all this trouble unless she wanted something.

She sat down next to Jide, not meeting his eyes, and began to tell him her plans and about the letter from Yetunde. He listened and then asked her to bring him his briefcase. He opened it and took out a large brown envelope.

"Here, my wife. Open the envelope."

Kemi gingerly held the envelope, opening it carefully. The look on her face as she took out the contents was of pure joy, for the envelope held two Nigerian passports. All the worry was erased from her face as she looked lovingly at her husband.

"Ah, ah, *oko-mi*, you surprised me."

She rushed to his lap, kissing him all over his face. Her kisses turned to passion as his hands began to touch her body and arouse her. The one thing Jide loved about his wife was her ample bosom. He buried his face in it. When he came up for air, he began to touch her nipples until they peaked. His hands were all over her. She looked knowingly into his eyes and neither of them spoke. They just got up and went into the bedroom. In seconds, her wrapper lay on the floor as Jide pulled her *buba* (blouse) off and her breasts fell freely into his waiting hands. Kemi was always shy with her lovemaking, never initiating; always letting Jide take control. She was raised to be modest and brought that modesty into her marriage.

But that did not stop Jide, who was very amorous. He strived to bring pleasure to his wife in any way possible. He kissed her neck and trailed his lips to her breast, then pulled off her scarf, freeing her braids. He reveled in the softness of her skin and the faint scent of musk. He lay on her as she arched her back to receive him.

Kemi radiated with the pleasure that her husband was giving her. He held back as her fingers massaged his buttocks and back. Kemi was feeling adventurous tonight. She kept pace with her husband, meeting his every thrust instead of lying passive and submissive. He was surprised at her ardor and was enjoying it more. The more she participated, the more he experimented.

When Kemi could hold back no more, she moaned with ecstasy as the two of them burst with a passion never known before in their marriage.

Jide lay over Kemi, looking deeply into her expressive eyes. He whispered, "I love you, Kemi. You are my lover for life."

Kemi held her husband tightly to her chest and affirmed, "Yes, my, darling, forever."

*****

Olufemi went to his meeting at the chemical company. He finalized most of his business that morning and that gave him more time to spend with Lola, showing her around London. He took her shopping on Liverpool Street. She commented on the lovely lace materials the shops carried and the fine selection of Italian handbags and shoes. This afternoon they would go to Buckingham Palace and to the London Tower to view the Queen's jewels before going to dinner at Bankole's house. When he arrived back at the hotel, Lola was on the phone. She had called her friend, Kemi, to tell her about London, and Kemi was telling Lola her good news.

"Oh, Omolola!" Kemi exclaimed. "I am so happy."

"Kemi, how did you convince Jide?" Lola asked surprised. "I thought he would be the last man to leave Nigeria for any reason."

"You know our men, Lola. A good meal and a little love, and they are like putty in our hands!" Kemi exclaimed delighted.

"I beg to differ, Kemi. Not all Nigerian men. Some are not that easy to charm." Lola was thinking about Olu, who, since Janice left, had been difficult to please.

Lola looked up to see her husband walking into their hotel suite.

"Kemi, I will talk to you later. Olu has just come in; *odabo,* my friend."

"Ekabo oko-mi. Welcome my husband. How was the meeting?" Lola greeted her husband effusively.

"Things went well. The shipment of chemicals will be leaving in two days for Nigeria. We will meet the ship by the time we return. Taju will be pleased that things went so smoothly."

"I'm glad, my husband. I have some good news for you. I was just talking to Kemi, and she told me she and Jide are going to America to study. Can you believe Jide agreed to go?"

Olu looked astounded at his wife. "You mean that typical Nigerian Jide agreed to go to America to seek his fortune?"

"Yes, isn't it wonderful?"

"Well, that remains to be seen. It's hard for me to think of Jide and Kemi in America. What will they do? They have no skills."

"I'm sure that they will be all right," Lola said, defending her friends, while at the same time, surprised at Olufemi's attitude.

The couple left to go sightseeing. When they returned, Bankole was waiting in the lobby. Olu introduced him to Lola, and she greeted him in the traditional way. The three of them left for his house. He lived in a newer London suburb. All the houses were small, three-bedroom cottages.

Lola was introduced to Bankole's wife, Patty. The short, chubby woman smiled nervously as she shook Lola's hand. She had a small baby in her arm. The baby's name was Shade, and she was a beautiful child. She had her mother's hazel eyes and soft, light brown, curly hair. She was almost a year old. Patty put her in her walker and showed her guests into the parlor.

Bankole was the talker. He welcomed Lola and did everything to make her feel comfortable. Patty, on the other hand, was slightly standoffish; she was polite, but Lola could sense her uneasiness. Olufemi caught it all. He walked into the kitchen while Patty was putting the finishing touches on dinner.

"Patty, thank you for being nice to my other wife."

Patty looked sternly at Olufemi, and then turned abruptly to stir the dish on the stove.

"Femi, I liked Janice. I feel very uncomfortable with what you are doing. I saw my friend, Jean, destroyed when her husband, Akim, took another wife. She left him and came back to England. I hear Janice has left you, too."

Olufemi cleared his throat, embarrassed to admit the truth.

"Janice is such a nice girl. How can you do this to her?"

"You know the story, Patty. I fell in love with Janice, even though I was already married to Lola. I miss Janice so much."

"That's good for you," she snapped. "You deserve what you get. Lola may be a nice person, but I met Janice first and this is unfair to me. I am being courteous for Bankole's sake. I just hope he doesn't get any ideas."

Olufemi laughed uncomfortably, trying to make light of the situation. But Patty's words could not be denied. Trying to allay her suspicious feelings, he said, "No, Patty, you are the only woman for him."

Lola reached for the baby. She was holding her in her arms as Patty and Olu returned with a tray of drinks.

"She is beautiful, Patty. Shade is such a lovely name."

"Thank you," she replied politely. "We plan to have another soon. What about you and Femi, Lola?"

Lola was embarrassed as she looked at her husband. So he answered for her.

"We don't know yet. I am so busy at work. Maybe in a year or two we will start a family."

The couple did not miss the look of surprise on Lola's face, but before Lola could respond, Patty announced that dinner was served.

After dinner, Patty put the baby to bed and the couples played cards for a while. Patty slipped once and mentioned the party that Janice and Olufemi attended while on their honeymoon. Olufemi looked apologetic at Lola, and Bankole censored his wife, who got up to take empty glasses to the kitchen. Lola followed her, sensing her embarrassment.

"Patty, don't be embarrassed. Janice is not a problem for me. She is back in America now, and I am Olu's only wife."

Patty turned to Lola and angrily said, "I did not hear that Femi divorced Janice. In fact, I hear she is pregnant."

Lola stepped back, stunned by the venom in Patty's words. Fighting back the tears, she left the kitchen and told Olufemi she wanted to go home, that she was not welcome there. Bankole apologized to Lola about his wife's behavior and said that it would not happen again.

Back at their hotel, Lola told Olu about her conversation in the kitchen with Patty, and how Patty insulted her with the fact that Janice is pregnant.

"I'm sure she did not mean it, Lola," Olu said, trying to console his wife. "But she met Janice first, and it is difficult for her. She is afraid that the same thing might happen with her."

In bed, Lola reached out for her husband. He turned away from her, feigning tiredness because of the long day. Lola felt hurt and vowed that Janice would not take him away from her again.

Olufemi was silently crying for both of his wives and the mess he created by his lies. He loved Janice and Lola, but he was thinking about Janice, the wife he wanted to be with tonight.

6

*J*anice walked into the doctor's office and took a seat. Her mother was concerned that the shock of the telephone call with Femi may have hastened the baby's birth. It took a lot for Edna to persuade Janice to see the doctor, but when she finally agreed, Edna was relieved. Janice had been having pains in her lower back and abdomen and could not sleep. The nurse took her blood pressure. It was elevated, and her feet were swollen as well. After the doctor examined her, she waited for his diagnosis.

"Janice, you will have to come into the hospital for some tests. It appears the baby may be breached. If the baby does not turn around on its own, then we may have to perform a caesarian on you. Now that you are in your last month, it's important that we do a scan to see if the baby can be delivered normally."

"Have you told my mother, Dr. Mason?"

"Yes, Janice."

"When do you want me to come in for the tests?"

"Tomorrow will be soon enough."

The ride home from the hospital was quiet. Janice went to sit in the yard, and her neighbor, Karen, came outside to join her.

"Jan, have you seen my boys?"

"No, Karen. Did you check the park?"

Not answering, Karen came and sat next to her instead.

"You look ready to have that baby, Janice. It won't be long now. Your mother told me the problems you are having."

Janice nodded her head. "Did she also tell you about Femi and what happened in Nigeria?"

"Yes, Jan, she told me."

Karen had experienced a bad marriage. Her husband deserted her and their three boys after 15 years together, and she was raising them alone. She worked with Edna as a social worker for a Human Services Agency.

"What are you going to do?"

"I don't know, Karen. I'm so confused."

"You still love him, don't you?"

Janice rubbed her round belly as the baby began to move. "Yes, I guess I do. How do you do it, Karen, raising those boys alone?"

"It's not easy, Jan. I mean I get lonely for a man sometimes, especially when the boys get overactive. Their father, Ted, remarried; his new wife can't have children. Now, all of a sudden, he wants to see the boys. I'm afraid he will try to take one of the boys to have a family."

"Oh, Karen, how horrible. I know he can never win. After all, he deserted you."

Janice felt like crying, and she thought Karen sensed it. She put her arms around Janice, giving her a hug.

"I know how you feel, Janice, but don't give up on him. He must care about you."

The tears began to fall down Janice's face.

"Karen, I love him and miss him so much. I really wanted him to be here when the baby comes. I don't want to do this alone."

Karen stood up in front of Janice, shaking her finger and shouting in anger.

"Then don't! Don't let her win, Janice! Fight! You gave up too easily. You have more to lose than she does. Certainly, she is Nigerian and from his culture, but that does not give him the right to hurt either of you. You ran away, Janice; she stayed. You let her win. You need to regroup. What better way to win a man back into your heart, then that he should be here when his baby is born!"

"But, Karen, when he called me, I was so angry. Lola was in London with him."

"Oh, stop whining, Janice. Of course, she was with him. You left, remember. Girl, if you don't want to raise this child without its father, then you need to fight for your man."

Just as Karen finished preaching to Janice, the sound of footsteps running towards them caught their attention. It was her boys, thinking she was shouting and complaining to Janice because they were not home.

"We're home, Mom. See, it's not ten o'clock yet."

Janice and Karen began to laugh at their innocence. It was a loud, joyous, happy sound.

The following day, Janice entered the hospital for the ultrasound scan. She lay on the table with her belly exposed and covered with gel. The nurse ran the scanner across her stomach, and the picture of the baby came into focus. She was lucky. The baby was not breached, but she was further along than expected.

"Janice, are you sure you counted correctly. Your baby appears large for its gestation period. Nevertheless, you should have a normal delivery." Then the doctor inquired about Femi.

"He is overseas, working," she lied, not wanting to share the pain with anyone else.

Janice wanted more than anything to have Femi at her side when she gave birth to their child. But, her mother was not so sympathetic. She held off her wedding plans, waiting for her daughter to give birth.

Janice wanted to call Femi, but instead, she called Dominique and told him what was happening. He wanted to fly to New Orleans, but she told him not to. It was just nice talking to someone who knew about her problems.

Next, she called Melinda. Bill answered the phone.

"Hi, Janice. How are you and the baby?"

"I'm due any day now."

"Really, Janice? Let me call Melinda to the phone."

Melinda came to the phone, and Janice told her what had happened with Femi and Lola in London.

"You mean he had the nerve to call you with her there?"

She also told her about the conversation she had with Karen.

"But, Janice, I don't agree with that. Jan, have some pride," she said.

"Mindy, I do have pride; that's why I lied in the first place. But now, I have to think about the baby. What kind of life will my child have without a father?"

Mindy was quiet after that remark, but then she retorted, "Don't you mean, what kind of life will you have without Femi?"

"So you do understand, Melinda. I still love Femi, even though he hurt me. A person does not stop loving overnight, you know."

"Janice, think about what you would be doing if you take him back. Remember, you will be taking Lola back as well."

"No, Mindy, I will fight to get him back. They were separated for two years and Femi loves me. I know he does. And soon, we will have more than ourselves to think about. We will have the baby."

The next few days in London went along fine. Lola and Olufemi spent their time shopping and dining out. They visited Aduke's brother, Tunde. Tunde introduced them to his fiancée, Terry. Terry had met Tunde's family. Everyone except Tunde's father blessed their marriage. He believed, like Emmanuel, Femi's father, that Nigerians should marry Nigerians. Terry was white, and even though Terry's family loved and accepted Tunde into their family, in Tunde's family's eyes, their marriage was out of the question. Olufemi and Tunde slipped off into the kitchen to have a private chat.

"Olu, how are things with Lola?"

"Okay, I guess."

"You don't sound too happy, Olu."

"I'm not. I miss Janice, Tunde. I feel I should be there with her when she has the baby."

"Then why are you here, Olu? Didn't you tell me she was due this month?"

"I'm worried about Lola and what she will do if I go to Janice."

"Come on, man. You can't have it all. You can't make everyone happy. You must be prepared to give one of them up, Olu. Stop being greedy. Which one means the most to you?"

Olufemi leaned on the kitchen wall, deep in thought. "Tunde, I do believe Janice means more to me. But I feel I owe Lola something."

"Whatever it is you feel you owe her can wait. You need to be there when the baby is born, or you can kiss Janice good-bye forever."

The men rejoined the women in the den. They discussed Tunde and Terry's wedding plans in detail. Tunde wanted Olufemi to be his best man. But Terry did not offer Lola the same. She knew she could not in this present situation.

"My sister is going to be matron of honor," she offered.

Both Tunde and Olufemi breathed a sigh of relief at her announcement.

Lola and Olufemi returned to their hotel and rested soundly that night.

Lola saw all the sights there were to see. The two of them attended several Nigerian parties, and she got to show off her latest lace and Italian shoes. She was sorry that she did not hit it off with Patty, but she could tell they would never be friends. Even after she gave her all the nice gifts for the baby, all Patty could say was thank you. Lola was happy that she got along with Terry though. Whatever feelings Terry had about her situation, she, at least, had the courtesy to keep them to herself.

Olufemi was very quiet and reserved for the rest of the trip. Lola attributed his moodiness to the business he was conducting. Their return flight from London went smoothly. Bisola and Taju met them at the airport. Taju was anxious to get the report on the shipment of chemicals. He had the driver drop Bisola and Lola off at the house in Surulere. Grace was waiting at the door for her mistress.

"Ekabo, Madame. Welcome home. We missed you, Madame."

"Thank you, Grace," Lola said as she walked into the parlor. Grace's husband carried the luggage inside.

"Lola did you and my brother enjoy the trip?"

"Yes, we did, Bisi. London is so different from Nigeria. I got to see the Buckingham Palace and the changing of the guards. I bought gifts for everyone. Grace, bring me the large black bag."

The maid brought the bag, carrying it as if it were made of gold. Lola opened it and pulled out a lot of packages. She gave Bisola one, as well as one for each of her children. Bisi thanked Lola. Grace stood nearby, waiting for her mistress to give her a gift too.

"Did you think I could ever forget you, Grace?" Lola pulled out a large box, wrapped in paper. Grace curtsied as she took the package.

"Thank you, Madame. I am very grateful."

Then she left the room, looking back at her mistress thinking, *my mistress does not seem too happy.*

"Did you meet Patty, Lola?" Bisi asked.

"Yes, I did. She is a nice girl, and her daughter, Shade, is a doll."

"Did you like Patty?"

"To be honest, she did not welcome me. Since she met Janice before me, she had already formed an opinion about me."

"I think you are just imagining it, Lola," Bisi replied. "I think that you are just sensitive to anyone who had any contact with Janice. I can understand your feelings."

"Thank you for being there for me."

The two women sat and compared stories about London, while Grace was in the kitchen preparing lunch for them. *It is just not fair that my mistress, Lola, is not happy,* Grace thought to herself. *I thought with the oyinbo gone, things would get better between my mistress and her husband. I must go to see my preacher. I will ask him to say strong prayer for Mr. Olu to forget the oyinbo; then Mistress Lola will be happy.*

Olufemi sat in Taju's office, briefing him on the business that he transacted in London for the company. When the meeting was over, Taju sat back in his chair and asked Olufemi about the trip with Lola.

"Olu, did Lola enjoy London?"

"Yes," Olu replied, distracted. "Taju, I cannot stop thinking about Janice. I called her from London."

"Oh?" he said surprised. "Lola does not know, does she?"

"No, Taju, she does not. I would never let her know anything about Janice. She is very sensitive on the subject. But, I found that I am still very much in love with my other wife. What can a man do in my situation?"

Taju got up and walked to the window, adjusting his *agbada*, gracefully throwing the robes over his shoulder, and freeing his arm. He said positively," What a man does in this situation is to choose, Olufemi. A lot of men would love to have your dilemma, to have two beautiful women in love with you. Come on, man; it boils down to which one do you love the most, and what do you stand to lose by any decision you may make? You must ask yourself these questions, Olufemi. Remember, I told you in the beginning, it takes a special man to maintain more than one wife successfully!"

Olufemi jumped up, agitated, and began pacing the floor. "But Taju, you do it. You still keep Abbe in the village."

"Yes, I do, Olu. But even I am a failure at polygamy. I cannot keep both Bisi and Abbe happy. Every time I come back from the village, I have to go through a confrontation with your sister."

"And what about Abbe?" Olu asked quietly.

Taju sighed, "I have just as much trouble with her. My father gave me no choice, Olu. I did not want to abandon Abbe, but I wanted children. You know how our culture is — a man without a son is not a man."

Olufemi nodded and thought about Janice and the child she was carrying. Even though he had been with Lola for three months, she had not become pregnant.

"Thank you, Taju. You have made my dilemma easier to bear."

"How is that, Olu?"

"Well, Lola has not conceived yet, and Janice is due to deliver our child any day now. I need to be there with her. I must make up to her and beg for forgiveness. I love her and my child."

7

*G*ace entered the hut in the back of the village. The old *babalawo* came into the dimly lit room. She knelt on the floor, continuing to greet the old man, and then sat on a mat near the door.

"Ekabo, Grace. How can I help you?"

Grace began wringing her hands as she told the story of Olufemi, Janice, and her mistress Lola. He listened patiently, holding his peacock feather fan in one hand, and a leather-bound stick with a tail of horsehair that he used to flick off the flies that buzzed around his face in the other. The old man practiced the local religion, which included the use of ritual prayers and black magic. Grace would often go to him when she needed advice and an herbal solution to a problem, such as the one she had with her former employer.

The old *babalawo* was of medium height with brown skin weathered from many years in the hot African sun. He wore a cotton wrapper draped in Roman toga style, leaving one arm bare.

Grace told the story from her own point of view, purposely leaving out a lot.

The old man just nodded his head saying *"O ye'mi* (I understand)."

When she finished her narration, he asked her what she wanted him to do to help her.

Grace said, "I want my mistress, Lola, to have a baby so that will take Mr. Olu's mind off the *oyinbo*. I also want you to make Mr. Olu love Mistress Lola again. The *oyinbo* used powerful magic to take him from my mistress. I want to stop her and make her never want to come to Nigeria again!" Grace was sweating profusely as she finished.

"I will do this thing you want, Grace, but it will be very expensive."

Grace smiled. "How much, *Baba?"*

The old man told her to bring 20,000 *Naira*.

Grace agreed. "*Baba,* first you must tell me if you can do this thing that I ask and tell me the future."

The old man reached behind him, not even uncrossing his thin legs, took a straw plate and placed on it an assortment of bones, stones, and feathers. He said some words in prayer over the items, and then closed his eyes, going into a trance. He began to shake and shiver; even Grace began to be afraid, but she kept reminding herself that this was for Lola.

Then to show Grace his power, he began to speak: "The other wife is named Janice. She is in America. She loves her husband and is very hurt. Soon she will give birth, and she wants him back. Lola will have a child too. I can see it in the oracle. I see her with a child." Then he stopped talking.

"*Baba*, what do you need me to do?" Grace asked excited.

"Bring me something from Omolola and Olufemi."

Grace wrote down the list of things that she was to bring.

"I will also need something belonging to the other wife."

"But, *Baba*, she is gone back to America. How will I get something from her?"

The old man rubbed his chin, thinking. "Then bring me her picture." After that, the old man gave Grace some herbs to put into Olu and Lola's food.

"What will this do, *Baba*?" she asked.

"This one for Omolola will make her become pregnant; the one for Olufemi will make him love Lola."

"Thank you, *Baba*." Then Grace gave him an envelope containing the money. She bowed as she left the room. It was almost time for her to prepare supper. She wanted to test the herbs on her employers. She knew she would not fail.

Grace's husband was suspicious of her, so he had followed her.

"*Now wayo!* See, this woman, she is going to make me lose my job. I must stop her." He said out loud, "Grace!" He shouted, "Stop, stop this thing!"

Grace turned to see her husband and became angry. "So, you de follow me. Do not interfere!"

Ayo grabbed her bag.

"Woman, what thing you go do now? You almost killed the lady at the other job. Why do you have to interfere with this one?" he asked angrily.

"You are wrong, old man. Do you think I have 20,000 *Naira* to give away? No, my husband; this came from Mrs. Shodeye and Omolola herself. I got the instructions from her mama to help her daughter."

Grace's husband sighed. "You mean her mama wants you to help her."

"Yes, you foolish man. Now let's go. I have much work to do."

Grace was lying to keep her husband from being angry. She knew he would not go against Mrs. Titiloye Shodeye, Omolola's mother.

*****

Lola and Grace had gone to Ilesha to see her mother. Titiloye welcomed the two of them. She was very happy to see her daughter. Lola brought her mother a lot of gifts from her trip.

"How is Olufemi, Daughter?"

Sadness came over Lola's face. "He is fine, Mama."

Titiloye could sense all was not well with her daughter. She could see she was not happy. "I can see you are not fine, Daughter. Tell me what is wrong."

Lola walked over to the window, looking out into the yard. Two chickens rushed across the grass as Segun's dogs barked and chased each other. When she turned to her mother, the tears were already flowing down her cheeks. She rushed to the comfort of her mother's arms.

"There, there child. Tell your mama what is the matter."

Lola told the story of how in London she did everything to make Olufemi happy. "Oh, Mama," she sobbed, "I am not pregnant with his child. I want to have his baby, and then maybe he will come back to me. Even though he does not discuss it, I know that he still thinks about his child and Janice."

Grace then spoke. *"Iya,* Lola, maybe I can help. I know this *Baba* in the village. He has helped many women become with child. He also makes men love their wives."

Lola was horrified. "No, Grace! If Olu does not love me now, no *ju-ju* can make him do so."

Titiloye smiled at her daughter's naiveté. She had tried to shield her from that part of their culture. Lola had no idea that her mother sought help with her marriage to Olufemi. *We had a lot of help*, Titiloye thought to herself. *I wanted my daughter to marry a rich man and never be unhappy, but it seems that nothing that I prayed for is happening.*

"Grace, Lola is right."

Grace and Titi exchanged knowing looks then changed the subject.

"Everything will be all right, Lola. I will speak to Emmanuel Adegoke. Maybe he can talk to Olufemi and make things better."

Lola went for a walk in the village. While she was gone, her mother and Grace planned what they would do.

"Grace," Titiloye said, "my daughter will have a child, and Olufemi will never see Janice again. Here is more *Naira.* Go to the old *Baba* and give him these instructions." And so Grace was happy that she had already carried out her friend's instructions to the letter.

She prepared a special meal for her two unsuspecting employers, singing to herself. *Pepper soup, fish pepper soup, and jollof rice, with moyin-moyin; the pepper soup must be spicy to mask the flavor of the herbs.*

When Olufemi arrived at the house in Surulere, it was filled with a tantalizing aroma. He walked into the kitchen and found Grace hard at work.

"E-ku-se', well done, Grace. It smells delicious. I can't wait for dinner."

He went upstairs to shower and change for dinner. Lola was in the garden. She came in when she heard the car in the driveway. Also smelling the aroma of the food, she asked Grace what was the occasion for such special dishes.

"Nothing special, Madame. I just felt like preparing fish."

"I am sure it will taste as good as it smells."

Olufemi and Omolola sat at the dining table, eating the special food prepared for them. While they ate, Grace said prayers that the *Babalawo* gave her to assure that his herbs had power. The husband and wife ate with relish, asking for seconds. After dinner, Olu asked Lola to accompany him to the Ikoyi Club. She agreed, since he had not asked her out since they had returned from London. He was still quiet, keeping to himself. Olufemi had been thinking about Janice and the baby and trying to find a way to get to her without hurting Lola. Every night, Lola tried to make love to him, but Olufemi kept putting her off.

The car drove through the night traffic. Lola looked at the people going home from their shops. It was 8 p.m. and Lagos was still hustling like it was 2 in the afternoon. Hawkers were carrying *suya, akara,* and *ati eke* on their heads, selling it to people on the street.

The couple entered the club. Olufemi held Lola's arm and led her to a table. They were joined by some of Olufemi's associates, who started talking about business and the economy. Lola was bored with all this talk and excused herself to go to the ladies' room. She wished that she had stayed home. When she came out, Olu was waiting for her at the door.

He whistled, flirting with her, bowing elegantly. "May I have this dance, Madame?"

She curtsied. "Yes, you may, sir."

Laughing and holding hands, they went to the dance floor. The music playing was American. Lola was not used to dancing to it. She preferred Fuji music or the sounds of Sunny Ade. It was a slow one, and soon she found herself caught in the rhythm. Olu held Lola, looking into her eyes. He felt like it was the first time he ever saw her and her copper skin, with large, almond-shaped eyes peering dreamily into his. She felt chills run up her spine as his hands massaged her waist. Olufemi stood tall over Lola, his hips moving closer as they swayed to the music. She could feel his arousal. His cheek was moist, and she smelled the scent of his cologne. She was reveling in him, enjoying the moment. It had been so long since he showed her any appreciation. He held her tight, and when the music ended, he looked into her eyes and said. *"Mo-fe-be'sun,* (I want to make love to you)."

"Patience, *o-lo-lu-fe'mi* (my lover). We will be home soon," she replied.

The couple returned to their table. One of Olufemi's friends who had been observing the couple on the floor had a smirk on his face; he was remembering when Olufemi danced like that with Janice. Olufemi and Lola decided to leave and bid everyone good night. They walked silently to the car and drove home, each in anticipation of what would happen when they reached their destination.

Lola and Olu held hands as they walked into the parlor. They did not know that Grace was watching them through the curtains of the servant's quarters. She was happy to see that the magic appeared to be working. Olu grabbed Lola by the shoulders and kissed her passionately. She stood there, as if in a trance, wondering what had come over her husband. They slowly climbed the stairs to the bedroom. Then Olufemi grabbed his wife and pulled her to him. Lola opened her mouth to protest, but was silenced by her husband's kisses on her neck. She moaned sensuously as he massaged her buttocks, pulling her skirt up over her panty line. Lola's head dipped back as his hands found her moistness, and she panted softly as he moved his fingers around, bringing her to the peak of arousal. He pulled her towards the bed, and she lay on top of him. Olu turned her over and began to remove her clothing. As each piece of clothing left her body, Olu's mouth kissed that part of her body, sending tiny shivers of pleasure up and down her spine. Lola knew that Olu had learned how to make love from some of his foreign acquaintances, but never before had he tried those moves on her.

He was like a hunter, and she was his prey. He was slowly wearing down her strength until the chase was over. Olu put her firm breast into his mouth, flicking the hard nipple with his tongue, and then filling his mouth with it. Lola squirmed under her husband, her hips rising to meet his as he entered her body gently. They wrestled with each other, rolling on the bed, struggling with insatiable passion.

She whispered into his ear, "I love you, darling. Let this be the night for our son, Olu."

He rode her like the wind, with Lola holding on, enjoying every moment. She wrapped her long, bronze legs around his body, assuring that he pushed deep inside the warm recesses of her body, lost and drowning in her until he could hold back no longer and let go. He never felt this way before. It was as if thunder was clapping inside his head, and lightning was the answer! Lola whimpered, crying in ecstasy as he held her, sighing with release. Olu lay there motionless, thinking, *Wow, that was the best sex I have ever had!*

Lola lay there beside him, holding her stomach and praying silently, "Dear God let Olu's son be inside me, please."

The couple did not venture from their room. They made love all night and into the morning.

Olu called Taju and told him he would not be in to work. The only work he wanted to do was on Lola. It was as if he could not get enough of her. He kissed her long, brown legs to her toes, licking each one with hunger. Lola squirmed under his kisses and moaned with pleasure. She pushed him back on the bed and climbed on him and took control of the moment. She was magnificent! He moaned and felt the pressure of her loins as he released himself into her. He was surprised at his own prowess. Lola had never aroused him like that before. He was certain that she drained every ounce of him.

Lola got out of the bed by mid-afternoon and stretched like a cat. She looked at her sleeping husband and smiled. *This is where I want you, Olu, in my bed forever.* Even she was not aware of the changes in herself. She had lost all her shyness to passionate abandon. She tried things with him that she had read in her romantic novels, trying to be more like the woman that left Olu. She went into the bathroom to shower and was surprised when Olu joined her there. They washed each other and made love again. It was as if each time Olu touched Lola, he could not resist her. He left the bathroom, clean, and satisfied.

Lola stayed behind, holding herself in awe and disbelief, for they never made love in the shower before. It was a new and thrilling experience for her. She loved Olu, and she loved their sex. If only she could have a child now, her life would be complete.

8

*G*race could not wait to report to the *Babalawo* the success of the medicine and prayer. She traveled to the village and entered the hut. The old man was pleased and asked for more payment to ensure that Lola became pregnant and Olufemi never thought about the *oyingbo* again.

"Okay, *Baba-lawo*, I will go to my mistress's mother and ask her for more *Naira* (money)." The old man nodded and gave Grace more herbs to feed her mistress to ensure her pregnancy. Grace backed out of the hut and rushed back to Titiloye's house to report the conversation with the *Baba* and to ask for more *Naira* to pay him.

As Grace entered Titiloye's house, Segun, Lola's brother who was visiting, greeted her in the traditional way.

"*Ekabo,* Grace, welcome," he said.

"Segun," Grace returned his greeting carefully. She was surprised to see him.

"My mother is still at the store. What brings you to the village?" Segun asked, looking at the older woman who appeared ill at ease.

"I came to see your mama. I hope she won't be long. I need to get back to Lagos."

"How are my sister and her husband?" he asked.

"Fine, Segun. They are both fine."

Titiloye walked into her home and was welcomed by her son.

"Welcome, Mother. You have a visitor."

Titiloye nodded, seeing that Grace was waiting in the parlor, and then she put her packages on the table.

Segun was standing cockily in the corner, waiting for the women to begin talking.

"Segun, my son," Titiloye spoke softly, "may I have a moment alone with Grace?"

He excused himself and left the room, but he stayed by the door to listen, unbeknownst to either woman. What Segun heard his mother and the servant Grace, discussing made him angry. He was surprised that his mother did not trust his sister enough to handle her own affairs. The fact that he warned Titiloye about Grace did not seem to matter at all. Segun was especially appalled at the fact that his mother had used the services of a *ju-ju* man in the past to secure Lola the favors of Olufemi in the first place. Everything became very clear ... everything, especially about Janice. *I hope they did not do anything to the oyingbo, and I hope that Lola knows nothing about this,* Segun thought to himself. He slowly crept away from the house before his mother saw him.

Segun drove to Lagos, hoping to beat Grace. He wanted a chance to discuss what he had heard with his sister. Sometimes he did not approve of the old ways. He felt people should be left alone when it came to affairs of the heart. He swore to have only one wife, and he prayed that witchcraft had nothing to do with Janice leaving, so that Lola had no involvement in this. He was not sure he could forgive Lola if he found out that she was involved. Segun was really upset and couldn't believe that his mother would resort to using *ju-ju* to get Lola a husband.

He reached Lagos in a few hours and went straight to the Adegoke home in Surulere. Lola answered the door.

"Segun, *ekabo, kini-kong (*welcome brother).*"

Segun returned the greeting to his sister as they hugged in the hallway.

"I was just preparing dinner. Grace is off today, and Olu is working late. Come and have dinner with me."

Segun went into the bathroom and washed for dinner. He sat down at the table to eat the plantain and bean stew that his sister prepared. After dinner, the two retired to the parlor with their soft drinks and began to talk about things that occurred since they last saw each other.

"How are things between you and your husband, Lola, since the *oyingbo* is gone?"

Lola shifted uncomfortably. "Well, brother, let me be honest with you. Things have not been good. Even our trip to London did not go as I hoped, but now we are doing fine."

Lola smiled, hugging herself with satisfaction. Segun looked at his sister. He saw nothing unusual — no guilt in her eyes, only love for her husband. He was now convinced that Grace and his mother were the only ones behind any deceit.

"Lola, I saw Grace with Mama this morning in Ilesha. They were discussing you and your husband. By any chance, are you pregnant yet?"

Lola blushed. "No, brother, not yet. But I am sure that it will not be long before I give Olu a child."

Segun did not want to alarm his sister since she was so happy. He decided to keep his information to himself and just watch things for the moment. If he sensed anything that would hurt Lola, then he would expose them.

Over the next few days, Olufemi discovered a new love for his wife, Lola. Every evening he brought her a gift on his way home from work. Segun was staying at their house while he was in Lagos. He was watching the two of them for any signs of trouble.

Grace prepared a special dish every night. Olufemi was happy and content and his life and marriage with Lola was settled and calm. No thoughts of Janice even came into his mind.

Olufemi's mother and father were in town staying with Bisola and Taju, so Bisi invited Olufemi and Lola for dinner. Lola told her that Segun was visiting and wondered if she could bring him along. Bisi said yes and told her that Aduke was visiting from America on holiday from school, and Bisola had invited her over for dinner, so Segun would be a welcome addition.

Lola checked her appearance in the bedroom mirror as Olufemi finished putting on his cap. The couple looked splendid, wearing a matching ensemble of gold and green guinea brocade with beautiful embroidery in the front. Lola wore matching shoes and a handbag she brought from London. Segun had also taken particular care about his attire tonight. He was dashing.

"Segun, you look fine, my brother. I am pleased you decided to join us."

The trio got into the car and drove through the Lagos traffic to Ikoyi. The night air was very humid, and they were glad for the air-conditioned car.

Olufemi drove into the gates of the estate and parked under a row of palm trees. Taju and Bisola's house was one of the most modern homes on the oceanfront. The white marble and stonewalls gleamed under the security lights, as the guard closed the gate behind the car.

They walked to the door and rang the bell. Joseph, the steward, answered the door. He led the trio into the parlor. After exchanging traditional greetings, they were served drinks. Lola sat on the leather sofa next to Olufemi; Aduke, wearing the latest Venice lace, was standing in a corner of the room having light conversation with Bisola. When she saw Segun enter the parlor with Lola and Olufemi, her curiosity was immediately piqued.

"Bisi, is that Lola's brother, Segun?"

"Yes, Aduke, it is, he looks different now, all grown up, huh?"

"Yes," Aduke said amazed. "I didn't know he had become so good-looking."

Bisola smiled. "Are you interested, Aduke?"

Aduke just laughed.

When Segun heard the joyous sound, he turned towards it. That's when he saw her, standing in the corner with Bisola.

"Aduke Bakare," Segun said in awe of her and silently to himself. Lola looked over at Aduke.

"Yes, Segun, that is Aduke. You remember her after all these years?" she asked, smiling at her brother.

"I could never forget."

"Well, let's go over and reacquaint you two," Lola said, grabbing her now shy brother's arm. "She *is* single."

When Lola and Segun reached Bisi and Aduke, Aduke and Segun just stood staring at one another. Lola broke the silence.

"Aduke, you remember my brother, Segun?"

"I sure do," Aduke said rather seductively, then snapped out of it. "How have you been?"

Segun grabbed her hand and kissed it, his dark, sensuous eyes never leaving hers. "Much better now that I will have the privilege of being in your company this evening."

Aduke blushed. Bisi and Lola looked at each other and started giggling.

Before any more could be said, Joseph called the family to dinner. Segun was seated intentionally next to Aduke. Emmanuel said the blessing, and the family started eating.

He and his wife were pleased to see all the children together, but Abimbola could not help missing Janice and the grandchild she was carrying. Earlier, she asked Aduke if she had seen Janice. Aduke told her that she had seen her recently. Janice was living with her mother in New Orleans, and they came to Chicago for a visit. She was due to have the baby in a few weeks. Sadness came across Abimbola's eyes as she watched her son and Lola together. She was happy that they appeared to be settling into their marriage; still, something was not right.

Aduke was talking to Segun through each mouthful of food.

"I'm an M.B.A. student at the University of Chicago. I'm home on holiday. What about you, Segun? What do you do?"

Segun almost choked on his food. *What should he do*? He was ashamed to tell her.

Lola saw his discomfort and rushed to his aid. "Aduke, my brother helps our mother run the store in Ilesha."

Olufemi, hearing the exchange, blurted out, "He drives a taxi."

Segun darted a hateful look at his brother-in-law, who sat back smiling smugly.

Aduke saw Segun's embarrassment at Olufemi's outburst. She was disappointed that the handsome man only drove a taxi; nonetheless, she was still attracted to him.

She smiled. "Segun, since I am going to be here for a few weeks, I need someone to take me around. Can you do that?"

Segun was grateful for her intervention and understanding. He knew his brother-in-law would stop at nothing to humiliate him. Their relationship had been strained ever since Olufemi's American wife, Janice, left Nigeria.

"Certainly, Aduke. I will be at your beck and call," he responded warmly.

After dinner, Taju called Olufemi into the den.

"Olufemi, I received a call from Houston today. They are ready to sell us the chemicals. I need you to travel to the United States to purchase them as soon as possible."

"Okay, Taju. I'll tell Lola."

When he did not mention Janice, Taju asked, "Have you heard from Janice, Olu?"

Olufemi's eyes became clouded. "Janice? Uh, who?"

Taju looked at Olufemi, surprised at his attitude.

"Janice, Olu ... remember — your other wife!"

Olufemi shook his head, as if to clear the fogginess from his brain.

"Oh, yes, Janice. Of course, I remember," he replied distracted. "No, I have not heard anything new."

Taju was concerned that something was going on at the Adegoke house that was not right. After the family left, he confided his fears to Bisi about his conversation with Olufemi and how he appeared to have forgotten about Janice.

"It was so strange, Bisi. When I mentioned her name, he acted like he had amnesia."

"That is unusual, Taju. Do you think that he has gotten over her already?"

"No, I don't. Not the way he loved her. No, dear. No man could forget a woman like Janice. Especially with her carrying his child. I fear that there is something else going on."

"Something like *ju-ju?*" Bisola asked.

"I'm not sure. But something."

On the way home, Segun could not stop talking about Aduke.

"She is so pretty. I think she likes me."

Olufemi laughed. "Segun, Aduke is an educated woman. She already has a B.S. degree. What could she possible want with a taxi driver?"

Segun felt his anger rise. Lola saw this and intervened between the two men.

"I think she likes you too, Segun. But don't move too fast. She will be leaving in a few weeks."

For the first time in his 27 years, Segun felt ashamed of his life. He would inherit his father's chieftaincy title in the village when his uncle died, but he had never thought about going to college, preferring to be the village lover and have all the ladies run after him. But Aduke was different. She was the first woman he knew that he would have to pursue.

*****

Olufemi arrived at his office late. He had spent a restless night tossing and turning in the bed. While Lola undressed for bed, he stayed downstairs in the parlor, sipping whiskey. As he stirred the ice in the glass with his finger, he thought about his conversation with Taju regarding Janice. Lola was already asleep by the time he went to bed. His dreams confused him. They were dreams of Janice calling to him with her arms outstretched, handing him a baby. He awoke in a sweat, shaking his head thinking, *Janice! Janice! Janice!* He knew it would not be easy going to America with Lola at his side.

He unlocked his desk and took out the photo album inside. The wedding and honeymoon pictures opened his eyes. There was his beautiful Janice. They were together, standing at the altar, kissing. He chuckled at the photo of Janice at Buckingham Palace's changing of the guard. She was standing next to one of the guards, trying to make him laugh. The next one had Janice posed seductively on the bed in a black negligee in a hotel in Paris. His memory of her and the good times they shared came tumbling down. The tears of love and regret fell silently, as he cursed his stupidity. *How could I have ever let you go!* He wiped his face roughly with his handkerchief and rushed across the hall to Taju's office. Taju, surprised at his abrupt entrance said,

"Olu, are you all right?"

"Yes!" he shouted. "Yes! When can I leave for America?"

"Did you tell Lola, yet?"

"No, I will tell her today. I have to be there, Taju. I want to be there for Janice and the birth of our child."

"Okay, Olu, I will make all the arrangements."

Taju called his wife, Bisola, after Olufemi left his office, and told her that he thought Olufemi would be all right. He went on to explain that Olufemi would be traveling to America and wanted to see Janice.

"Bisi," Taju said, "Olu said, and I quote, 'I want to be there for the birth of my child.' "

Olufemi made reservations at the local Chinese restaurant for dinner that evening. He picked Omolola up at work. Lola wondered what the special occasion was. After they finished dessert, Olufemi told Lola his plans to travel to Houston.

"When do we leave, darling?"

Olu cleared his throat before speaking. "Lola, I must make this trip alone. I cannot take you."

"Iro! (No!)," she shouted, oblivious to their surroundings. "No! I must come with you!"

She was furious, but since they were in a public place, she held back some of her anger and said through her teeth, "Olu, we will discuss this at home!"

"No further discussion is necessary, Lola. My decision is final."

Lola jumped out of her seat and ran to the car, her eyes blazing with fury. Olufemi followed, and the driver, Ayo, surprised that they left the restaurant in a hurry, took them home. They sat silently in the car until they reached their house.

Once inside the privacy of their parlor, Lola jumped right in on Olufemi.

"What kind of foolishness is this, Olu? Why can't I go with you?"

"Lola, this is a business trip."

"London was a business trip, too, but I went with you. You are going to see her, aren't you?"

Deciding not to hold anything back, Olufemi told her the truth. "Yes, Lola. I am."

Lola let out a scream that shook the windows of the house. *"Ero! O-ti-O!* You cannot go without me, Olu! I will not let you go!" The tears of frustration were running down her cheeks as she clenched her fist.

Olufemi stood rigid. Lola rushed at him, her nails bared, ready to claw at his face. He grabbed her hands, not allowing her to scratch him.

"Stop it, Lola! This is madness! You cannot go with me, and that is my final answer!"

Her eyes blazed with fury as she pulled her hands free. "You planned this all the time, Olu! What about the love you professed to have for me?" she said sobbing. "It must have been all lies! You never stopped loving her, did you!?"

"Lola," he said softly, "no, I never said I did."

He turned and walked up the staircase to the guestroom, leaving Lola alone with her fury.

She grabbed a pillow from the sofa and screamed into it. She was still sobbing when Grace came into the room.

"Madame, what thing be wrong?"

"Oh, Grace," she sobbed. "My husband is going to America and is not taking me."

"No!" Grace said angrily. "This cannot be happening. He promised this would not happen. He promised he would forget the *oyingbo.*"

Lola looked at Grace, questioning. "Who promised what Grace?" She wiped her eyes and asked again. "Grace, what are you saying?"

Segun, returning from a date with Aduke, walked happily into the parlor. Overhearing some of their conversation, he became angry and jumped in.

"I'll tell you what, Lola." Segun walked to the center of the room, looking at his sister. "Grace and Mama have been using *ju-ju* to make Olu forget Janice, and to make you have a baby."

Lola's eyes widened with horror. "You mean Olu does not really love me? That this was caused by witchcraft? I don't believe it, Segun! Please, tell me it's not true!"

"Ask her, Lola," he said, pointing an accusing finger at Grace. "Ask her why she was in the village with the old *Baba*. Ask her where she got the money to pay him. Go ahead; ask her."

Grace was trembling with fear as Lola turned her tearstained face towards her.

"Grace, is it true? Did you and Mama do this?"

Grace turned her face and looked helplessly at Segun. "Yes, Madame," she whispered, adding, "but we only tried to help you, Lola."

Lola covered her face with her hands as a fresh flow of tears streamed down her cheeks.

"Help me!?" she cried. "Yes, you helped me all right!" she said with sarcasm. "Look at things now. Olu is going to America to see Janice. He refuses to take me with him. All of you certainly did help me!"

She ran up the stairs sobbing.

Segun looked at Grace. He never trusted her. "You see, woman, what you did was wrong. You and my mother should stop meddling in Lola's life. You only made her situation worse. I know about how you and my mother schemed to get her married in the first place."

Grace was shocked to hear this and quickly turned away.

Segun went upstairs and knocked softly on Lola's door. "Sister *mi* (my sister), may I come in?"

Lola continued sobbing uncontrollably. Segun entered her room and put his arm around her.

"Lola, you must be brave. I will help you. Where is Olufemi?"

"He is in the guestroom," she said, weeping. "He won't talk to me, Segun. What am I to do? They have ruined things for me with their meddling."

Segun held his little sister and said, "Lola, I will help you get to America. Aduke is leaving next week. She has invited me to come and visit her. I feel that our relationship is getting serious. I believe it was fate that brought us together again. I love her and want her to be my wife. But I have nothing to offer her. We have been discussing my going to school and getting a degree. I want to study Pharmacy. She said she could help me get a scholarship to attend the university."

Lola dried her tears. "Oh, Segun, that is wonderful. If you can help me I would be grateful. We can travel together, and I can try to be with Olu. Thank you, my brother. You have saved me."

Grace entered the servants' quarters, her shoulders slumped, a sad look on her face. Her husband was waiting for her at the door. He had been listening at the window.

Pointing an accusing finger at his wife, he said angrily, "Now, you see, woman! See what you have done! You messed up her life! I told you not to do this thing! I don't want to lose my job here because you always mess in other peoples' business!"

Grace got ready to retort, but before she could, her husband, Ayo, pulled out a broom to beat his wife for her meddling.

"Ye! Ye!" she cried as he beat her.

"Promise me you will never go to the old *Baba* again."

When she refused, he whacked her again soundly on her buttocks.

"Promise me, Grace!"

She promised never to go there again, and her husband stopped beating her. She sat in a corner by the window, vowing vengeance

against Segun and her husband.

9

*O*lufemi's plane landed at Houston Intercontinental Airport, where representatives of the petroleum company met him. After a series of meetings, they finalized the shipment of chemicals to Nigeria. Olufemi was staying at a hotel near the airport. He sat there thinking about his argument with Lola. After he told her he was leaving, she went to his family to enlist their help to convince him to take her to America, for in Nigeria, the wife needs her husband's permission to leave the country. Olufemi's father summoned him to Ekiti to discuss his travel arrangements. Olu told them how he felt and what his mission was in traveling to America. He parents agreed with him.

"Son, you should be there for the birth of your child. Lola will have to bear it. You are still married to Janice," his mother said, secretly happy that he decided to go and see Janice.

"I know mother, but Lola is making my life hell now.""She will get over it," his father replied. "She had no right to interfere in the relationship between you and Janice. You need to reconcile with Janice so that you can claim your child."

Olu wished Lola could see it from his point of view. This was his first child and he would not miss its birth for anyone. But Lola would not give up trying to change Olu's mind.

Lola's mother, Titiloye, came to Lagos when Grace told her what had happened. Lola was furious at her and would not see her. Segun begged his sister to see her, telling Lola how hurt their mother was. Eventually, Lola backed down and saw her.

Titiloye also tried to talk to Olufemi, but she could see his mind was set. Though she understood their culture and felt it was better that Lola backed down and let him go, she reminded her son-in-law sternly, "Just don't forget Lola, Olufemi. And do not stay away for too long."

After his business in Houston was finished, Olufemi caught a late flight to New Orleans. While on the plane, he sat deep in thought. *What will I say to Janice? Will she forgive me?* He took a taxi to his mother-in-law's house on the East Bank after his plane landed at the airport.

As he walked towards the door, he was unaware that he was being watched. Karen was looking at the strange man from her window. Suddenly she recognized him from the wedding pictures that Janice had shown her and called from her window, "No one is home yet. Edna went to the store."

Olufemi turned, startled at Karen's voice.

"Hello, is Janice at home?"

"Who is asking?" she said.

"My name is Olufemi Adegoke. I am her husband."

Once Karen confirmed his identity, she invited him to have a cup of coffee at her house while he waited for Edna. She told him Janice was in the hospital.

"Why? What's wrong? I hope nothing is wrong with the baby!"

Just as Karen started explaining why Janice was in the hospital, Edna drove up in her car, so they walked outside to meet her.

"Hello, Mother," Femi greeted her with the deepest respect.

Edna, looking as if she had seen a ghost replied, "Femi! When did you arrive?"

She almost dropped her groceries, but he caught the bag and carried it inside for her. Karen followed them into the living room and sat down on the sofa; however, Edna remained standing, trying to keep her anger from coming to the surface over the way Olufemi treated her daughter.

"Femi, I trusted you with Janice. You promised to take care of her. Instead you did not tell her you were married. Now you come here to see her. Why?"

"Mother, please forgive me. There can be no excuse for what I did to Janice or to you. I just want to see her. I love her so much."

"You are right, Femi, there is no excuse for what you did to Janice. She still loves you. I don't understand why, but she is an adult and can do as she wishes."

Edna finally walked over to the sofa, sat down, and started fidgeting with her hands.

"Where is she, Mother?" Femi asked, trying to confirm what Karen had already told him.

Edna looked at Femi and sighed. "She is in the hospital, waiting to have the baby. She had some complications. I just hope your being here doesn't upset her more, Femi. She has been through enough."

She got back off the sofa and headed in the direction of the door. As much as she thought that Femi seeing Janice was not a good idea, she knew that there was nothing she could do to stop him.

The drive to the hospital was slow because of rush hour traffic that was lined up on the bridge to New Orleans. Arriving at the hospital, Femi talked to the receptionist, asking for Janice's room. He took the elevator to the maternity wing and walked into her room without knocking.

The nurse was taking Janice's blood pressure when Femi entered the room.

"Hello, Janice."

Janice took a deep breath, blinking with disbelief, as the nurse, puzzled by her rising blood pressure, turned to see her staring at a man.

"Femi? ... Femi! When did you get here?"

The nurse saw that he was the reason for the change in her patient's pressure so she smiled at the couple and left the room, closing the door.

Femi pulled up a chair next to the bed. He smiled blissfully at her as his eyes filled with tears. Then he embraced his wife.

Janice kept repeating, "Femi, Femi," over and over again, sobbing. She was filled with so much happiness at his unexpected arrival. Their tears mingled as the reunited couple exchanged a long, sweet kiss.

Femi rubbed his hands across her large abdomen.

"Janice," he said proudly, "the baby is so big now. You still look beautiful. I missed you so much. I am so sorry about all the pain I caused you."

"Femi, I am so happy to see you," Janice said, taking his hands to her lips and kissing them softly. "Let's put the past where it belongs — behind us. Let's move forward, my love, and start over again. Soon our child will be born and will need both its mother and father."

He laid his head on her abdomen and kissed her navel, causing her to quiver. It brought back memories of their lovemaking. Suddenly, Janice felt a sharp pain in her back. The contraction radiated around to the front of her body, causing her to moan with pain.

"What's wrong, Janice?" Femi asked concerned as another contraction went through her body.

"Femi, I think I'm having the baby now," she cried in agony, wincing with pain.

He reached for the call button on the side of the bed as Janice held on to the rails for support as the contractions increased. She shouted and lay back exhausted after each wave of pain.

The nurse came in and examined her. She then rushed to call the doctor. The room became hectic with people moving her to the delivery room.

Femi used the telephone in the room and called Edna. She said she would be there as soon as she could.

In the delivery room, they prepped Janice for her baby's birth, and then the doctor asked who Femi was. Janice proudly told Dr. Mason, "He's my husband."

They gave Femi a cap and gown and led him into the room with her. She was in great discomfort, becoming incoherent with each contraction. After a few hours, Janice was dilated enough to deliver the child. Dr. Mason returned to the delivery room.

Femi stood by Janice, holding her hand and encouraging her to push and breathe after each contraction. Before long, Edna came into the room and joined them. She saw Femi standing next to Janice, holding her hand, and her face filled with anger. But upon seeing their happiness, she decided to let her anger go and get ready to welcome her grandchild into the world.

"Push. Push! Okay, relax," Dr, Mason ordered.

"Janice, I can see the head! Now, on the next contraction, I want you to push very hard."

Femi sponged her face with cool water and held her hand, ready to encourage her to push their child out into the world.

The contraction came suddenly, and Janice had the urge to push. She grits her teeth and pushed with all her might, screaming as her child was born. Femi and Edna cried with joy as the doctor passed the crying baby to the nurse.

"It's a boy! You have a son, Janice."

Femi and Janice looked with love and amazement as the nurse placed the screaming infant on Janice's abdomen. Tears of joy flowed freely as they watched their gift of love cry out in his new environment. Edna cried with them.

"Thank God it went all right. You are parents now. You have someone else to worry about other than yourselves," Edna said.

But Janice and Femi were too lost in each other's pride and love to hear her. They were now parents.

Edna could not wait to call her sister Dotty, her niece Melinda, and her love James. She wanted to tell them the news of the baby's birth and Femi's sudden return to America. She left the two lovebirds and went to the lounge to make the calls.

"And you won't guess who is here, Sis."

"Who Edna? Don't keep me in suspense," her sister begged.

"Femi! He just turned up out of the blue. That baby boy seemed to be waiting for his daddy to come. It's almost a miracle. One more day and he would have missed the birth of his child."

After talking to her sister, she called Melinda to tell her the good news.

"How is Jan, Aunt Edna? How does she feel about Femi being here?"

"She seems to have forgiven him for all the lies. She loves him, Mindy, and now that the baby is born, the bond that is between them is strong again."

"Oh, I am so happy for her. I prayed that everything would work out for Jan. And now that it has, I also have some good news. Tell Janice that I am expecting too. Her baby won't be alone. He will have a cousin to play with real soon."

"How wonderful, Mindy. My sister will be ecstatic to be a grandmother. Have you told her yet?"

"No, Aunty, but I plan to tell her today. I wanted Jan to have her baby before I told anyone about mine."

Femi wanted to stay at the hospital all night, but the nurses assured him they would take good care of his wife and child. Edna had already gone home, and Janice was in a deep sleep. He reluctantly returned to the hotel and lay exhausted on his bed, thinking about the miracle he had witnessed today. *A son! A son!* he thought proudly. *Janice, I was so wrong to put my selfish needs in front of our son. Nothing and no one will ever take precedence over him again. He is a precious gift from God, and I will strive to be the best father imaginable.* He reached for the telephone to call his parents in Nigeria.

"Ekasan, Mama, this is Olufemi."

"Ah, ah, Olufemi, *se'dada ni?* (How are you) my son? Are you in Houston?"

"No, Mama, I am in New Orleans. I called to tell you that I have a son."

"Ye! Ye!" his mother shouted with joy. "Emmanuel, come quickly! A son! Congratulations, Olufemi and Janice! How is she?"

"She is well, Mama. She has forgiven me."

His father took the line, shouting, "I am proud of you, my son! I am happy and proud. Please give Janice my congratulations and greetings."

"Will you call Bisi and Taju and tell them the good news for me, Father?"

"Of course, Olufemi. You stay there and take care of your family, son. *Odabo.*"

Emmanuel was smiling as he replaced the receiver. Abimbola hugged herself, repeating, "A son, a son. Olufemi has a son."

They called Bisola and Taju. Bisi was ecstatically happy. She smiled at her husband, saying, "See, sometimes there is a happy ending."

"That remains to be seen, Bisi. Lola *nko?*"

"What about Lola, Taju? My brother made his choice and I believe that he is where he truly wants to be. Lola will just have to accept the fact that Janice and my brother have a baby. You know our culture. The one who has the child, especially a son, is put on a pedestal. I wonder what they will name him. I'm sure Father has a name already picked out."

They both nodded in agreement.

*****

Lola inspected the ticket that Segun brought to her. Her plans to follow her husband were now complete. All she needed to know was when they would leave.

"Segun, when do we leave for America?"

"Sister, be patient. I have not been approved for my visa yet. We will go as soon as they stamp my passport."

"Good, I want to get there before Janice has her baby."

The doorbell rang and Segun answered it. Kemi entered the parlor. She came over to tell Lola when she and Jide would be leaving for Chicago. After the traditional greetings, they sat down and talked about their plans to leave Nigeria for America.

"When are you and Jide leaving, Kemi?"

"Our flight is scheduled to leave in one week. We hope to see you while you are there visiting, Lola."

"Segun, will you be staying with Aduke?" Kemi asked.

"Yes, and so will Lola, at least until she can join Olu."

"Oh, does he know that you are coming with Segun, Lola?"

Lola hesitated to answer. She did not want Kemi to interfere with her decision to follow Olufemi to America, especially when she knew that he had forbidden her to travel.

"Yes, Kemi. He asked me to come before Janice has her baby," she lied.

"Where is Grace, Lola? I was surprised that she did not answer the door."

Segun answered for Lola. "That woman is back in the village where she belongs. She caused a lot of trouble between Lola and Olufemi."

Lola shifted uneasily in her chair. She, too, was glad that Grace was no longer in her house. If only she had known what she had been up to.

"Grace is gone and good riddance," she said with composure.

Then the three friends continued to talk about their plans to travel to America.

10

*J*anice sat up in her bed as the nurse brought the baby into the room to be fed. Holding the precious bundle carefully, she pulled back the cover to check that he had all his fingers and toes. *Perfect. He is so perfect,* she thought to herself. *He looks like both of us. Open your eyes, little one. Let me see them. What will we call you? Olufemi Jr.?* She smiled a mother's smile of contentment as she placed her breast to her little baby's mouth for feeding.

As he suckled, Olufemi came into the room.

He stood holding a teddy bear, balloons, and flowers, and silently watched Janice feed and talk to their son.

She noticed Femi standing at the door and motioned for him to join her on the bed.

"Come and say good morning to your son, Femi."

Femi walked over to the bed and sat next to Janice. *"Ekabo, ekabo, my pikin* (Welcome, my child)."

He watched his son suckling hungrily at his mother's breast. Then he looked at Janice's face with tenderness and love.

"Janice, he is beautiful, just like his mother. God, how I long to be the one at your breast."

"Oh, Femi, don't be silly," she smiled. "I missed you too."

"Janice, let this moment be our beginning, the beginning of our life together. Our family is all that is important to me. I want us to be together forever," Femi said with deep emotion in his voice. A lonely tear fell down his cheek as he held the baby's hand. He moved closer to Janice, and their lips touched softly. Then he pulled away gently, afraid that he would mash the baby.

"Don't worry, Femi. He's okay. You won't squeeze him. Go and put on a gown and hold your son." Femi rushed to the dresser and put on a paper gown.

"Gently, Femi. Now place your hand under his head. Remember, support his head."

"Don't worry, Janice. I have held Ajoke and T.J. when Bisola had them. I'm a pro at handling babies."

The scene that Edna saw when she entered the room followed by Karen was so loving. The two women looked at each other and walked silently out of the room to let the new family have some more time together.

"Edna, looks like they will be getting back together again."

"Yes, Karen. But Femi still has a lot of explaining to do. Janice went through too much for me to keep silent about his situation with his other wife."

"You may be right, Edna," Karen agreed, "but it seems to me that Janice has her husband back. I doubt that Femi will give up his child for Lola."

"I hope you are right, Karen. I hope so."

*****

Joseph answered the door at the Balogun residence and showed Lola into the parlor to wait for Bisola. Bisi was at the pool with her children, enjoying an afternoon swim. She told Joseph to send Lola outside to her.

"Ekabo, Lola. Long time no see. What have you been up to since my brother left for America?"

Lola was standing at the poolside. She removed her slippers and sat down, letting her feet play in the cool water. Bisola joined her, and then the children swam over to the women.

"Ekasan, Aunty-*mi!"* T.J. and Ajoke cried in unison. Lola shouted a greeting as they raced to the other side of the pool.

Bisola was surprised at Lola's visit. She had not seen her for a few weeks, not since her brother had forbade her to travel with him and Lola had tried to enlist her help and that of her husband, Taju, to get Olufemi to change his mind. Taju told Bisi not to get involved, that the situation was too delicate. They both knew he was going to America to reconcile with Janice.

"Have you heard from my brother, Lola?"

"No, not since he left. You know he was angry with me, Bisi. I wish he could understand my feelings."

"Then you don't know yet?" Bisola asked sadly.

"Know what, Bisi? Did something happen to Olu?"

Lola stood up and reached for a towel to dry her feet while Bisola tried to think of a way to tell her sister-in-law about the baby. Bisola walked over to her, and took her hand.

"Lola, Janice has had her baby! It's a boy! He was born yesterday."

Lola looked at Bisola and gripped her hand for support. Her mouth and eyes opened wide in shock. Bisola led her to a lounge chair. Lola just sat there lifeless, unable to speak. Suddenly, she jumped up and screamed.

"O-ti-o, Bisi, *iro ni!* I don't believe you! She was not due yet! Not until ... Oh, God, what will I do now? I wanted to get there before she had the baby."

"Lola, Omolola. What do you mean, 'get there'? Are you planning to go America?"

Lola began pacing in front of the pool, her hands wringing the towel roughly. She realized that she let it slip that she was going to travel to America without her husband's permission.

"Yes, I am," she finally said boldly. "I am traveling with Segun. He is leaving this Friday. Now it is too late."

"Lola, you cannot disobey your husband. You can't be serious. You know you risk his anger if you show up now. Accept what has happened and wait for him to return to Nigeria."

"No, Bisi. I cannot wait. What for? For him to tell me that he no longer wants me? I have no child." Lola began to cry hysterically. "I have nothing to hold him with anymore. Now he has a son. Oh, Bisi, what am I to do? I have lost Olufemi!"

Bisola took Lola into the house and poured her a stiff drink to calm her down. Lola gulped the drink through her tears. Then she turned and looked helplessly at Bisola, and a fresh flow of tears began to fall.

"You have not lost my brother. He is still married to you. You have to be strong and hold on, Sister. You are not the first woman to be in this position. Look at Abbe."

"Yes, look at her! What an example to use, Bisi! She is living in the village, barren, unable to have any children. If she is lucky, she gets to see Taju once a month. Is that what you want me to look forward to, Bisi?"

Bisola knew that she had said too much. She now regretted telling Lola about the baby. She tried to calm her down, but to no avail.

"Bisi, I bid you good-bye. I will see you when I return from America with my husband."

Lola stormed out of the house and slammed the door. Taju was just getting out of his car when he saw her speeding out of the gate. He walked inside the cool house and saw his wife in a chair, sobbing.

"Bisi, what is it? Wasn't that Lola I saw speeding out of the driveway? She didn't even stop to say hello. What happened to upset you?"

Bisi related the story to Taju, leaving out the part about her telling Lola about Janice having the baby. Taju was furious. He knew the reason that Olufemi did not want Lola to come with him was so he could reconcile with Janice.

"When are Lola and her brother leaving?"

Bisola wiped her face with her wrapper and gulped her drink. "She said they were leaving Friday."

"That does not give me much time to warn Olu. I will call him tonight. Did Lola tell you where she will be staying?"

"Yes, Taju. They will be in Chicago with Aduke. What are you going to do, Taju?"

"I am going to warn your brother that Lola is coming to America and advise him to stay in New Orleans."

"That's a good idea. I tried to convince Lola to stay, but her mind was made up. Now look at all the *wahalla* (trouble) she is going to cause."

"That's okay. Olu will be ready for anything that she can dish out. I'm hungry. What's for dinner?"

Bisola called Joseph to set the table for dinner and went outside to the pool to get the children. She thanked God for not letting Taju find out that she was the one who told Lola that Janice had already had the baby. She did not want to face her husband's anger if he knew she told Lola. They ate a quiet dinner and went to the club afterwards.

*****

Lola met Segun at home. He had moved into the house with her when Olufemi left for America because Lola did not want to be in the large house alone. She had asked her mother to take some time off from the store and come to visit, but Titiloye had refused and Segun came instead. Lola was sobbing bitterly.

"Segun, Janice has given birth to a son. I am ruined! All my chances with Olu are finished!" She cried harder, wringing her handkerchief in her slender hands.

"No, sister, they are not finished. You can still win. I am certain that Olu loves you."

"If he loves me so much, then why have I had no word from him? Why didn't he tell me about the baby? Oh, Segun, he has a son ... a son. I can never compete now."

Lola covered her face with her hands, while Segun held her, offering what comfort he could.

"Don't worry, sister-*mi*. We will be in America soon. Then you can see your husband has not left you. Go upstairs and begin to pack. I know you will be taking a lot of things with you."

Lola dried her eyes, red from all the tears. "Did you have dinner yet?"

"No, because I am taking you out tonight. So don't pack everything. You will need a nice dress to wear," he said smiling.

*****

Kemi served Jide his dinner. While eating, they discussed their plans to leave Nigeria. She told her husband about Lola traveling with Segun.

"Didn't my friend ask Lola to stay here?"

"Yes, he did, but she is adamant about going. I don't think that it is a good idea for Lola to disobey her husband. I guess that it's hard for her to be here while he's with Janice. She has had so much unhappiness."

"It looks like she is going to have much more. I love Lola too, Kemi, but I can't understand her going where she is not wanted."

"Never mind, my husband. Let's start packing tonight. I have already found a buyer for my shop. A friend of my mother's wants to pay me 10,000 *Naira* for everything. Do you think I should accept?"

Jide knew that his wife was a shrewd trader. She had started her business long before she met him, and her income surpassed his government salary. Yet, he was grateful that she asked for his advice.

"I think it's a good offer, Kemi. The profit will give us money to live on in Chicago, so we will not be wholly dependent on your cousin."

"Good; I will accept then. Let's begin packing our things. We are leaving in one week."

*****

Lola entered her office to find Alhaji Yaro had arrived early. He was in his office having a meeting with a woman she did not recognize. The strange woman left his office and entered the reception area, followed by Alhaji. She was tall with a fair complexion, wearing gold on her neck, arms, and fingers and was dressed in traditional Hausa attire — a two-piece dress made of brocade material. She was stunning. Her face was tattooed in the Fulani style, and her hands were stained with red henna.

"Mrs. Omolola Adegoke, I want you to meet my wife, Hadjia Fatima Yaro."

Lola nodded to the woman and said good morning, surprised that Alhaji had brought his wife to the office. He smiled at her and walked his wife to the door speaking in Hausa.

"Hadjia, tell Usman to take you to the market. Here is some money for you to shop. Buy what you want."

"Na-go-de, Alhaji, (Thank you)," she said, giving her husband a curtsy.

Lola watched the scene with interest as he escorted his wife into the hall.

Alhaji returned to meet Lola's stare. "So, that is one of your wives. She is pretty, Alhaji."

Alhaji cleared his throat before answering her. "Yes, that is my last wife, Fatima. She wanted to do some shopping. The three of them are having a dispute, so I offered her a day in Lagos to cool off."

Alhaji moved closer to Lola and placed his hands on her shoulders. "You look troubled, Lola? Is there something going on that I should know?"

"Alhaji, you were right all the time. Janice has had the baby and my husband is with her. I want to ask for time off again. I need to travel to America to make sure that my husband will return to Nigeria."

He began to massage her shoulders. Lola was beginning to relax and actually enjoyed his touch. She had been through so much with Janice and Olu that it was nice to be the center of attention for a change. She knew that she was treading on dangerous ground, but what more did she have to lose. Olu was with Janice and his new family, and she may need someone to fall back on in the future. Who better than Alhaji, a rich man who could keep her in the style that she had become used to. True, he had three other wives, but who was she to complain. After all, didn't Olu have another wife?

"Umm, Alhaji, that feels good. Do you give all your wives such nice treatment?"

"No, Lola," he said, his breath becoming ragged. "Only you. I have always wanted you, Lola."

He turned her around in her chair so that she was facing him. Lola needed the time off but she was not sure that Alhaji would let her go this time. She had taken a lot of time off lately and Alhaji did not replace her. However, she knew that he longed for her and now she would have to play that card in order to get the time she needed.

Her exotic eyes and long lashes fluttered seductively at him. He began to perspire in his heavy *baba riga*. She reached up and touched his cheek; he blushed. Taking her hands, he pulled her from her seat, her body pressing close to his.

"Alhaji," she purred, "you are so handsome. No wonder your wives fight for your favor. I will have to stand in line when I return from America. Will you wait for me, sir?"

Alhaji and Lola stood toe to toe. He towered over her slender body. Feeling his desire rising, he took her into his arms and embraced her body. She shivered and thought, *I wonder what it would be like to be with him. I have never had anyone except Olu. If this is what it takes for me to get to America, then so be it.*

"Lola, if I give you the time off that you want, what will you give me in return, my dear?"

His meaning was not lost on Lola.

"What do you want, Alhaji?"

"You know that I want to make love to you, Lola. Won't you let me?"

She smiled and rubbed her leg against his, pulling his head down to her face, then she kissed him gently on his mouth. Neither of them was prepared for the onslaught of their emotions as they were swept up in the storm of need and want. Alhaji's fantasy finally fulfilled, as Lola became his. He grasped her buttocks, lifting her off the floor in one swift movement. She gasped for breath as she felt her wrapper being undone and his hands groping under her *buba* to feel her breast. He made an agonizing sound of surrender as her hands found their way through his robes.

"Lola, not here. Let's go into my office on the sofa."

Alhaji reluctantly released her as she, clad only in her slip and *buba*, walked seductively into his office, trailing her wrapper behind her on the floor. Her round buttocks jiggled as she swayed to imaginary music inside her head. He was almost overcome with desire as he, like a puppy, followed right on her heels.

Once inside the office, Lola took a deep breath as he locked the door and removed his robes. Soon he was clad only in his pants, his curly hair plastered to his head. Lola ran her fingers through the soft curls and looked deep into his eyes as he removed her top, freeing her breasts. He held his breath at the magnificence of his capture.

Lola relaxed by degrees as she realized that her ploy worked. The way Alhaji looked at her made her melt inside, for she never believed that any man could arouse her like Olu. She was wrong. Lola's breath quickened with yearning as he filled her with his heat. She closed her eyes and reveled in ecstasy as their bodies strained and moved in rhythm together. She closed her eyes tighter, trying to picture Olu in her mind instead of her boss. He lowered his mouth to her breast and drank from it as though it were water in the desert. Lola moaned with excitement for she knew there was no turning back now. Once she made love with Alhaji, she knew she would never belong only to Olu.

Alhaji was a passionate man and very adept with lovemaking. He knew just what to do to arouse Lola and was using all his experience to bring her to the peak of excitement. Lola twined her arms around his neck, breathless, as they continued making love. She sucked in a wild breath of pleasure as his lips swept over her breast again and again. A delicious languor stole over her as rapture totally overwhelmed her. Alhaji moaned, ecstasy leapt through him, and hot, wild bolts of thunder rushed to his brain as he thrust deeply inside, riding on wave after wave of pleasurable sensations. Slowly they floated down from the clouds, lying on their sides, facing each other. Alhaji filled his arms with her and held her close to him.

"Lola, it was just as I imagined it to be. Darling, you are wonderful. I shall remember this day forever. Now that you have fulfilled my dreams, I will grant your wish. And when you return with or without your Olu, I will be waiting for you. Waiting to make more sweet, tender love to you."

Lola could not say anything. She was too overwhelmed with the feelings of guilt. She prayed silently, *Lord, I know I have sinned. But it was all for Olu and our marriage. Please forgive me, Lord* ...

11

*T*he sun was shining brightly, yet the air was cool for a New Orleans afternoon. The baby and Janice were going home from the hospital. Femi cradled his newborn child gently as Janice climbed into her mother's car. The main topic on the way home was what to name the baby. Until now, none of them had agreed on a name. Femi's parents had phoned Janice congratulating her on the birth and offering names for them to give the child, yet they still hadn't decided on anything. Femi sat next to Edna in the front. He turned to look at his son and wife on the back seat. Seeing that they were comfortable, he sat quietly while his mother-in-law drove over the bridge to Gretna.

They reached the house and Janice carried the baby inside, while Femi and Edna wrestled with all the bags filled with gifts that friends and family had brought to the hospital. Janice put the baby into his crib and sat down on the bed to watch him sleep. Femi stumbled into the room awkwardly with his arms loaded, trying not to wake the baby.

"Femi, come and sit by me," Janice said, patting the bed.

He sat down and took her hand and gently placed her palm against his lips. She shivered as memories of their past lovemaking once again flooded into her mind. Turning her face to his, she touched his cheek and kissed his lips with all the love and passion she had stored inside during their time apart. Her mother came into the room unannounced, interrupting the private moment.

"Femi, aren't you tired of that hotel food? I want you to go and pack your things and come stay with your family." Femi looked at his wife, waiting for her to tell him it was all right.

"Femi, please come. I need you. Your son needs you. We want you to be here with us. Let the past remain there."

"Thank you, my wife, for loving me enough to take me back."

When Femi reached his hotel, the desk clerk gave him a message. It was from Taju. He rushed to his room to call Nigeria to see what his brother-in-law wanted. The deal for the chemicals was finished, and they were on their way to Lagos via ship. Taju did not expect Olufemi to return to Nigeria until he reconciled with his wife, Janice, so Olufemi wondered what he wanted. He dialed the international operator and waited to be connected.

Joseph answered the telephone in Lagos, and he asked Olu to hold on while he called Mr. Taju to the line.

"Bawoni, Olufemi, is that you? Congratulations, Brother, on the birth of your son. Bisi and I want you to extend our greetings to your wife, Janice. Have you decided on a name yet?"

"Thank you, Taju, and to answer your question, no, we have not decided on a name yet."

Not wasting any more time, Taju started in with the news.

"Olufemi, there is something I must tell you. Lola is traveling to America with Segun. They are leaving on Friday."

Olufemi felt his anger rising.

"No! She would not dare come after I asked her not too! How did she get a visa?"

"I assume that Segun got her one. Olu, you have to be careful. She should not come to New Orleans and disturb you and Janice. And by the way, how are things going between the two of you? Have you reconciled?"

"Yes, I am happy to announce that we are getting back together. She has forgiven me. I will not let Lola come between us. We are a family now — Just the three of us."

"You will have to deal with Lola one day, Olu. I just don't feel that America is the place. She has no business traveling without your permission. I will try to convince her not to come."

"Thank you, Brother, for your help. Say hello to my sister and the children for me. *Odabo.*"

Olufemi sat on the bed, deep in thought, trying to decide on what to do about Lola. All of his dreams were finally coming true — he was the father of a beautiful son and his wife, Janice, had forgiven him and wanted him to come live with her. He would not let Lola ruin his chances with Janice. He picked up the receiver once more and dialed the international operator again.

"Operator, I'd like to make a call to Lagos. The number is 422-086."

The phone rang at his home in Surulere, and Segun answered it.

"*Ta-ni.*"

"Segun, this is Olufemi. I need to speak to Omolola."

"Olu, *kini-kan. Se'Alafia ni.*"

"Adupe, Segun."

"Hold on, let me call my sister to the phone."

Segun rushed to the kitchen to inform Lola.

"Omolola, you have an international call."

"Kilo-de' (who is it), Segun?"

"It is your husband calling from America."

Lola took the phone smiling, happy to hear from her husband who had not called since he left.

"Olu, how are you? Why haven't you called me for so long? I hope everything is all right? Are you calling from Houston?"

"Lola, what is this I hear about you coming to America after I asked you not to come?" he demanded angrily. "I told you that you could not come with me this trip. Why are you disobeying me?"

Lola was frightened. She knew that Bisi or Taju must have told him so now she had to talk her way out of this mess or lose the chance to patch up her marriage. With the thoughts of her love affair with Alhaji in the back of her mind, she began to plead softly with her husband, telling him how much she missed him and longed to be with him. Olufemi charged back that she was not to come. That's when Lola blurted out that she knew about the baby. Olufemi was shocked.

"So, that is the real reason that you don't want me to join you. You want to spend all the time with Janice and the baby. Oh, I forgot to congratulate you on the birth of your son," she said with sarcasm tingeing her words. "I know you will not return, Olu! That is why I am coming to be with you, my husband!" she cried passionately.

"Omolola, I warn you! If you come to the United States without my permission, I will not see you!"

Lola knew that he meant it. She knew that she was risking her marriage if she disobeyed her husband. But nothing would stop her from her mission. She would not allow Janice and her newborn son to take Olu away from her.

"I'm sorry, Olu. I am coming with my brother, Segun. We will arrive in Chicago by Sunday. I will call you then."

"Is there nothing that I can say to you, Lola, to convince you not to come?"

"No, Olu. No."

"Then so be it," and Olufemi slammed down the receiver.

Lola stood holding the receiver away from her ear. The shock of him hanging up on her left her numb, filled with helpless emotions. She knew she had crossed her husband and there would be hell to pay. She stood there with tears rolling down her cheeks as she envisioned Janice, Olufemi, and the child. *They are playing with the baby.* She shivered, gritting her teeth and clenching her fist in anger. Then Lola wiped away her tears on her face and vowed to keep her husband, whatever it would take.

Olufemi drove slowly back to his mother-in-law's house. He wanted all the anger to subside before joining his wife and child. As he reached the house, he parked in the driveway, and Janice welcomed him with open arms, the two of them embracing and kissing in the living room. Edna smiled at the scene.

"Come on, you two lovebirds; dinner is served. You better eat before the baby wakes up."

They all retired to the kitchen for the delicious dinner that Edna had prepared for them. Afterwards, she made a surprising announcement.

"James and I are going on with the wedding. We were just waiting for Janice to have the baby. He called me tonight and wants me to come to Chicago tomorrow. I know that the baby is too young to travel, so we decided to have a civil ceremony in Chicago, and then have a reception in New Orleans for the family."

"Mama, this is so sudden! When did you plan all this?"

"Just yesterday. We only wanted to see if you and Femi would reunite. Since you did, I know that you and Jr. will be all right."

"Thank you, Mama. Thank you for having faith in our love," Femi said, taking Janice's hand in his own.

"Now that that's settled, my flight leaves for Chicago in the morning," Edna said, as excited as she could be. "I'm already packed. I'm leaving the three of you to get to know each other. I will only be as far away as a telephone call. Femi, I trust you to take good care of my daughter and grandson."

"You can count on me, Mama."

Femi drove Edna to the airport the next morning. He didn't get much sleep because Jr. kept him and Janice up all night. The baby did not like the formula, preferring his mother's milk. So in order to get some sleep, Janice had to put him in the bed with them, and the baby slept, suckling his mother's breast.

Femi kissed Edna and wished her luck as she boarded the plane to Chicago. James would be waiting, and they were to be married the next day.

The next few days were blissfully happy for the new family. They decided to name the baby after Femi and Janice's late father: Olufemi Augustus Charles Louis Adedeji Adegoke. They christened the child in the local church and planned to have a traditional African naming ceremony when Edna and James came to New Orleans. Karen was appointed godmother for the Christian ceremony and Aduke would be godmother for the African ceremony. Baby Charles, wrapped in white, was quiet during the ceremony, but burst out crying when anointed with the holy water.

They had refreshments at the house and were joined by Aunt Dotty, Karen, and a host of friends and well-wishers from Janice's past who were curious to meet her husband.

Though Janice was happy, she missed her home in Nigeria. She missed the sounds and smells of Lagos. She wished her mother-in-law could be at the naming ceremony. She looked over at Femi, who was deep in conversation with one of her former classmates, and thought *he is so handsome. I am very lucky to have a man like him. He dotes over his son and is devoted to me. He never even mentioned Lola. I wonder how she let him go. I must ask him about it later.* Feeling overwhelmed, Janice pushed all thoughts of Lola out of her mind and walked over to join her husband and the party.

*****

Their plane landed at O'Hare Airport. Kemi and Jide were grateful to finally arrive in America. Yetunde and her husband picked them up, and they drove through the heavy traffic to Hyde Park. Yetunde had a large apartment near the university, where she was studying to become a doctor. Her husband, Fatayi, had already earned his degree from another school and drove a taxi for a living.

"So, this is America. Oh, Jide, it's wonderful. So many people," said Kemi excited.

"You have not seen anything, Kemi. Wait until I take you shopping downtown. There is so much I want you to see here," replied Yetunde.

They arrived at the apartment and Yetunde showed them to their room. Tired and weary from all the excitement of the trip, they laid down to rest while Yetunde prepared dinner for them.

*****

Lola and Segun had arrived in Chicago the day before. Aduke picked them up from the airport and took them to her place. She also lived near the university. They entered her flat and she showed Lola to the room she would be using.

"Welcome to America, Lola. I hope that you will enjoy your stay here."

"Thank you, Aduke," Lola said and went into the room.

Aduke was ready to show Segun where he would sleep. She had been so happy to see him when he arrived at the airport, but she was horrified to see Lola following close behind. Now she was curious to know why Lola was traveling with him and thought that this was the time to ask. She pulled him aside.

"Segun, why is Lola with you?"

"She was determined to see her husband. What was I to do? She begged me to bring her with me. Is it all right if she stays with us, Aduke?"

"Segun, you should have called me. I am Janice's friend. How will she feel if she knows that Lola is staying in my apartment?"

"It will be all right. After all, she is my sister and will be related to you soon. Let this time be happy, Aduke. I am so happy to see you."

Aduke smiled and they embraced each other. She told him to follow her.

"Segun, this is your room. We cannot sleep together until after the wedding. I will let you and Lola get settled. Dinner will be served in a little while," she announced.

By the tone of her voice, Segun knew that Aduke was not pleased with him bringing his sister, so he followed her into the kitchen. Standing tall over her, he grabbed her from behind. She giggled and turned to face her handsome fiancé.

"Segun," she said smoothly, "you are a naughty boy. You know that Femi does not want to see Lola. Anyway, he is not in Chicago, so she cannot reach him."

He pulled her to him, gently kneading her buttocks and pressing hers into his. She sighed and rubbed her breasts into his chest.

"Segun, in America, men kiss their women like this."

She pulled his face to hers and kissed him passionately. Segun, not used to aggressive women, pulled back, looking into her eyes. Seeing the laughter in them, he took her into his arms and pressed his lips to hers, searching for her tongue. Aduke moaned with pleasure as the sensations rushed from her lips to her loins. She purred like a kitten as his hand reached under her skirt, searching for her heat. Realizing that they were standing in the kitchen, she pushed him gently away.

"See, Segun, if we were alone, no telling what would have happened. There will be plenty of time after the wedding, darling. I am saving myself for it. Just be patient."

"It will be hard, Aduke. You are a very desirable woman, but I will be patient as long as my sister is in the house to chaperone."

Lola paced the room. She had unpacked her bags and was trying to think how she could get to Olu. She knew that he must be in New Orleans with Janice. *Aduke must be very angry with Segun for bringing me. I know she is Janice's friend. But I am married to Olu too. I will not let her stand in the way of my happiness,* she thought to herself.

While helping Aduke with the dishes after dinner, Lola tried to have a friendly conversation. Staying away from the subject of Janice and Olufemi, they talked about Aduke and Segun's wedding plans, while Aduke put the last of the dishes away.

"Lola, Segun and I plan to wed in a civil ceremony. Later we will have a big wedding in London. He needs to register for school this semester, so we cannot afford to have a large wedding now."

"Aduke, I am so happy for you and my brother. I know you will make him happy." Lola was desperate to ask about her husband and Janice.

"Aduke, have you heard from Olu?"

Aduke stiffened and put up her guard. "Yes, he is with Janice in New Orleans. Lola, you know that Janice had the baby."

"Yes, I do," Lola, replied sadly. "Yes, I know. I found out in Nigeria. That is why I came. I want to be with them."

"Lola, you know that is out of the question. Janice would not permit that. Save yourself some grief, girl, and return to Nigeria before it is too late for Femi to forgive you!"

"I cannot do that. If I do, I will lose my husband forever!"

"If you stay, Lola, you may lose him anyway."

Lola knew that trying to convince Aduke was pointless. She knew that Aduke's first loyalty was to Janice. To soften things between them, she said, "I will stay away from them until I am invited to come. After all, Aduke, I am still his wife."

Aduke nodded in agreement, while knowing that she must warn Janice that Lola was in America and that she must be on guard at all times. She did not miss the disdain in Lola's voice when she mentioned Janice and the baby.

Kemi had given Lola Yetunde's phone number before leaving Nigeria. Lola called her to let her friends know that she had arrived. Even Kemi had misgivings about her friend's decision to follow her husband to America, especially after he had forbidden her to come. Happy to talk to her friend, she told her about the conversation that she and Aduke had.

"What did you expect, Lola? Aduke and Janice have been friends for a long time. Remember, she was expecting Segun, not you. You have crashed in on their reunion. I'm sure that she did not plan on that."

"Maybe you're right, Kemi. But I could not have traveled without Segun. Guess what? Segun and Aduke are getting married soon."

"Oh, how wonderful. Your mother must be very happy. Aduke is beautiful and comes from a good family."

"Her parents live in London. They are going there when school breaks to have a large wedding ceremony."

"I have to go now, Lola. We are going shopping for some new clothes. I will be looking for a job and cannot wear a wrapper.

Talk to you soon and, Lola; please be careful what you do. Don't alienate Olufemi."

"Thanks, Kemi. I will try not to."

Lola replaced the receiver and got dressed to go out with Aduke and Segun. They were going to the university to register him for classes. He would be going to Chicago State University instead of University of Chicago because he could not pass the entrance exam. Lola rushed to keep up with her brother and Aduke, while taking in all the sights. The campus was large and they had to do a great deal of walking to get from building to building. When they completed the registration process, they went to lunch at McDonald's. Lola had never had a hamburger before and delighted in the taste.

"I like this American food. It's delicious," she exclaimed.

Segun wolfed down two Big Macs and a chocolate shake. Aduke was amazed at his huge appetite. She smiled and teased him while ordering refills. After lunch, the trio went shopping and to a movie. Aduke and Segun wanted to be alone and Lola could sense this; she felt she was in the way.

"Why don't you drop me at the apartment so that you two can spend some time together, Aduke?"

"Are you sure you don't mind, Sister?" Segun asked, afraid of offending her.

"No, don't worry about me. I will look at television or read a book while you are gone."

They took Lola back to Aduke's apartment, and then the couple left to spend some time alone. Lola paced the living room floor, all the time wishing that Olufemi would call her. But she knew that was wishful thinking. She spent the night alone until

Aduke and Segun returned to prepare for bed. She pretended to be asleep, not wanting Aduke to see her crying bitter tears of loneliness.

12

*A*duke went to class feeling sad. Unable to concentrate on the lecture, she decided to skip her next class. She wanted to tell Janice so badly that Lola and Segun were in Chicago. She did not want to alarm her, but she felt somehow that Lola's motives were not good. She ran into Melinda in the hall and decided to tell her what was going on and let Melinda tell Janice.

"What do you mean Lola is in America, Aduke? What can she possibly expect to gain by coming after Femi?"

"Melinda, all Lola thinks about is Olufemi. She does not care who she hurts. I believe that she is obsessed with him and will stop at nothing to get him back to Nigeria."

"Aduke, I must warn Janice. Do you think that Femi knows she is here?"

"I cannot say, but I think that if he does, he is not happy about it."

Melinda decided to give her cousin a call after work and warn her about Lola.

Femi and Janice were very busy taking care of baby Charles. It was a full-time job just changing diapers, but Femi was enjoying every minute of it. He was concerned that Lola would spoil his bliss, so while the baby was napping, he decided it was time to tell Janice his worries.

Janice sat back on the sofa and looked at her husband. His brow was filled with lines, and he looked tired as he told her about his last conversation with Lola at the hotel.

"Janice, I tried to stop her. I did everything in my power to keep her from traveling to America. She came with Segun and is staying at Aduke's house. I wanted to be the first one to tell you."

Janice was silent, trying to digest the disturbing news. She walked over to her husband and smoothed the lines from his brow.

"Femi, I understand. She feels threatened now that I have the baby. Everything depends on you. You know how I feel about you now and you know that I love you and our son and want us to be a family. But I want to put the past behind us and go on with our lives. I cannot live with Lola. Even though I cannot ask you to divorce her, especially since I accepted your marriage to her when I left Nigeria, I had hoped to give you and her time to be together, and you time to forget me."

"Janice, I could never forget you. I fell in love with you, and I want you and my son. Lola will just have to deal with the fact that I love you and Charles and will not let you go."

"She will never understand, Femi. She will not let you go easily, nor will she want me to be your wife. She does not want to share you, and I don't blame her. But I, too, am not going to give you up, Femi. You are the father of my child."

The couple sat silently, holding each other, not knowing what to do. Olufemi did not want to hurt Lola, but he knew that it could not be avoided. Now that he had a son, he was certain that things could never be the same again.

"Let's not let Lola spoil this special time together. I told her not to come to America, but she decided to come at her own risk and now must face the consequences."

Melinda phoned Janice to see how she was and to tell her the news that Lola was in Chicago. Janice informed her cousin that Femi had already told her.

"What do you think she will do, Janice? I am worried that she will try to do something to break you two up."

"The only way that can happen is if Femi allows it. He loves me, Mindy, and had forbidden her to come. He refuses to talk to her, so she is wasting her time here."

"How long before you return to Nigeria, Janice?"

"It will be a few months before the baby is old enough to travel. Plus my mother wants James to come and see the baby."

"I saw her the other day, so radiant and happy. James is very good to her."

"I know, Mindy. I am so glad that she has him. How is Bill doing?"

"He is getting used to the fact that he will be a father soon. He wants to visit Nigeria too. You may have houseguests after the baby is born."

"That would be great, girl. Then our children can spend time together like we did, growing up. I always looked forward to spending the summers in Chicago with you and your mother."

"Janice, I don't mean to pry, but is Femi going to remain married to the two of you?"

Melinda knew that she was opening up a delicate subject, but she felt she had to know if Janice was going to still have to share Femi with Lola.

Even though Janice had gotten over the initial blow of Femi's lies and deceit, and even though she had accepted his decision to have two wives, that was in Nigeria. In America, she knew she could never share him with another woman in public or in private. They had rediscovered the special feelings that brought them together in the first place, and neither of them was willing to lose it again.

"Melinda, Femi has a difficult choice to make. I would not like to be in his shoes for anything in the world. And whatever he decides to do, I will abide by his decision."

*****

Lola walked in on Segun and Aduke. Both were rushing to leave for classes. Lola was bored and tired of waiting for Olu to call her, and even Segun was getting tired of Lola's sullen moods. He then decided to take matters into his own hands and call his brother-in-law in New Orleans to tell him that his other wife was in America.

Femi and Janice had just come in from walking the baby in the park when the phone rang. Janice answered it. She did not recognize the voice on the other line, but she knew it was for Femi.

"Hello, Janice. This is Segun, Lola's brother."

"Oh, Segun," Janice said cautiously.

"May I speak to Olufemi?"

"Sure, hold on."

She called her husband to the phone. He saw the look on her face and, at first, thought it was Lola.

"Ta-ni? Segun, *bawomi?"*

"I am fine, Olu, but Lola is not. She wants to speak to you."

Olufemi spoke in Yoruba so that Janice could not understand. "Segun, I told her that I would not talk to, nor see her. She should not be here."

"Oh, come on, Olu. She is miserable. I cannot continue to be responsible for her. I have started classes at the university and do not have time to spend with her."

"That is your problem," he retorted angrily. "She should return to Nigeria, where she belongs. Tell her I don't want to see her!"

"You can tell me yourself," Lola's tearful voice sounded into the receiver. "Olu, my husband, why have you treated me this way? I am your wife, and I miss you so much. It's killing me. Why do you want to kill me?"

Femi looked at Janice sitting quietly, watching him. Her expressive light brown eyes were mirrored with concern. She was testing him now, trying to see how he would handle the situation. Lola's words were tearing at his heart. He did not want to hurt her the way he did when he told her about his decision to marry Janice, but now that Janice has given him what he wanted, a son, he was not quite sure how to deal with the situation. Janice left him because he was not faithful to their relationship — breaking his own rules, allowing his male weakness to lead him astray and break the agreement. Janice had tried so hard to live in polygamy. She had given their culture a chance; now he was going to have to decide to give hers a try. Whatever he said to Lola at that moment would be the turning point in his relationship with Janice.

"Lola, I am going to say this only once, and I want you to understand me. I am now with Janice and my son. We are trying to give our marriage the chance that it did not have in Nigeria. Your coming here against my wishes has helped to make up my mind. I love Janice, and I want us to be together as one family. *I no longer want to have two wives*. It is too complicated for me. Lola, you have shown me by your coming that you care not for my feelings. I am certain now that I want Janice. I have made my choice."

Lola heard the words, but did not believe that he said them. She held the receiver, numb from shock, as Olufemi hung up the phone. She just stood there with silent tears making rivers onto her chin.

Janice could not believe her ears. She rushed over to her husband and cried softly into his chest. It took a few seconds before she realized that he, too, was sobbing.

"Femi, shh, it will be all right. I know it was not easy for you to do that," she said, consoling him.

"Oh, Janice," he sobbed, "When you left Nigeria, I thought I would die. I tried to be a good husband to her. I tried to forget you. But your memory burned in my mind. Every time I closed my eyes, I would see your beautiful face, and I would long to caress your soft skin and feel your hair on my face and smell its scent. I went through hell without you. When I came to Houston, I came for you, my love. I did not want to hurt her, but, Janice; I could not bear the thought of life without you anymore."

"There, there, my darling. It will be all right. She will survive. Someday she will get over you, Femi. It will take time, but I am certain that she will go on with her life. Now we must go on with ours."

Lola's scream could be heard throughout the apartment. Aduke and Segun rushed to her aid.

"What is it, Lola? What has happened?" Segun asked.

Lola stood there, crying hysterically. "Oh my God, he has left me! I have lost my Olu forever! Oh my God, he is gone! I cannot bear it!"

Then the room began to spin around her as darkness overtook her consciousness.

Lola awoke to strange surroundings. She was in a hospital. Aduke and Segun rushed her there when she would not respond to their ministrations. The doctor said she was in shock, and it would be a few days before she would be normal. He also told them that she was a few weeks pregnant, and that contributed to her delicate condition. Aduke and Segun looked at each other in shock because now Lola no longer had a husband.

Segun called Kemi and Jide, who spent many hours at the hospital with Lola. She wouldn't talk to anyone; she just kept calling Olufemi's name over and over again. The doctor told them that if she did not wake up soon, he would recommend that she be transferred to a psychiatric hospital that specialized in this type of problem. Segun was very concerned and called Nigeria to inform his mother of what had happened.

Titiloye was distraught and went to see Olufemi's parents in Ekiti. When she told Abimbola and Emmanuel what their son had done to Lola, they were upset and could not believe that Olufemi could be so heartless to leave her when she was carrying his child. Not knowing what to do, they called Bisi and Taju to see if they could shed some light on the matter. Bisola told her parents that her brother had forbidden Lola to travel to America, that he had gone there to reconcile with Janice and did not want Lola to interfere. Since Lola went anyway, she had gotten what she deserved.

"I must go to my daughter, Emmanuel. Your son has done a terrible thing. It is not fair for him to leave her for Janice and the child, especially now that she too is pregnant."

"Now, now Titi, Lola was told not to go to America," said Emmanuel. "I know my son. He tried to have them both, and it did not work. It was only a matter of time before he had to choose one of them. But if it will make you feel better, I will book you a flight for Chicago and you can see to your daughter. My advice to you is to bring her back to Nigeria. Maybe in time he will forgive her."

So that is how it is, Titiloye thought to herself while preparing for her journey. *They have accepted the news that their son has abandoned my daughter. We shall see about that.*

Lola stayed in the hospital for three weeks. She was thin and tired with dark circles under her eyes. Her mother arrived, and as soon as she spoke to her daughter, Lola snapped out of her delirium and came around. Her mother said special prayers with Segun, Aduke, Kemi, and Jide. The doctor was happy with her progress, so he decided to release her into the care of her mother.

Lola recuperated slowly. Her mother took good care of her while Segun and Aduke attended classes and went to work. Segun had found a job at a local parking garage. He found American life tough, but knew he must study hard to maintain his grades.

Aduke breezed through her classes and rushed home every day to cook for her husband. During Lola's illness, Segun and Aduke didn't want to wait any longer. They decided to get married at City Hall. Kemi stayed with Lola in the hospital. Titiloye was present and Jide stood in as best man. Aduke's mother was unhappy that her only daughter rushed into marriage. Her father gave his blessing and soon his wife came around. Aduke could not even invite her best friend, Janice, since Lola's mother was going to be at the wedding.

Lola's morning sickness hindered her recovery. She lost even more weight and everyone was worried about the baby's health. The doctor assured them that this was normal and that they should not worry. After a month of her mother's care, Lola's color became normal and she was able to leave her bed and sit on the balcony. No one mentioned Olufemi or Janice. Aduke received an invitation to Edna's reception, but had to call Janice to decline.

"Janice, my mother-in-law is here. She is taking care of Lola, who has been very sick since Femi broke up with her."

Janice was sorry to hear that Lola had been sick.

"She is better now. But since I am married to her brother, it would not be good if I came to your mother's reception. I hope you understand."

"Yes, I do, Aduke. I miss you, girlfriend. I still want you to be the baby's godmother. Femi's family is coming here to America for the official naming ceremony. Can I expect you then, Aduke?"

"Of course. I would not miss that for the world, Janice."

Janice and Femi were very happy. They made love almost every night and planned to have another child soon. The money in the bank account was getting low, so Femi took a job at Dillard University, teaching engineering, while Janice stayed home and took care of her two men. The couple had decided to continue living at Edna's house while she was in Chicago with James. They began to make friends with other couples and became adjusted to their newfound happiness.

Every weekend, they would go out to dinner or to a show; Karen would baby-sit. She enjoyed taking care of Charles and had the help of her children. This gave Janice and Femi time to be together without the baby between them. It was during those times that they would slip off for a romantic evening in the French Quarter to listen to New Orleans jazz, then go to a hotel and make love. One such night, outside under the stars, they shared a bottle of champagne and ate oysters Rockefeller until they were full. Afterward, they went to a small guest inn where Femi asked for the bridal suite. Once inside the room, he ordered another bottle of champagne. Janice kicked off her shoes and sat on the edge of the bed. Her tall, handsome husband removed his tie and jacket. She lay back, watching him undress, his muscles flexing as he bent over to remove his shoes. Janice drew in her breath when he removed his pants, leaving him in his bikini shorts.

"Just stand there, Femi. I want to admire you," she said in a sexy tone.

He smiled seductively and struck pose after pose as if he were modeling for a Mr. Universe pageant. Janice felt herself become aroused with desire and motioned him to join her on the bed. She looked deep into his eyes, smoldering with passion. Femi kissed her deeply. *Oh sweet mercy,* he thought. *The taste of her was so intoxicating.*

He undressed her slowly until she was naked, and then filled his mouth with her breast, while his hand sought her heat below. Janice moaned with ecstasy as he massaged her gently. The pleasure was exquisite as she pulled him over her, guiding him inside her. Together, they moved, riding each other to oblivion. They were intoxicated with love. She arched against him as he thrust, scalding himself in her heat. They reached their peak together and came tumbling down, clinging to the other tightly.

He lay on the bed beside her, running his fingers through her long hair, damp from their passionate lovemaking. Janice put her head on his chest, and they slept for a few hours before going to Karen's to pick up Charles. Edna and James were married at the City Hall in downtown Chicago. Her sister Dotty, Melinda, and Bill stood with her. They were leaving for the Bahamas for a weeklong honeymoon. Janice, Femi, and the baby went to the airport with the couple. Before her plane left, Janice told her the news about Lola. Edna cautioned her to be careful, that a woman scorned was dangerous, and not to let her guard down. She also told her to watch out for her husband.

Janice asked James to take care of her mother and looked forward to their return. She was planning their reception to be held in two weeks, after which her mother would move to Chicago and live with her new husband. They flew back to New Orleans that evening.

At work the following day, Olufemi received a call from Jide, who told him about Lola and her stay in the hospital. Jide told Olu that he was to blame for everything, but did not mention the fact that Lola was pregnant. Olufemi was upset by this news, and told Jide that he would discuss this with Janice and see if there was anything that could be done. Jide told him that because Lola's mother was in Chicago, it might not be wise for him to come at this time.

Olufemi told Janice the news about Lola. Janice was suspicious, but remembered how she felt when she caught Femi and Lola together at Surulere. She, too, had ended up in the hospital.

"Do you want to go and see her, Femi?" Janice asked, afraid that he would say yes.

"No, her mother is with her, and Jide says she is going to be all right. She just had to get over the initial shock of our breakup."

Janice was not convinced. She knew that no woman would let go of a man like Femi without a fight.

13

Omolola sat in the bed while her mother fluffed the pillows. She rubbed her hand across her flat stomach, remembering the doctor's words in the mist of her delirium:"You appear to be pregnant. I cannot tell without an ultrasound, but you seem to be around eight weeks," she recalled. She now had fulfilled her dream of having a child for Olu. Her mood darkened as she remembered her love affair with her boss. She could still see his handsome face and feel his hands on her body. She gave credence to the fact that the child might be his. *But as long as I am still married to you, Olu, this baby is yours,* she thought confidently to herself. Her mother brought her some food."Omolola, you must finish it all. You need to get your strength back so that your baby, my first grandchild, will be healthy."

"Sounds good, Mother; your first grandchild. I am hoping for a boy."

Aduke entered the bedroom full of cheer and merriment. She knelt down before her mother-in-law and greeted her in the traditional way. Then rising, she turned towards Lola.

"E'karo, sister *mi.* How are you feeling this morning?"

"I am better, Aduke. I am sorry to be so much trouble."

"You are not in any trouble. We were just sorry you missed our wedding ceremony."

"Where is Segun?"

"He has already left for work," Titiloye broke in. "Aduke, you look well today. My son made a good choice."

She hugged Aduke, then the three Nigerian women continued to talk about the traditional wedding planned for London before Aduke bid them farewell and rushed off to her classes.

Everyday, Lola got stronger. She was given a clean bill of health when she visited the doctor for her checkup. He told her that the baby was growing, and he asked her for the date of her last menstrual period, so that he could narrow down the delivery date. Lola said she could not remember, so he concluded that an ultrasound should be scheduled in a few weeks to determine the gestation period.

Titiloye called Emmanuel and Abimbola and kept them informed of Lola's condition. She wanted to talk to Olufemi, but after the incident with Grace, where she had interfered in the couple's marital affairs, she decided to remain silent. Although her daughter was hurting from Olu's decision, she felt that at least with Lola having his child, she could bear it. At least she would not be treated like Abbe, Taju's other wife, and be sent to the village because she was barren.

Still, Lola would not give up so easily. She was prepared to do anything to get her husband back, even if it meant continuing to share him with Janice. She wanted her child to be raised with its father. Though she was not sure that he was the father, no one had any idea that she had slept with Alhaji before she came to America. She lay back, remembering Alhaji's passion and the pleasure he gave her. She knew that if anyone found out, her chances of going back to Olu would be finished.

Her mother tried to convince her that she should accept the fact that Olu no longer wanted her living with him and accept the arrangement of him supporting her and the child. She reminded Lola that Olufemi comes from a rich family, and that they would do anything to see that Lola and the child were cared for in elegant style. She would keep the house in Surulere and be able to provide for her mother in her old age. But Lola was adamant about getting him back into her bed as her husband and would not listen to reason. Even Kemi tried to talk to Lola, telling her how lucky she was to be pregnant.

"Just think, Lola, in a few months you will be a mother and have a child to pour your love into. You know how our men are. They like to play around. Let Olufemi take care of you and the baby, then go find a lover to take care of you when he is not around. Stop being a baby, Lola. That is what our women do. I have a cousin who is the fifth wife. She has a lover who takes care of her needs when her husband is with the other women."

Lola wanted to tell her friend about her affair with Alhaji. She longed to share her secret with someone. She looked at her friend who was so happy and content with her marriage. Kemi and Jide were set on their course towards success in America. Lola would miss them when she returned to Nigeria.

"Kemi, if I tell you something, will you promise not to tell anyone, not even your husband?"

"Certainly, Lola; you know you can trust me."

Lola lowered her eyes. Her long lashes glimmered with unshed tears as she told her friend about the love affair with her boss.

"It only happened one time, Kemi. I was afraid that he would not give me the time off to come to America."

Kemi stared at Lola, her mouth open wide with amazement. Then she began to laugh. "Lola, I'm not surprised. Alhaji was always attracted to you. He always wanted you, and now you have given in. So why are you running after Olufemi? Why don't you let someone who really loves you take care of you?"

"I don't want to be part of his harem. With Olu, at least there is only one other wife."

"That is true, Lola, but how do you know that Olu will stop there?"

"I don't, Kemi. But I can only hope that he will."

"When are you going to tell Olu about the baby?"

"As soon as he will take a call from me. My mother wants to talk to him about our breakup, but I don't want her to interfere."

"You have to be strong, Lola. Strong to bear whatever the future may bring."

"And I pray that it will bring me Olu."

*****

Melinda's rise to motherhood came suddenly one night. Bill rushed her to the hospital just in time. Their daughter was born in less than an hour. The whole family was present except Janice. Edna phoned her, telling her the good news about her cousin. "Jan, she really missed you. The baby is fine, and they want you to come for the christening."

"Tell Mindy that I will call her soon. How are you and James?"

"We're fine, but I'm missing my grandson. Is Femi treating you right?"

"Yes, Mom, he's wonderful. But I found out that Lola is in Chicago."

"What! Why is she here, Jan? I sure hope she doesn't cause any trouble and that she stays away from you all. Have you spoken to her?"

"No, but Femi did. He told her he did not want to see her. I was happy that he finally made the decision to keep only one of us. I just wish that he had done it before I left Nigeria. It would have made things so much easier."

"Well, I hope he sticks to his guns for Charles' sake. I'll call you tomorrow."

When Femi came home from work, Janice told him the good news about Melinda and Bill's new baby girl. He went into the bedroom to see Charles, and then sat down for an intimate dinner with his wife. He decided that this was the time to tell Janice his feelings about returning to Nigeria and his job with Taju.

"Jan, I just want the baby to get older before we return. Taju needs me, and my father needs me too. I cannot stay in America too long."

"I know, Femi. I miss Nigeria too. Not the bad memories, but the good ones. Since my mother is married now, there is no reason that I cannot return with you. I won't let you go alone."

"Good, I'm glad that's over," Femi sighed, reaching out for his beautiful wife and covering her mouth with kisses. Just at that moment, they heard Charles on the monitor and both began to laugh.

"He must be hungry. Go and give him his food. I will just have to wait until later for my feeding."

Janice smiled a knowing smile at her husband and kissed him on his cheek.

"There is enough for the two of you, my love."

*****

Lola tried everything she could, short of flying to New Orleans, to see Olufemi herself. She felt he was a coward not to face her. Now that she was pregnant, she fully intended to use her condition to get him back.

Her mother was at a loss of what to do with her. She could not understand her daughter and got frustrated when Lola refused to return to Nigeria with her. Titiloye finally gave up trying to convince her and left for home. The first thing she did was to go to Emmanuel and Abimbola to tell them the news about the baby. Bimbo was upset because she knew that her son had decided to divorce Lola and have only one wife. She longed to see her new grandson.

Lola overheard Aduke talking to Janice one day on the phone. They were discussing the christening for Melinda's son. Janice and Olufemi would be coming to Chicago for the ceremony. *So they are coming,* she thought to herself. *I will get Segun to take me there.*

The day was sunny and cold. Winter was coming and soon a blanket of snow would cover Chicago. Janice pulled the blanket over Charles as she and her husband arrived at O'Hare Airport. Edna and James picked them up and drove directly to their home in Hyde Park. The christening would be held at Bill's parents' church on the far south side of the city.

Aduke and Segun were invited. They did all they could not to let on to Lola that Olufemi and Janice were coming to Chicago. Segun had tried to convince his sister to return to Lagos with their mother, but she was adamant about seeing her husband. She had not even told him about the baby yet, and she was almost four months along.

Lola had been in contact with her boss, Alhaji Yaro, who was very angry and disappointed in her. But just hearing her voice brought back the memory of their lovemaking and made him long for her again. He had to hire someone to do her work, and now Lola did not have a job anymore. She began to blame Janice and Femi more and more each day. She stood looking in the mirror naked, seeing the changes in her body. She was a strikingly beautiful woman and the pregnancy only enhanced this fact by giving her face a noticeable glow. She rubbed her protruding stomach. The baby was moving inside her. She smiled thinking, *soon, my child. Soon. We will once again be a family with your father.*

Lola dressed and hired a taxi to take her to the church. Aduke and Segun had left earlier. They told her they were going to visit friends and then go to dinner. The taxi drove south on the Dan Ryan expressway to 95th street, where the church was located. There was a large crowd of well-wishers and family going inside. Lola stood nearby, trying not to be seen by the others.

Janice and Femi arrived and entered the church quickly to protect the baby from the cold. Melinda and Bill were at the altar with the pastor. When Janice saw Aduke, she waved. She was named the godmother and Bill's friend, who was the best man at their wedding, was the godfather. The child was christened Jenoa Marie.

Lola slipped in the rear of the church and sat quietly, observing Janice and Femi until the ceremony was over. When the family was leaving the church, Lola stood up and blocked Femi and Janice's departure.

"Lola!" Olufemi shouted, surprised. "What are you doing here?"

Everyone turned towards them. Aduke and Segun were astounded that Lola would have the nerve to show up at the church.

"I came to see you, Olu. Please talk to me."

Janice stood beside him, wondering what he was going to do. Lola looked in the direction of Charles, who was asleep in his mother's arms. Edna, sensing danger, came forward and took the baby from harm's way.

"Lola, you should not have come. This is a private ceremony. Please, let's go outside and talk," Janice said quietly.

"No, I don't want to talk to you, Janice. You stole my husband!"

Lola began to cry, the hot tears making trails on her face. Olufemi was uncertain about her motives, but he knew he had better do something fast. The other guests were leaving and they would surely witness a scene if he didn't act fast. Everyone was invited for dinner at Melinda and Bill's house. Aunt Dotty, with Edna's help, had prepared a feast.

Edna looked at Janice.

"Go on, Mom, with the others. We're all right. Take Charles and we'll join you later. Melinda and Bill, we'll be there soon."

Aduke and Segun stood beside Lola.

"Janice, I am sorry. I don't know how she found out about the christening," Aduke said.

Even Segun was upset at his sister's behavior. He reached for her arm to lead her outside, but she pulled away from him.

"I will not leave until I talk to Olu."

"We have nothing to talk about, Lola. I think you should leave with your brother," Olufemi replied, trying to control his temper.

"No, I won't leave. Not until I tell you about our child."

A hush fell over the room as Lola opened her coat to reveal her shapely body in the early to middle stages of pregnancy. Janice looked at Femi in horror as Femi turned to her. Her light brown eyes opened wide with disbelief as Lola paraded her pregnancy proudly.

"Femi, did you know about this? Please tell me this is not happening!"

"Janice, I didn't know she was pregnant!"

Then she directed her question to Aduke and Segun, who stood silent, not knowing what to do.

"Aduke, why didn't you tell me? Why?" Janice asked.

Aduke looked helplessly at her friend. She knew she should have told her, but Lola was now her sister-in-law and she could not betray her.

"I am sorry, Janice. I didn't think that it mattered."

"How could you think that it would not, Aduke?"

Femi sat down defeated in a church pew. He did not know what to do. He could not believe that Lola was pregnant. They had tried so hard to conceive a child in Nigeria, but had no luck. Segun looked at Lola and saw how much damage she had done. He also saw how much Olu loved Janice.

"Listen, Lola. You should not have come here. This was not the place for you to tell Olu about the baby."

"I know, Segun, but he refused to talk to me. I had to do something drastic or risk having this child alone."

Femi felt as if all the plans that he and Janice had made were over. Now they would have to resume the triangle that he had dismantled. Janice decided to keep quiet and not let Lola feed on her anger. She whispered to Femi,

"I'll see you later at Melinda's. I want to give you two some time to talk," she said more diplomatically than she felt.

The three of them left Lola and Olufemi alone. They walked slowly to the car and sat inside. Segun turned on the engine and started the heater. It was beginning to snow.

"Olu, I miss you. Why did you treat me this way? All I wanted was your love. Will you abandon me and our child?"

"Lola, this is a shock to me. Why didn't you tell me you were pregnant? Why wait until now? When is the baby due?"

"It's due in a few months. Will you take me back? I love you, and your child needs you."

Olufemi did not answer her and drove towards Aduke's apartment. When they arrived, he parked and walked with her inside. She took his coat, and they sat down on the sofa. Lola offered him a drink, but he declined.

"Lola, I will take care of my child. But I told you, I don't want to have two wives."

"But Olu, this is what we both prayed for — a child of our own to complete our family."

"Lola, I already have a child. Why are you doing this to me? I asked you not to come to America. Why didn't you wait until I returned to Nigeria?"

"I missed you so much, Olu, and I was afraid that you would not return once Janice had the baby."

"Lola, you're wrong. Janice and I are planning to return to Nigeria once Charles is old enough to travel. So you should have been patient and waited."

Lola looked at the man she was married to. She could see his love for Janice was stronger than his commitment to her. She knew she was fighting a losing battle trying to get Olufemi to accept her and take care of her like he did in Nigeria. Maybe Kemi and her mother were right. Maybe she should think about Alhaji. At least she would have someone who cared about her.

"All right, Olu, I will return to Nigeria and wait for you to come back. I know I was wrong to come, and I hope you can forgive me."

"Only time will tell, Lola. But I don't think that things will ever be the same between us. As I said before, I do not want to have two wives anymore. But I will take care of you and the baby in Nigeria."

Olufemi rose and took his coat. He was walking towards the door when Lola rushed to him, holding him, pleading.

"Olu, please! Everything I did, I did out of my love for you! Please don't close the door on our marriage like this!"

Olufemi stood there, his arms hanging loosely at his side, refusing to return her embrace. His hand on the doorknob, he looked down at Lola's beautiful face, her eyes shedding bitter tears.

"Lola, I don't want to do this anymore. We will discuss the arrangements when I return home."

He pulled himself free from the pleading, crying woman, and left. Slowly, Lola slipped to the floor.

She lay there on the floor where he left her. She knew that he was truly gone. She knew that he had chosen Janice over her. The hold that Janice had on him was stronger than hers. She could not think of anything else to say that would convince him to keep her as his wife.

She cried out loud, "Oh God! What have I done to deserve this? My husband has abandoned his child and me! What have I done?"

14

*J*anice paced the floor at Melinda and Bill's house while her mother and Aunt Dotty prepared the table for dinner. Feeling uncomfortable after the scene that Lola made at the church, Segun and Aduke decided to leave early. Janice took Charles and sat down in the dining room, waiting for Femi to return.

The doorbell rang; it was Femi. He walked towards his wife, whose eyes were filled with questions. Edna and James carried the last of the dishes to the table and sat down, waiting for the others to join them. Everyone wanted to know what had transpired between Lola and Femi, but they all remained silent as Femi and Janice sat down at the table, trying not to mention the incident.

After dinner, Janice took Charles into Melinda's nursery and laid him on the bed. She smiled, as she looked at her cousin's daughter asleep in her crib. "Well, Mindy, they will grow up together just like we did. I want you to let her come to Nigeria to visit me during the summers."

Melinda rushed over to Janice and hugged her. "Jan, I don't want you to go back. It is not safe. That woman may be dangerous, especially now that she is pregnant."

Melinda's words stunned and filled Janice with the memory of what happened in the church this morning.

"Mindy, I will be all right as long as I know that my husband loves me and Charles."

"Come on," Melinda said, taking Janice's arm in hers. "Let's rejoin the others."

They returned to the living room to find everyone deep in conversation. Edna had gotten up the nerve to ask Femi what he and Lola had talked about. Femi told everyone that he had not changed his mind about anything, and that Charles and Janice were his family. He had told Lola that he was not going to have more than one wife, but that he would take care of his child. Janice took a deep breath and looked proudly at her husband, and then she took his hand and held it tight. He gave Janice a look that brought tears to Edna's eyes, for she knew that they loved each other — a love that transcended culture and tradition. Femi was willing to make that sacrifice for Janice and Charles. He was determined not to lose Janice again and would reinforce his decision once they returned to Nigeria to live.

*****

Lola sat alone in the apartment, waiting for Aduke and Segun to come home. They came in angry.

"Sister, what has come over you?" Segun asked, not waiting for an answer. "You had no right to come to the christening. I was so embarrassed."

"I'm sorry. All I wanted to do was to talk to Olu. I didn't mean to hurt anyone."

Aduke had been pacing the floor, listening to the exchange between Segun and Lola. She was tired of the way Lola disrespected Janice and Femi in the first place and could not hold her own anger back any longer.

"Lola, I don't believe you. I feel that you would do anything to get Olufemi back, even try to break up their marriage. Olufemi has made a decision. He does not want you anymore. You need to show some pride and let go gracefully, even if you are pregnant. You know that he will take care of the child!"

Segun looked at his wife, surprised at her outburst. He knew that her friendship with Janice had become strained since their marriage, but he could not let her take out her frustration on his sister.

"It's all right, Aduke. I'm returning to Nigeria in a few days. There's no reason for me to stay in America. Olu no longer wants me here."

"I think that is for the best, Sister. I'll phone Mother and let her know that you are coming."

*****

Janice and Femi entered the guestroom at Melinda and Bill's. Charles shared the room with his new baby cousin. Janice sat on the bed, brushing her long, brown hair while her husband watched her. She saw his look and patted the bed next to her for him to sit down.

"When will we be leaving for Nigeria, Femi? I know that your family is anxious to see the baby."

"I'm planning to leave next week, Janice. That is, if it is okay with you."

He took the brush from her hands and began to brush her hair. She moaned with pleasure at her husband's touch. Femi put down the brush and took hold of her chin, pulling her face to his. He covered her mouth with his full lips, kissing her. She looked in his eyes with yearning as his hands found her breasts and began kneading one gently. Their kisses became more demanding as his free hand reached under her nightgown, massaging her body. His lips kissed her throat and her exposed breasts. Janice flung her head backward and moaned with pleasure as Femi's fingers continued to stroke her moistness. They parted only to undress and lay naked on the bed, touching and massaging each other's bodies. He kissed each and every sensitive part of her, reveling in her sweetness. Her hands massaged him as he entered her body, thrusting with purpose. Their bodies entwined in a quest to reach the pinnacle of pleasure as she whispered in his ear endearments of love, while he pushed his manhood deeper into her. Janice bit his ear and clawed his back with her long nails as she reached the clouds and came with pulsating ecstasy. Femi lay on her breathing heavily, his hands entangled in her long hair. They slept together, naked, legs and arms entwined, until the morning sun crept over the windowsill, and the cries of their son wanting his breakfast awoke them.

Femi wrapped a towel around his naked body and crept quietly into the nursery and took his son to his mother. Janice sat up on the bed and breastfed the hungry baby, while his father watched the scene with love and affection. They later dressed and had breakfast with Melinda and Bill before going to her mother and stepfather's home in Hyde Park.

Edna wanted Janice to come over and see them before they returned to New Orleans. She knew that they were going back to

Nigeria and wanted a chance to say good-bye to her new grandson. She did not want Janice to go back, but she knew that she could say nothing to change her mind. Her handsome son-in-law had a love-hold on her daughter that she knew could not be broken.

"Janice, James and I will come to Nigeria to visit in the spring when he is on vacation."

"Yes, Mother, I think that will be great. I will be sending you pictures and videos of baby Charles' development. I will also keep you informed of the Lola and Femi saga."

"That is one chapter that I hope will close soon. She should let you and Femi get on with your lives."

"In time, Mother ... in time that will happen."

*****

Kemi and Jide had settled well into American life. Yetunde was very helpful in getting Kemi a job at the store where she worked part-time while studying nursing. Jide drove a taxicab. They would share the apartment with Yetunde and her husband just until they had saved enough money towards their own flat. Jide was taking night classes at the local community college while Kemi had been admitted into the nursing program at Chicago State University.

Lola took a taxi to Hyde Park to tell her friends that she was leaving for Nigeria in a few days and wanted to wish them good luck with their studies and new life.

"Lola, I will miss you. Will you be all right without your daily ride to work?"

"No, Jide, I won't. Things just won't be the same without you and Kemi."

Kemi stood nearby, wiping a tear from her eyes with the corner of her wrapper. Even though she was comfortable in American fashions, she still preferred to wear her African attire at home.

"Lola, now that Olu knows about the baby, is he going to take you back?"

Lola lowered her expressive eyes, blinking back the tears that threatened to overflow onto her copper cheeks. "No, he said he does not want to have two wives anymore. He said that he will take care of me and the baby, but he won't live with me as my husband anymore."

"That's not fair, Lola," Jide said angrily. "You have gone through too much with your husband. I wanted to speak to him about his treatment of you, but he refused to talk to me. Will you be all right?"

"I have to Jide, for the baby's sake. I must be strong."

"I will take you home, Lola. Just let me get my car."

When Jide went to the garage, Kemi asked Lola about the baby and if Olu suspected that the child may not be his. Lola told her that he didn't but it made no difference anyway. Olufemi was determined to shut her out of his life.

"Kemi, I will say *o'daro* until we see each other again," said Lola. And she was gone.

Segun and Aduke drove Lola to the airport to catch her flight to London en route to Nigeria. On the way home, Segun breathed a sigh of relief at his sister's departure. He wanted to get on with his life and to begin enjoying his marriage to Aduke. They had made a lot of plans, which did not include his sad sister, and so he was glad that she decided to go back to Nigeria and let their mother take care of her.

"Well, Segun, we are finally alone. What will we do with all this freedom?" asked Aduke.

Segun looked over at his beautiful wife and smiled.

"Ah, Aduke, just you wait until we get home. I will show you ways that freedom can be used constructively. You won't be disappointed, I assure you."

Aduke purred and leaned back into her seat. She was happy that Lola was gone and Janice was in control of her marriage again. She still believed that she and Olufemi belonged together. Although, she felt sorry for her sister-in-law, Lola was a beautiful woman who would have no problem getting any man she wanted. She just needed to let go of Olufemi.

They parked the car and walked into their apartment, heading straight for their bedroom to enjoy making love the way they had longed to do in private. Without Lola or Titiloye present in the home, Aduke was able to release her passion like she never could before.

"Oh, Segun, *Olo-u-fe-mi*, I love you, my dear," she cried out with ecstasy as he pushed her to the stars. They lay beside each other in total peace as they slept, dreaming about their future in America.

15

Titiloye was in Surulere, preparing the house for her daughter's return. She had met with Abimbola and Emmanuel in Ekiti about the marriage of Olufemi and Omolola. Things were going to be difficult since Lola was pregnant — Titiloye used that fact to get Emmanuel to agree that since Olufemi did not want Lola to be his wife, she should be able to keep the house and Olufemi should assist Lola with bringing up their child. Titiloye's daughter was unaware that her mother had been negotiating behind her back.

Lola took a taxi from the airport. Since Grace and her husband were no longer in her employ, she did not have a chauffeur. She would need to get servants to help her maintain her home; she knew that she could not do it alone, especially now. Lola was having morning sickness daily and did not feel like doing much of anything, so she laid her head on the car seat watching the familiar Lagos traffic — a boy chasing a hen across the busy street and a woman hawking wares on her head to passers-by.

A tropical afternoon shower fell, making the air more humid and unbearable. Lola wiped her face with a handkerchief, trying to think of what she could do to change the way things were going for her. Olufemi and Janice would be returning to their house in Ikeja. The only difference was that Olu would not be spending every other week with her. She bit on her lower lip, drawing blood, as she tried to stem the tide of tears that threatened to flow from her large, expressive eyes. She caught the driver looking at her through his mirror.

"Kilo nwo? What are you staring at?" she snapped at him.

The driver quickly lowered his eyes, looking away from the mirror. The elegant woman sat upright and wiped her eyes with her handkerchief thinking, *enough of this weakness. I must be strong. I cannot let them win. I cannot...*

*****

Bisola sat by her pool, enjoying the tropical sea breeze while alternately reading magazines and watching her children swim in the water. Joseph came out to announce that she had a visitor. When she turned around, her brother and Janice were coming to the poolside.

"E'kabo, Olu welcome home!" she shouted, jumping from her chair. "Janice, how are you? You look wonderful! Who is that you are carrying?"

"Hello, Bisi, I'm fine. I want you to meet your nephew Charles."

Bisola took her sleeping nephew into her arms. Ajoke and Taju Jr. rushed from the pool to greet their aunt and uncle.

"Let me see the baby, Mommy. I want to hold him," Ajoke cried with glee.

"Now, now. Go and change into dry clothes and meet us in the den."

The adults retired to the den and sat down while Joseph served them refreshments.

"Why didn't you tell us you were coming? I would have sent the driver."

"It's all right, sister-*mi*. We took a taxi. I will call Taju to let him know that we are back. How are Mother and Father?"

"They are fine and anxious to see all of you, especially little Charles. Oh, you guys, he is adorable."

"Thank you, Bisi," Janice said with pride.

"Janice, let me look at you. You look great. Your figure has already returned. I'm impressed. Aren't you nursing?"

"Of course, I am, and thank you for the compliment," Janice said, tossing her long hair from her face.

"Bisi how is our house? Is Peter still there?"

"Yes, and he already has the house ready and waiting for you all."

They went on to talk about Aduke and Segun's marriage, and Janice gave the children their gifts. Bisi did not want to share Charles with anyone, not even Ajoke.

Ajoke was thrilled to have a baby cousin. "Aunty Janice, may I come over and help you with the baby?"

Janice smiled and took her niece's hand. "Yes, you may. I need all the help I can get with him."

"Janice, I will give you the name of the nanny who took care of Ajoke and T.J. I'm sure that she will be available for you."

"I think that Peter's wife will be good enough for now. If she does not work out, then I will definitely call you. When are your parents coming to Lagos?"

"My father said on Friday. That will give the two of you time to get settled before you have a house full of people."

Olufemi was on the telephone talking to Taju, who was glad that they were back. He really needed Olu to help him run the company. In fact, he wanted him to start back to work right away.

"This will be the challenge I have been missing, Taju. Teaching school is okay, but nothing like negotiating business deals."

"Great, Olu. Then why don't you come into the office tomorrow and familiarize yourself with what has transpired since you have been away. I assure you, I have a lot for you to do."

Olufemi replaced the receiver and went back to his wife and sister, who were chatting about the house in Ikeja.

"Janice, it is just as you left it. As soon as we heard you were coming home, I had Peter and his wife clean the house and make it ready for you."

"That was so nice of you, Bisi," Janice said, hugging her sister-in-law. "It makes things so much easier for us. I missed Peter. I really could have used him in America."

"I'll call Adisa, our driver, to take you home when you are ready."

Janice sat on the sofa nursing Charles, while Olu and Bisi talked about recent events happening in Nigeria. The political climate was not good at the time. There had been another military takeover since he left for America. But even that news did not stop Janice from returning to her second home. She loved Nigeria now and wanted to stay there as long as her husband wanted to. She was happy and felt it was a good place to raise her son and the other children she planned to have.

*****

Titiloye Shodeyi sat in the kitchen on a stool, preparing food in the traditional way. She was not used to the conveniences that Lola had in her modern kitchen. She used the broomsticks to whip the *ewedu* (jute leaves) until they were drawing like okra. She cooked the meat without the pressure cooker and took her tomatoes and pepper to be ground at the local pepper mill, instead of using the blender. She was making dinner for her daughter, Lola, who had been suffering from morning sickness. Dinner was the only meal that she could keep down. She served two plates of *gari* (ground cassava) and carried them on a tray to the dining room. Lola was upstairs and smelled the delicious food.

"Lola, Omolola, *wa jeun* (come and eat)."

"I'm coming, Mother."

The two women sat at the table, and Lola ate with relish. When they finished, they washed the dishes together. Lola was sad, and her mother felt powerless to help her. She wanted to go to the village to consult her *juju* man, but she did not want to leave Lola alone. All Lola's close friends and her brother were now in America, and Lola did not make friends easily. Titiloye wanted Lola to come back to the village with her until the baby was born, but Lola objected to leaving Lagos for anything she also wanted to return to work. So Titiloye gave the store to her brother-in-law to run for her while she stayed in Lagos. She knew Lola would need her when the baby was born.

Abimbola and Emmanuel came to see Lola to confirm that she was pregnant when they visited Lagos. Titiloye was happy that at least they took an interest in her daughter. Olufemi seemed to have abandoned her. Emmanuel gave Lola a large sum of money to run her household. He did not tell her that it really came from his son. Abimbola told Lola to be strong, and that she was sorry that the marriage between her and Olu was not working. This made Lola angry. She felt that his parents were protecting him and pushing her out. She had a plan and would surprise all of them when the time was right.

Every night she would lay in bed thinking of the life she had with Olu before he went to America. Everything was good until he met the *Oyinbo*. I wish he had never met her. I would still have him with me. Lola rubbed her stomach. Her usually flat stomach was beginning to have a nice roundness to it. She could feel the baby inside kicking. She would cry herself to sleep, wishing her husband were lying next to her. *Oh, Olu, I still love you so. This life is so unfair. Oh, God, what am I to do?* She thought.

*****

Janice was rearranging some of their things in the bedroom when Femi came in adjusting his tie. He was returning to work today. The house was just as they left it. Peter had done an excellent job in maintaining their home. The baby was in his crib in the nursery and was being taken care of by Peter's wife, Eno.

"Have a good-day, Femi. I know that Taju will welcome the help."

Femi walked over to Janice, stood behind her, and kissed the top of her head while wrapping his strong arms around her.

She leaned back and sighed. "I am so happy, Femi. This is how our lives should have started off in the beginning. Just you, and later Charles, and me, I could not wish for a happier marriage."

She turned around to face him, looking into his warm, dark-brown eyes. They kissed a deep, satisfying kiss.

"This will have to hold you until you come back this evening, darling. I love you, Femi."

"And I you, Janice. Let me go now, or I will be late."

Femi rushed into the kitchen to eat his breakfast. Peter was standing at the table, waiting to serve his employer.

"Eggs and toast, sir?"

"Thank you, Peter. Oh, Peter, I want to thank you for the wonderful job you did maintaining the house while we were away."

"You are welcome, sir."

After breakfast, Femi drove himself to work. He merged into the Lagos traffic with ease and took the expressway to his office on Isolo Road. The air was cool, but he knew that by noon, it would be very hot and humid. He always believed that the weather was one factor that affected productivity in Nigeria. When the weather was hot, people were too tired. A lot of the factories were not air-conditioned. He was glad that their factory had the latest technology; it was a new building, fully air-conditioned.

Taju was waiting for him, and they convened a small meeting to familiarize Olufemi with the jobs at hand. Olufemi met his new secretary, a middle-aged woman named Alice. His former secretary was on maternity leave. He sat in his office, looking over contracts when his brother-in-law joined him.

"Olu, have you seen Lola since you returned to Lagos?"

"No, Taju, but my parents paid her a visit. My mother and father are coming to spend the weekend with us. They will probably fill me in on what is happening with her."

"How do you feel now that Lola is pregnant? Do you think it will affect your relationship with Janice again?"

"No, Taju. Janice and I have a very strong foundation. Even stronger than the one that Lola and I had. I will never leave Janice for another woman. She and Charles are my life now."

Taju and Femi went to lunch around noon. The Ikoyi Club was crowded as they found a table with an ocean view. Femi ordered pepper soup and *moyin-moyin,* while Taju ordered pounded yam with *egusi* soup. Alhaji Yaro, Lola's boss, was also having lunch at the Ikoyi Club. He was sitting at the next table and decided to say hello to Olufemi.

"Sannu, Mr. Adegoke. Welcome back to Nigeria."

Olufemi turned around to see who was greeting him. He was surprised to see Lola's boss standing there, looking splendid in his *baba riga*. Olufemi stood up and shook his hand.

"Alhaji, good afternoon, sir. How is business?"

"It could be better if your wife were at the office again. I've never had a more efficient secretary than Lola. How is she?"

Alhaji was digging for information. He had not heard from Lola, but found out from one of the other office staff that she had returned to Nigeria. She had not called him, and he wondered why.

"I guess she is fine. I have not seen her since I returned. We are separated, Alhaji."

Alhaji was surprised. "Really, I thought you two were happy."

"Things just did not work out for us. I have another wife now."

Alhaji rubbed his chin. He did not like this man very much. *How can he be so cruel to Lola? She really loves him,* he thought to himself.

"Well, if you see her, let her know that her job is waiting for her. Good afternoon, gentlemen."

Alhaji tipped his hat and left the restaurant. He was worried about Lola, especially after their affair. But he was a patient man. He truly believed that someday she would be his.

"Olu, I didn't know that Lola worked for that Alhaji Yaro," Taju said. "He comes from a very wealthy and influential family in Kano. He is a very powerful man."

"Oh, yes, she has worked for him for several years now. I believe that he has a thing for her. But he already has three wives and knowing Lola that would be too much for her. She would not become involved with a man like that."

"Well, what does that matter now, Olu? You no longer want her anyway."

Olufemi watched Alhaji leave the restaurant and get into his chauffeured Mercedes Benz. A twinge of suspicion went through him for an instant. Then he shook his head and continued eating his lunch.

*****

Janice was feeding Charles when Peter came to announce a visitor. It was her good old friend, Linda Hassan.

Linda walked in, looking as beautiful as ever, wearing a white linen pantsuit. Her long, black hair in a ponytail bounced as she walked gracefully into the den.

"Linda!" Janice shouted, surprised and happy to see her friend.

"I heard you were back from the states, girl. I can see motherhood agrees with you. How are you, Janice?"

"I'm fine, Linda. How is your husband and children?"

"They are fine. The children are with my mother-in-law in Bauchi, and Ali is in Switzerland on business. I expect him to return tomorrow. Let me hold the baby."

Janice led her to a chair and Linda took Charles from her arms.

"Oh, Janice, he is so cute. Hello, Charles. I bet you call him Chazz."

"How did you know, that?"

"I have a brother named Charles, and that's his nickname. Janice, how are things with you and Femi? I couldn't believe that you came back after all you went through."

Janice told Linda what had happened between her and Femi since she left Nigeria. She told her how Lola followed them to America and tried to cause problems. She also told her about Lola's pregnancy.

"But, Janice, how are you going to handle that? She will always be in your life now because of the baby. Ali's new wife is expecting too. But my situation is so different from yours."

"I will be fine, Linda. As long as I have Femi, I will be fine. Have you seen Sharon? I miss her. I intend to call her today."

"Sharon and Ngozi are all right. Uche is now the chief accountant for his firm. Sharon no longer has to work. She decided to stay home and have another baby."

"I'm planning a dinner party and will invite all of my friends and renew acquaintances. Will you come and bring Ali?"

"I can't promise Ali, but you know that I will be there."

They spent the rest of the afternoon catching up on what had been happening in Lagos and their women's club. Janice put Charles down for a nap and the two women went for a swim in the pool. Linda left right before dinner.

Janice saw that Linda's life had not changed. Linda was satisfied living in polygamy. Her husband was a very rich and powerful politician. He already had two wives, Linda and Yasmin. But before Janice left Nigeria, he took another wife from India, a young woman named Leti. The three women were able to live together in harmony because they were all from different cultures. Yasmin was Egyptian, Linda, an American, and Leti was from India. They each brought something special to their house, and this enabled them to not compete as much. Their husband, Ali, would not tolerate any problems anyway. He ruled his household with an iron hand. They just hoped he would not bring in another wife.

16

*L*ola wanted to return to work. Her morning sickness had subsided, and she was bored staying at home. She took particular care with her appearance, wearing a new wrapper she had made recently, and she wore her hair in braids that hung down her back. Her figure was fuller now that she was pregnant, and her skin glowed with her approaching motherhood. She walked into the reception area of the ministry and met a strange woman at her desk.

"I'd like to see Alhaji Yaro."

The woman eyed her with suspicion.

"Do you have an appointment?"

"Just tell him Mrs. Omolola Adegoke is waiting."

The secretary buzzed Alhaji on the intercom. He rushed out of the office to Lola's surprise.

"Sannu, Lola, welcome back! How lovely you look today. Come inside my office so we can talk."

Alhaji put his arm around Lola's back and led her into his plush office. He watched her sit down on the sofa as he stood, absorbing her beauty.

"Lola, you look wonderful. How was your journey? Are you coming back to work soon?"

Lola fiddled with her hands in her lap, trying not to meet Alhaji's eyes. When she finally looked up at him, she saw the desire they held for each other. He had noticed how she filled out and asked her if she was she gaining weight. She told him she was in the early stages of pregnancy. He was surprised, and said he hoped that would not keep her from returning to work.

"Oh, no, Alhaji. I came hoping that I could get my old job back."

"Of course, Lola. I told you your job would be waiting for you. I saw your husband at the Ikoyi Club a few days ago having lunch. He told me he was with his other wife and that you and he were no longer together."

Lola was embarrassed that Olu would make it public already that they were not living together any longer. She did not want Alhaji to be proved right and rub it in.

"Yes, Alhaji, it is true that we are not living together. He decided to stay with the *Iyawo*, but I am pregnant with his child and I expect him to come back home when the child is born."

Alhaji was not pleased with her words. He had been longing for her since that day in the office when they made love. He never felt that way about his other wives and wanted Lola to fill the void in his life.

"Lola, why do you persist with this? Your husband has said publicly that you are no longer man and wife. In my culture, when a man announces his desires, it becomes law. Can't you understand that he does not want you? I want you, Lola. I will do anything to make you happy. Can't you at least give me a try?"

Lola looked into Alhaji's dark, handsome eyes. She knew that he was sincere and that he loved her. He proved it the afternoon they spent together on the very sofa she was sitting on when they made love. His motives were genuine, while Lola's were for her own benefit.

"Alhaji let me think about it. I need some time to get over Olu. Can I begin work tomorrow?"

"Yes, Lola. You know there will always be a place in my office and in my heart for you."

Lola went home and told her mother that she planned to return to work. Titiloye was not pleased with this. She wanted her daughter to remain at home and let Olufemi take care of her now and after the baby was born. They were still married, and he owed an obligation to Lola and her unborn grandchild. Lola knew that it was not going to be easy working with Alhaji now. She knew that he was going to try to win her heart, but her heart had hardened to men and she was determined to get Olu back.

Lola had another friend who worked in the market named Yinka. She sold china and glassware in the Balogun market in Lagos. Kemi had introduced them, and they became good friends. Yinka had two children by her husband, who lived in Abeokuta, but she preferred to live in Lagos because he had several wives. He had wanted her to move her business to Abeokuta so she would be closer to him, but she dared not, for to do would mean giving up her independence, and she had worked too long to do that. She knew she was more successful than all of her husband's other wives, who depended on him for support, and she also knew that if she moved to Abeokuta, he would try to control her money and movements.

And so, she just saw him twice a month and she always paid a visit to his mother and father in the village nearby.

Lola had confided in Yinka about her problems with Olufemi, and Yinka proved to be a good friend and confidante, consoling and advising Lola as to how she should deal with the issue of Janice. After she left Alhaji's office, she paid Yinka a visit.

"Let him have her. Just make sure that he sees you regularly," Yinka told Lola sternly. "You see, Lola, you messed up when you made demands on him by saying that he had to live with you. Let him stay with her so long as he makes regular visits. Really Lola, the sex is better when you have not been together for a while."

"But, Yinka, I feel that he is shutting me out of his life. Now he won't even speak to me!"

"That is temporary, my friend. Believe me, when he sees his child all that will change. Trust me he will come running. Right now she has the upper hand because she has a son for him. But wait until you have yours, Lola. He will come running. Our Nigerian men don't like the idea of another man raising their children."

So Lola did like her friend said. She returned to work and tried to live her life without Olu in it. She now took a taxi to work every morning and even stayed at work and worked overtime. Still, Alhaji, hard as he tried, could not persuade her to have lunch or dinner with him, so he finally decided to give things a rest and wait; he was certain that Lola, being young and lonely in spite of her pregnancy, would come around ... he hoped.

*****

Abimbola welcomed her daughter-in-law by giving her a big hug as she walked into the living room. Janice looked around and sighed at the homey feeling that the room had. Emmanuel threw his *agbada* over his shoulder and held his arms open for Janice to come to him for a hug. Janice was surprised and happy that her father-in-law had finally accepted her. She knew that the birth of a grandchild meant a lot in their culture. Abimbola hugged and kissed Janice again and inquired as to where their son was. Then Olufemi came into the room, smiling and holding Charles for them to meet.

Janice and Olufemi stood back and watched the years fall off his parents as they played with Charles. Peter took their bags into the guestroom and showed their driver to his quarters. Eno served drinks while Abimbola held the child in her arms.

"Oh, Olu, he looks like you. All except his eyes and hair — that is his mother," she said.

The baby did have Olufemi's features and Janice's light brown eyes and curly hair. He was a happy baby who smiled at his grandparents, making them feel glad he was a part of their family.

"Most babies cry at strangers when they are this age," Abimbola said joyfully while bouncing him in her arms. "He is such a happy baby, Emmanuel."

She was tempted to put him on her back like she did Olufemi when he was a baby, but instead, she looked at Janice and asked her if she had tried it.

"Yes, I have. And as soon as I put him on my back, he would be asleep in an instant," she responded.

They all laughed.

Soon it was dinnertime, and Eno came to take Charles. The family went into the dining room to eat. After dinner, Olufemi took his father to his club while the women bathed the baby and put him to bed. After kissing him good night, Janice and her mother-in-law went to sit by the pool and watch the sun go down.

"Have you seen Lola, Janice?"

Janice was surprised by her mother-in-law's question. "No," was all she answered.

"I have seen her, and we are doing what we can for her. She is back in the house in Surulere, where she lives with her mother."

A tear slid down Janice's cheek slowly, followed by another. She walked inside silently, her mother-in-law close behind her.

"Why did you bring up her name and spoil our reunion, Mama Femi? Lola is no longer a part of our lives. We are happy. I am happy, and your son can be happy, if you all let him."

"Janice, I did not mean to upset you. But you know Lola is a problem that will not go away, even though you are married to our son. She carries his child, just like you did, and she deserves better treatment than this. After all, she is his first wife."

Janice wiped her tears and raised an eyebrow at Abimbola's use of *is*. Then they walked into the luxurious living room decorated with the latest modern decor.

"What do you want me to do? I cannot live the way we lived before. I cannot accept the fact that Femi is still married to her and me, especially now that Charles is here. Femi promised me he would not take her back. He realized that he made a terrible mistake not divorcing her before he married me. I forgave him for all that. Now, I just want us to be happy."

Janice stood up and began pacing the floor. Abimbola sat stiffly, not saying what she really wanted to. She and her husband had taken over their son's responsibilities where Lola was concerned.

"Janice," she began softly, "Olufemi has a responsibility to Lola until the baby is born. Then his responsibility for Lola will end. I am not asking him to take her back. I know that he loves you. I see the way he looks at you and you him. I know that Lola cannot make him happy anymore. But you must understand our position. I don't want to lose my grandchild. I thought I had lost that angel in the other room when you left Nigeria. We have a lot of money, Janice; money is no object. However, Lola will not go away. She does not want the money ... She wants Olufemi. I fear that she will stop at nothing to get him back. Janice, I want you to be careful where you go. Always take a driver with you and stay away from the local market without an escort. A jealous woman is a dangerous woman, but a woman scorned..."

She did not even need to finish. Janice knew all too well what a woman like Lola could do to someone she wanted to hurt.

"I understand, Mama Femi. But I am not afraid of her. She hurt me once. She will never hurt me again."

Olufemi and his father sped towards the Eko Hotel in Victoria Island in Lagos. Emmanuel was not used to the nightlife of Lagos. Outside of a few parties and cocktails, he and his wife usually turned in early when they visited the city. Olufemi knew this and was pleased when his father accepted his invitation to go out. He gazed at his father, who looked splendid in his native attire, appearing younger than his 52 years. His hair, graying at the temples, stood out under his hat. *He is still a strikingly handsome man,* thought Olufemi, who was settling well into his 32 years, *and I am a lot like him.*

They made quite a pair as they walked inside the lobby towards the hotel lounge. Olufemi found a table near the bar, and they ordered drinks. Emmanuel was glad to have the time to talk to his son.

"Olufemi, your mother and I visited Lola last week. I am unhappy with the way you have abandoned her when she is expecting your child."

Olufemi sipped his drink, not looking at his father. He realized now why Emmanuel wanted to come with him.

"Father, I asked Lola not to follow me to America. I forbade her to travel, but she chose to do so anyway. Aside from that, I did not know she was pregnant. I was in Houston for two months before I even went to New Orleans to reconcile with Janice. In fact, Janice refused to even talk to me. It was very difficult for me to convince Janice that I loved her, and then Lola comes to America to spoil everything I repaired. I was shocked that she came, disobeying me. I warned her that if she did, I would not speak to her again."

"Son, I understand your reasons for being angry with her, but to divorce her? When we arranged your marriage to her five years ago, you said you loved her. Why did you marry her if you didn't? No one was forcing you!"

Olufemi looked at his father incredulously. He could not believe what his father was saying. Had he forgotten the threats to disinherit him if he married a foreigner?

"Baba mi," (my father), he began passionately, "I know you and Mother did not want me to marry a woman who was not from our tribe or culture, but what you refuse to understand is that you cannot control the human heart. I didn't go looking for love with Janice; it found me. True, I grew to love Lola; what man would not? She is a desirable, beautiful, and a fascinating woman. But I fell in love with Janice. I was faithful to Lola until I met Janice. Janice is the best thing that has ever happened to me. I cannot and I do not want to live without her. I could not bear it. When she left, I felt like my whole world had ended. With Lola I was half; with Janice I am whole. I know how you and Mother feel about her being a foreigner, but she is of African descent. She is learning every day about our culture. She wants Charles to speak our language, and she wants him to be raised African. What more can I do?"

Emmanuel again nodded in agreement while sipping his drink. He looked around the room filled with people then looked back at his son, choosing his words carefully.

"Olufemi, you are an Adegoke. Our family has always upheld its honorable name. Maybe your mother and I were wrong to deny your marriage to the English woman, but we felt we had your best interest at heart. I still believe that we made the right decision at the time. I did not understand the kind of burden I put on you when we arranged your marriage to Lola. Our people want the best of the western society without compromising our cultural heritage. Your marrying a white woman would have changed the entire makeup of our family. At least with Janice, she has African ancestry, even if she is mixed with the European races."

Olufemi nodded in agreement with his father. *"Baba mi,* I will do what I can to make Lola comfortable until she has the baby. This pregnancy came up so suddenly. I was in complete shock when she told me, especially since I had just reconciled with Janice, but I will do the honorable thing. I will not shame the family."

Emmanuel and Abimbola spent the rest of the weekend with their children, doting on their new grandson. On Sunday afternoon, they packed their bags and returned to Ilesha. Janice and Femi breathed a sigh of relief as the driver took them to the airport. Femi joined his wife on the sofa and sat playing with her hair.

"Let's spend the afternoon in our room doing some catching up," he suggested.

Janice looked at Femi's handsome face and drew her finger along his cheek gently. Then she moved closer and pulled his face to hers, kissing him full on his lips. He sighed and pushed his tongue into her ready, waiting mouth. They sat there in a passionate embrace, when Eno, holding their son, Chazz, interrupted them.

"Oh, I am so sorry, Madame, sir. I should have knocked," Eno spoke, blushing with embarrassment.

Baby Chazz was smiling, bouncing in his nanny's arms as Janice and Femi readjusted their clothing, smiling at each other at Eno's obvious discomfort.

"It's all right, Eno. Give me the baby and take the rest of the afternoon off," Olufemi said, taking his son into his strong arms.

So instead of making love all afternoon, the two new parents spent the day playing with their son and loving each other with their eyes. Janice put the baby to bed around 6 p.m. and served dinner at 7 p.m. The loving parents then went to bed early to finish up where they left off that afternoon.

Their lovemaking held the heat and excitement of the day they first met. Femi was so masterful with his touch, able to arouse Janice to her peak instantly. She was so excited by the time he entered her that she reached her new heights of ecstasy as he plunged into her hot, moist depths, filling his lips with the tan tips of her breasts. She shouted aloud with exquisite pleasure as he rode her to oblivion. They slept close together, he lying behind her with his arm around her body, holding her tight.

*****

While in another part of Lagos, Lola spent a restless night alone in her bed. She laid naked, rubbing her hands gently across her rounding abdomen, feeling the child moving and fluttering like a butterfly. A lonely tear fell across her bronze cheekbones; she closed her eyes, her long, black lashes fanning her cheek. Her full lips pouted as she tried to hold back the emotional dam that threatens to burst.

"Olu ... oh my Olu," she spoke to herself with hope in her heart. "You will come back to me when our child is born."

Deep inside, Lola really believed that she could win back the heart of her husband. Then in the next instant, bitterness took hold of her heart, and she squeezed her beautiful eyes into slits of anger.

"She will not win. No, she cannot have him. If I cannot have him, then no one will!"

17

Sharon and her steward set the dinner table for four, and then he rushed into the kitchen to check on her roast. She was serving a traditional American dinner of roast beef, potatoes, carrots, salad, and rolls, with peach cobbler and ice cream for dessert. She had invited Janice and Femi to join her and Uche for dinner to celebrate Uche's promotion to chief accountant of Peugeot in Lagos. It was a very high-level promotion that Uche truly deserved. He had worked for the company since graduating and returning to Nigeria. They were also celebrating Sharon's news that she was expecting a baby in the spring. Their daughter, Ngozi, was now five years old and they did not want her to grow up an only child. Uche wanted his wife to stop working and concentrate on raising his children, which Sharon was ready to do now since her husband's new job gave them more money than they needed.

Her husband Uche, hailed from the eastern part of Nigeria, Imo state he was from the Ibo tribe and Sharon was from Virginia. The promotion came with lots of perks, including a car, chauffeur, and a new house on Victoria Island. Sharon was thrilled that she was going to be living in the same style as many of the American women in her club. She planned to ask Janice to help her decorate the house because she had such good taste.

They had dessert and Sharon was showered with praises over the peach cobbler. Janice and Femi raised their glasses in a toast to their host and hostess. It had been a long time since Janice had seen her friend. Sharon had given her support at a time when Janice's marriage was in trouble. The couples then retired to the living room with their wine glasses and talked about their children. Femi bragged about Charles, who had tried to stand up and was already eating table food.

"They grow so fast, Femi. Maybe it is time for you to have another one," Sharon said, pointing at her stomach.

Even though Femi did not react, he began thinking about Lola and the impending birth of their child. He remained silent, and Janice noticed his mood.

"Is everything all right, honey?"

"Fine, Jan. I think I just drank too much wine."

They left around 11 p.m. and drove through Lagos to Ikeja. After they got home, they rushed in to check on Charles sleeping in his crib with Eno nearby. She rose and left for her quarters to join her husband, and the proud parents stood around the crib, looking at their sleeping child, holding each other's hands.

"Femi, let's not wait too long before we start planning another baby. I don't want Charles to be an only child like me."

But Femi did not comment. His mind was not on Janice's needs at the moment; instead, he was thinking about Lola and her pregnancy.

*****

Lola's return to work was met with joy and celebration. Alhaji was so overjoyed; he even gave her a raise. She took over her duties from her replacement, who was not happy to be given another assignment. Lola was never late and every morning she met him with his tea. She missed Jide taking her to work in the morning because she hated the taxi she had to use. Her mother had suggested that she should ask *Baba* Femi to give her a car and driver. She decided to, and he agreed to find her someone as soon as possible, but then he changed his mind and agreed to pay for a taxi driver to come every morning and take her to work.

Lola tried to ignore her boss's flirtation with her. Alhaji had tasted her fruit and wanted more. She had known that it was going to be hard to restore their relationship to the way it was before they slept together, but still she was going to try.

"Lola, no one can even tell that you are pregnant. You don't even show. Please accompany me to dinner tonight."

"Alhaji, you know that I cannot. I will not do anything that will make Olu think that I have betrayed him."

"But Lola, you said yourself that he has not called for two months. You need some excitement. Come out with me."

Lola was adamant. She was not going to make the same mistake again with Alhaji. Though he was handsome and desirable and an excellent lover, she wanted to remain celibate.

"No, Alhaji. I will not jeopardize my chances with Olu again."

Alhaji was incensed. Though he wanted Lola, he wanted her to become his willingly. "All right, Lola, but Olu will find out one day," he forewarned, then he turned abruptly and left, his robes rustling as he walked with dignity into his office.

Lola breathed a sigh of relief. She knew that Alhaji loved her, but she could not give him what he wanted. Right now, all she wanted was her husband back.

Taju and Femi sat together going over their reports on the company when Taju put down his papers and looked over at his brother-in-law.

"Olu, have you heard from Lola?"

Olufemi looked with surprise at Taju. "No, I have not. Should I?"

"Bisi saw her at the market yesterday. She told her that she had returned to work. My wife was a bit embarrassed to run into her, especially since it is your parents who are taking care of Lola. She told Bisi that your father has given her a car and a driver."

Olufemi was startled and a bit angry that his father was being so generous with his other wife.

"I think that my father has gone too far with this, and Lola is taking advantage of her situation. Taju, I don't feel like being the father to her child. I am blissfully happy with Janice, and this is the only shadow hanging over our happiness."

"I know, Brother, but Lola is still legally your wife and you must take care of her until that changes. After all, it is your child."

"I know, Taju. I fully intend to be responsible for the child, but I cannot take care of Lola anymore. Janice does not like it, and I will not do anything to hurt her again. She has suffered enough already. We are also thinking about having another baby soon."

"That is wonderful, Olu. Then Janice intends to make Nigeria her home permanently. Not many women can give up their country and family, you know."

"Yes, Janice agreed. We intend to go twice a year to see her mother and her other relatives. She does not want to leave Nigeria. She is making this her home and the home for our children."

"Splendid, Olu; that is splendid. I pray that everything will go as you plan. I do believe that Janice is special. I know of several Nigerians who have had foreign-born wives for many years. Take my physician, Dr. Mimi, for example. He and his wife came here from London. She is British and white. They have been here for twenty years, and she has raised their children here, who are now in college in London."

"Janice loves Nigeria, Taju. If it were not for the situation that I created, she would never have left."

That evening, Olufemi told Janice about his conversation with Taju. She saw the concern in her husband's eyes and assured him that she would not leave him again.

"Femi, I am very happy. I have friends here, and I am devoted to you and our son. I intend to make Nigeria my home for as long as you will have me."

He took his wife into his arms, holding her tightly. His nose tingled with the smell of her freshly washed hair. He ran his fingers through the long, brown locks, pulling her face to his and brushing her lips gently with his before raining passionate kisses onto her face and neck. Janice's body quivered with passion as she returned his kisses with adoration. They looked deeply into one another's eyes, and no words were needed as Femi lifted Janice into his strong arms and walked silently into the bedroom.

He laid her on the bed and began to undress her. Piece by piece, he removed her clothing until she was naked on the cool sheets. The room held the soft glow of moonlight as his eyes held a mystical glow of their own. He quickly removed his clothes and joined his beautiful wife on the bed. For a few seconds they did not touch; they were becoming aroused just looking at each other. Janice's eyes shone with flecks of fire as her passion smoldered, waiting to be ignited. She did not have to wait long, because Femi took her fingers into his mouth and began kissing each one, ending with the palm of her hand, then he rolled his tongue gently around in circles, igniting the fire in her loins. He covered her mouth with his while his hand covered her breasts, tickling her nipples until her body tingled with excitement. His fingers then sought her moistness as she arched her hips to meet him.

She moaned softly, pulling him closer to her as he pushed his tongue into her mouth, kissing with tenderness. Her hands sought his manhood to guide it into her pulsating heat. They molded together, fire into fire, hot and demanding flames shooting one another with the searing sparks of ecstasy, giving and receiving pleasure, pushing to the limits of passion. Janice cried out, her fingers kneading his back as he filled his mouth with her breast. He thrust deeper into the heat; bursting with release as together they whirled into the vortex of ecstasy, feeling the pleasure pulsating over and over inside cooling the fire. They lay together, not speaking, just holding each other until they fell asleep peacefully in the night.

*****

Lola awoke each morning filled with purpose. She was happy to go to work — it kept her busy and didn't give her time to think about Olu. Meanwhile, Lola blossomed into motherhood. Her stomach was much larger than that of a woman five months pregnant, and lately, she was eating a lot more. Everyone asked her if she was carrying twins, even her mother. Alhaji would tease her, but she would just laugh it off, while deep inside, she was filled with fear that she could not pull off her deception.

One evening at home, Lola's mother commented on her size. "Lola, it will be a double blessing if you were to have twins. I would be so proud. Your brother, Segun, wrote me another letter asking about your pregnancy. I will write him back and tell him what I predict."

Lola turned her bloated body around in her chair to face her mother. "You will do nothing of the kind. Don't get him worked up, thinking that I am having twins. I am just having a big baby, that's all."

Titiloye was puzzled by her daughter's behavior. Lately she had become irrational and overly emotional. Her mother worried about her mental health so much that she decided to give Olu a call to beg him to at least talk to Lola and ask about the pregnancy. His father sent money every week to pay for her expenses, but Lola wanted it to come from Olu.

Olufemi told Janice about Titiloye's request. Janice was amazed that Lola's mother would have the nerve to approach Femi with such a request. Janice knew that Olufemi no longer loved his first wife, but still she did not trust him being alone with her.

She could not hide her worry from her voice. "Femi, if you feel that you need to see her, then do so, especially if her health will affect the child. I will not stand in the way of you fulfilling your obligation to her."

Janice could not meet his eyes because she knew he would be able to see she was not sincere.

"Jan, I have been thinking about paying her a visit at work."

Janice's heart leapt. She was glad that he was not going to see her at the house in Surulere.

Femi called Lola at work that morning and asked if he could come by her office. She was annoyed that he wanted to meet her in a public place, and she hoped that Alhaji would be out on business so she could meet him in private.

Femi entered her familiar office. He could hardly recognize her. She had blossomed. Pregnancy definitely agreed with her. Her bronze complexion glowed under her long braids that were held together with a colorful scarf that matched her cotton caftan. She had gained most of her weight in her round belly. It protruded in front of her like it was in the way. Lola stood, looking at the handsome man who had forsaken her, and her eyes began to fill with tears.

"O ... O ... Olu," she whimpered, reaching out for him. He cringed, his eyes filled with guilt as he held her shuddering body, grateful for the baby that kept her from getting too close. He handed Lola his handkerchief and led her to her desk chair. She sat down, dabbing daintily at her expressive, brown eyes, looking at him deeply. There could be no mistaking her love for him. He cleared his throat and began speaking.

"How have you been, Omolola? Your mother said you wished to see me."

Lola stared incredulously at her estranged husband. She could not believe that this attractive man sitting in front of her was Olu. All she could see was how distant he had become. Her full lips turned slowly up into a seductive smile as she told him about her health, while trying to think of a way to lure him back into her arms.

"I am well, Olu. The baby is strong. I am growing larger daily," she said, patting her round abdomen. "My mother is taking good care of me."

Then when she saw no change in him, her voice became impatient. "She is doing what you should be doing, Olu. Why do you persist in this? We are still married, and I am entitled to see you. I refuse to be treated like Taju treats Abbe, pushed into the background and forgotten." Her voice rose in anger.

Olufemi remained calm and explained his position to Lola again. "Lola, I told you that I no longer want to have two wives, and I have chosen Janice. I know that you do not want to understand, but I will do what I can for you and the baby. The child will have all it needs."

"Yes, everything except its father! Olu, who will be its father?" Lola was shouting and rose from her chair to confront him. They began arguing over responsibility.

Outside in hall, Alhaji heard Lola's voice raised in anger. He had seen her husband's driver outside the building. He nosily put his ear to the door and listened to their argument.

"Lola," Olu began, "I am sorry that you do not agree with the arrangement. If you want to file for divorce, I give you my permission."

Olufemi stood firm, holding her angry gaze. His eyes held a vacant look and she saw no love in them for her or for her unborn child. She began to shake with fear as she thought; *I don't know this man standing before me. I have truly lost him.* Her eyes filled with angry tears as she shouted accusations to his face, pointing out that he was abandoning his child. Then her stomach began to hurt as the child kicked her mercilessly. She leaned back against the desk and held her abdomen. Olu, seeing her face pale, asked if she was all right.

"How can I be all right? I thought that if I left you alone, you would come to your senses and take me back. Olu, what have I done to make you hate me? What spell has this woman cast on you that would make your love turn away? I agreed to have a mate, and now you discard me. How can I raise this child alone without a husband, Olu? I will never let you go, so go back to your other wife and tell her that. I will never divorce you!"

A look of fatigue appeared on Olufemi's face as the truth of his actions came to bear down on him. He knew that all this was his fault, and he had no one to blame but himself. He only looked with guilt at his first wife, for he knew that he was just using her disobedience as an excuse to leave her. He knew that his decision to stay with Janice would mean divorcing Lola, because he was more than certain that Janice would never agree to him taking care of her and the child. His situation was not at all like his brother-in-law Taju's, whose wives were both Nigerian. Olufemi regretted his decision to keep Lola a secret from Janice, and he did not want to go back to living with both women again. Now his heart was with Janice and Charles. Still he did not want to jeopardize Lola's health by asking her for a divorce in her current condition. So he walked over to where she stood, sobbing, and took her by the shoulders. She turned into the shelter of his arms, reveling in his masculinity.

"Oh, Olu, I love you. Please take me back. I will die without your love," she cried desperately. "It has been so long since you held me like this."

She snuggled deeply into his chest, wetting his shirt with her tears. He felt a stirring of guilt, not love. His mind began to see Janice and her pleading eyes when he told her he was going to see

Lola. He knew he had a difficult choice to make, and, in the end, there would be no winners. Olu pushed Lola gently away.

"All right, Lola. I have to go to work now. I will stop by and see how you are doing in a few days."

Reluctantly, Lola released him, her lips quivering. Olufemi took a deep breath and turned towards the door.

Alhaji, still listening to their conversation, heard Olu say that he was leaving, so he rushed downstairs pretending to have just come inside. He met Olu on the stairs, and the two men greeted each other.

"San-nu, Alhaji, *Lafiya?"*

"Ah, Mr. Adegoke; long time no see. Did you travel?"

"No, Alhaji, I have just been busy. Well, good day to you."

Alhaji watched Lola's husband leave the building and enter his car, his eyes closing together like a cat, observing him, and envying him. He thought to himself, *Olu is a very lucky man. He has the one thing that I cannot seem to win ... Lola's love.*

Alhaji entered the office and Lola was looking out the window, also watching her husband drive away.

"Lola, I met your husband in the hall. Is everything all right now?"

She turned around, her beautiful face filled with pain. The tears began to roll as she twisted Olu's handkerchief in her hands. Her body shuddered, filled with sobs, and she spoke incoherently.

Alhaji was deeply moved and took her into his arms, attempting to console her. He spoke softly. "Lola, you are a beautiful and desirable woman. Any man would be a fool to let you go."

He felt her child move against his body and pressed closer, while she allowed him to caress her cheek. Then he kissed the tears from her face. She looked into his eyes and saw the pain of love in them and sobbed even harder for she knew that though he was offering her what she needed, she couldn't accept it. Gently pulling away, she blew her nose and wiped her face.

"No, Alhaji, I cannot do this. Olu has said he would take care of the child and me. He will try to visit me more often."

"And when the child is born, Lola, will Olu be its father?"

"He said he would, Alhaji. But only time will tell."

Alhaji knew better. If what he heard transpiring between them was any indication of her husband's acceptance of his responsibility, then Lola was a fool. But he wouldn't tell her that now. He would wait for her to finally come to her senses and understand that she would never be first in her husband's life again. Then he would make his move.

*****

Peter served Janice and Sharon lunch outside by the pool. The cool, tropical breezes blew through the palm trees that lined the yard as the two women talked about the last meeting of the women's club and the party they were planning to give. Sharon was on the refreshment committee, while Janice was responsible for the decorations. They had decided to hold the party at Janice's home. She was more than happy to accommodate. She loved parties, and this would give her a chance to show off her home and her handsome husband.

"Sharon, I am glad you are feeling better. Morning sickness is no joke."

"Girl, who are you telling? I was so sick every morning; everything I ate would come right up. Uche was so concerned, but I assured him that it was normal. He had forgotten that I was sick like that with Ngozi. It's a blessing that she is in school now. I have more time to prepare for the baby. Jan, I saw Lola in the market on Saturday. She recognized me from the airport. She was friendly enough, but I could not believe how big she was. She looked like she was nine months instead of seven. That is how far along you said she was, didn't you?"

Janice looked at her friend, surprised. "Yes, that is what Femi told me."

"Janice, I'm sorry to tell you this, but unless she is carrying twins, she looks further along than that."

They finished their lunch and took Charles, who was sleeping in his stroller, inside. Then they turned on the latest video from London.

Janice left shortly after and took Charles to pay a visit to Bisola. They entered the cool house and met Ajoke, who was more than happy to take her cousin off to play. Janice found Bisola in the kitchen cooking, something that her sister-in-law rarely did because she had a full-time cook.

"Bisi, you are in the kitchen cooking! I am impressed," Janice said smiling.

Bisola laughed and finished the last of the *moyin-moyin* she was preparing. She then put the molds into a large pot and gave instructions to her cook to watch them until they were firm.

Bisi hugged Janice, and the two women walked into the den.

"Where is my nephew?" Bisi asked, looking around the room for Charles.

"You're too late. Ajoke has taken him to play."

"I am happy to see you, Janice. You look well. How is my brother?"

"He is fine, Bisi, just fine. Bisi, I have something to ask you. When was the last time you saw Lola?"

Bisola was surprised by the question and stopped what she was doing to look at her sister-in-law.

"I saw her last week. Why do you ask?"

Janice told her about Sharon's observations. "You know, Bisi that Sharon is a nurse and would know about these things. If Lola is seven months, then she should not be so large."

Bisola was silent, thinking about Lola and how upset she was when she saw her last. She was very unhappy that Olufemi only came to see her at the office, instead of at home.

"Come to think of it," Bisi wondered to herself, "she does appear to be larger than a woman in her seventh month."

"Maybe she is having twins, Janice; that could be the reason that she is so large."

Janice pushed her long hair away from her face, looking at Bisi and thinking, *they always stick together.* She stood up and began pacing the floor.

"Bisola, the only thing standing in the way of my personal happiness is the fact that Lola is pregnant. That ties her permanently to Femi. We will never be free of her. He will have to be responsible for her and their child and Lola will forever be in our lives."

"Now, Janice, I thought you were over that. I thought you accepted that fact. It is our culture. Olufemi will not abandon his child. Your situation changed when she became pregnant. He has an obligation to the child."

"Yes, to the child, not to Lola!"

Bisola walked over to Janice, placing her hand on her shoulder, trying to calm her.

"He has a certain amount of obligation to his first wife, too, Janice."

The words stung even before she said them. His first wife ... his first wife — the words reverberated in Janice's brain. She placed her hands over her ears as if to shut out the sounds.

Shaking her head, feeling defeated, she asked, "Bisi, will I ever have peace in my marriage? I love Femi and I know he loves me. Will I ever be free of this curse?"

"Only if the child is not my brother's. Then he would be released from all obligations to Lola and her family."

The wheels began to turn in Janice's brain. She spent the rest of the afternoon with Bisola, enjoying the food she prepared. Then she went home and phoned Sharon to tell her of her suspicions. If her memory served her correctly, Femi was in Houston when Lola became pregnant.

"Sharon, Femi told me himself that he had not been sleeping with Lola before he came to Houston. They had been quarreling about his traveling alone."

"Are you sure, Janice? Those are some pretty heavy accusations. You have to have proof. How will you get it?"

"You can help. Didn't you tell me that you are friends with the nurse at the maternity hospital and that you and Lola have the same obstetrician?"

"Yes, we do," Sharon, agreed reluctantly.

"Then you can find out her due date. She told Femi it's in two months."

"Janice, I'm surprised at you. You know that information is confidential. I can't ask the doctor that."

Deflated, Janice sat quietly for a moment, rethinking what she would ask Sharon, for Sharon was her only hope of getting information on Lola.

"Then just ask him if she is having twins. That will be enough. Because if she is not, then why is she so big?"

Sharon agreed to do that. She hoped it would help her.

A few days later, Sharon had her doctor's appointment and Janice accompanied her to the maternity hospital. They entered the waiting room and found among the women waiting to see the doctor Lola, sitting in the corner reading a magazine. The two ladies sat in another area of the waiting room where Lola could not see them.

"Mrs. Adegoke, you may see the doctor now." Instinctively, Janice stood up when her name was called.

Sharon grasped her arm and whispered, "Not you, Janice — Lola."

Janice watched Lola struggle from the chair and enter the examination room. She could not believe her eyes — Lola appeared near term. She did not look at all like she was in her seventh month. Janice's heart began to beat faster as she thought about the prospect of Lola having twins. She looked at Sharon, who nodded in agreement that she was further along than seven months.

"Sharon, I will go and wait in the car. I don't want Lola to see me here when she comes out."

Janice walked outside into the sunshine and sought the shade of a coconut tree.

The doctor was examining Lola. He felt her stomach and listened to the baby's heart. When he was finished, he told her everything was progressing well and she should deliver in a few weeks. Lola was unhappy with that news. She had hoped to carry the child at least another month, so that an early delivery would not appear suspicious to anyone. She thanked the doctor and left the room.

Janice watched as Lola came outside and rushed into the busy street to hail a taxi. She then returned to the cool, air-conditioned waiting room and sat down to wait for Sharon.

While being examined by the physician, Sharon casually inquired about Lola, telling him she was a friend of hers.

"We have known each other for years, Dr. Mimi. I saw her in the waiting room. She is so big; she must be having twins!"

"No, she is having just one. As a matter of fact, Sharon, Mrs. Adegoke is due in a few weeks."

An astonished look appeared on Sharon's face. She could not wait to tell Janice the news. When Sharon came out into the waiting room, she told Janice that she was given a clean bill of health and the baby was due in a few weeks. Janice congratulated her friend, but was anxious to hear what the doctor said Lola.

"Janice, the doctor said *she* is due to deliver in a few weeks. Lola could not possibly be seven months pregnant!" reported Sharon.

Janice was astounded that Lola would go to such lengths to keep Olufemi.

"Are you sure, Sharon? That cannot be possible. If the child is not Femi's, then who is the father?"

"Jan, I don't know, but I would not care to be in Lola's shoes if she lied about the baby."

The two women entered the car and drove to the Balogun market to shop. They walked through the stalls and came upon Yinka's shop. Sharon was fingering some material for a dress when Yinka approached Janice.

"Well, if it isn't the other Mrs. Adegoke. The *Iyawo* (the younger wife)."

Janice was startled by the strange woman's tone. She looked at her. "Excuse me. Do I know you?"

"Ha, ha! No, but I know all about you, the woman who stole Omolola's husband. Why don't you go back to America and leave the woman's husband alone?"

Yinka began walking menacingly towards Janice. Sharon stood between them as the other traders began to crowd around them, hoping for a fight.

"You foreign women, you come here to take our men. Why don't you just leave them alone," she shouted, pointing at the Janice and Sharon.

Soon other women in the crowd began to support Yinka. They began shouting, "*Oyinbo! Oyinbo* pepper! If you eat pepper, you go yell mama!"

Janice was angry and afraid. She did not want trouble, but she knew that their position was not good as the local Nigerian women surrounded them. Their car was not far away, so they started backing out of the market with the crowd following them.

Janice could feel Sharon shaking. In all her years in Nigeria, she had never been harassed in the market before.

"Look, lady, I don't even know you. How do you know me?"

"Omolola is my friend. I know all about you, O*yinbo.* All that I need to know. Why don't you go back to America and leave Lola's husband alone!?"

Janice whispered to Sharon. "Let's make a run for it."

Before Yinka could hit Janice, the two women turned and rushed for their car, screaming for the driver. Sharon's driver heard their cry and met them at the gate. He saw the crowd of women running behind them. He opened the car door, and then the crowd surrounded the car as they rolled up the windows. He got out, taking a large stick and brandishing it at them. A policeman directing traffic saw the commotion and rushed to the scene. Everyone was yelling. Sharon and Janice cowered inside the vehicle, wishing the driver would get in the car and take them home. Then the officer brought Yinka to the car and asked Janice to step outside.

"Did this woman threaten you, Madame?" the officer asked.

Janice looked at Yinka, feeling more confident now that the police were there. "Yes, she did. We were just shopping in the market, and she started insulting me and my friend."

He looked at the market women, fuming. "Is this how we treat visitors to our country? Chase them from our market?"

The other women lowered their eyes guiltily.

"Do you wish to press charges against this woman?" the officer asked.

Janice looked at Yinka. She had calmed down considerably, especially since the policeman held her arm tightly.

"No, let her go."

Yinka looked at Janice with surprise. The policeman dropped her arm roughly and began to disperse the crowd.

When Janice got home, she told Femi all about what happened. He was shocked, but he scolded her for going to the local market alone.

"Do you know this woman named Yinka, Femi?" Janice asked.

"Yes, she is a friend of Kemi and Lola. Janice, you could have been hurt. Please, next time take the driver inside with you. Is Sharon all right?"

"Yes, Femi. And there's something else. I saw Lola today at the clinic when I went with Sharon. She did not see me though."

"Did she look well?"

"Yes, she did. Femi, when did she tell you the baby is due?"

He looked at his wife, wondering why she was asking about Lola. "She told me in two months. Why?"

"Oh, no reason. Just asking."

Janice left Femi standing in the living room to see about Charles. He poured himself a glass of whiskey. The spirits brought tears to his eyes as he swallowed it quickly, then poured another shot and downed it. He could not fathom why Janice was concerned with Lola, especially when he was more worried about Janice's safety. He also knew that Lola wanted him and would even go as far as trying to drive Janice away from Nigeria. He knew that sometimes his Janice was naïve about his country, and he would have to take greater steps to protect her from harm.

Janice sat in Charles' bedroom in a rocking chair, singing him to sleep. She kept thinking about what Sharon had told her about Lola and what her husband had said about Lola's due date. *I must pay Lola a visit very soon*, Janice thought; *very soon.*

18

The Muslim call to prayer sent Alhaji Yaro to the mosque every Friday for Jumat prayer. He would dress in his finest attire to answer the call to prayer. He left the office early and returned around three in the afternoon to resume work. Sometimes he would take the rest of the day off. His senior wife was concerned that he had not been to her or his other wives lately. He would go to his club after work and stay until late in the evening and come home tired and go to his room without seeing any of his wives. One evening his eldest son, Abu Bakar, met him at the front door. Abu Bakar was sixteen and became the man of the family when his father was not at home. He knew that in their culture, the women never questioned their husbands' behavior unless they were not taking care of the family. Alhaji always made sure his household was well provided for, even if he did not spend time with them. Abu Bakar's mother, Aisha, was concerned that maybe her husband wanted to take another wife. She shared her feelings with the other wives, and they decided that since Abu Bakar was the eldest son that he should ask his father why he was not coming to see them.

Abu Bakar met his father at the door one evening when he came home late and asked him why he stopped coming to his mother and the other wives. Alhaji was surprised at the maturity that his son possessed and so confided in him instead of becoming angry that he should even ask.

"My son, I have fallen in love with a woman who is so special, that I cannot rest until she is mine."

"But father, you already have three beautiful women. Why do you need more?"

Alhaji Mohammed looked at his son and smiled. "You may not understand now, Son, but someday you will also know the ways of men and women, if you do not already. I have seen the way you look at the housemaids."

Abu Bakar blushed. "Father, my mother is concerned that you do not want her. I hope that is not the case."

"No, son. I intend to take this woman as my wife, after your mother and my other wives agree with my choice. I need a woman who can travel with me and understand my business. One who can communicate with me on equal terms."

"But Father, a woman like that will be difficult to control. Why would you want such a woman?"

Alhaji's eyes took on a far away look as a picture of his beautiful secretary, Lola, came into focus. A thrill went through him as he remembered their lovemaking.

"Abu Bakar, she is not a Hausa woman, but is from the Yoruba tribe. Nor is she a Muslim. But I will present her to my family when she consents to being my wife."

Alhaji's son was astounded at his father's revelation. He knew that the family frowned on marrying outside the Hausa tribe and a non-Muslim, why he had been forbidden to marry a woman who was not of the faith.

"But Father, it is forbidden is it not? I mean to marry an outsider?"

"Not in my case, Son, because I already have three wives who are from my culture and religion, so if I so desire to take another, I only need my wives' permission."

"And if they do not agree, Father, what then? What will you do?"

Alhaji had not thought about his wives not accepting his decision. He did have trouble with Aisha accepting his second wife, Hanna, but getting their approval for Fatima was easy. The senior wives felt secure because they both had given Alhaji sons. But still, he was breaking tradition by wanting to marry a non-Muslim and a Yoruba woman.

"Father, whatever you decide to do, I am with you, even if she is Bature (a foreigner)."

"No, Son, I don't think that they would accept a foreign woman, and I would not insult them by asking them to."

*****

Titiloye watched her daughter struggle to get out of bed to go to work. She tried to keep Lola home, but she was a determined woman. Not wanting to make anyone suspect that she was more than seven months pregnant, she would get up every day and dress in her loose caftans and catch a taxi to her office. Alhaji noticed her fatigue and told her to take the rest of the day off. She refused because she knew that Olufemi was coming to the office to take her to lunch. She looked forward to those times that they spent together. Lola avoided everyone she knew. She heard about the incident at the market with Janice and Yinka and had to caution her friend to stay out of her affairs. That it only made matters worse.

Emmanuel and Abimbola paid Lola a visit, and Abimbola was surprised at the size of Lola. She, too, became suspicious and spoke to her husband about it. He answered that all pregnant women looked alike, and he could not see any difference in Lola. But Bimbo was not to be put off, so she went to see her daughter, Bisola, and asked her if she had seen Lola. Bisola said no, that Lola had been avoiding her lately. None of this fazed Titiloye, who went about preparing for the birth of her first grandchild as if nothing was wrong. She did not care whether Olufemi came to live at Surulere or not, just so long as he kept taking care of her daughter. It was more than she could hope for, and at least Lola was not banished to the village like so many other forgotten first wives.

But for Lola, it was not enough. She wanted a full marriage. She wanted Olufemi back at home with her again.

Janice did not know that Olufemi was meeting Lola for lunch that afternoon as she maneuvered the car through the traffic. All she could think of was why Lola would lie about how far along her pregnancy was. Janice chose her outfit carefully. She was wearing a two-piece white linen pantsuit with matching white sandals. Her hair was up in a French roll for a change, allowing the breeze to cool the sweat on her brow. She was thinking how she would approach the subject. Janice parked her car in front of the ministry and walked up the three flights of stairs to Alhaji Mohammed Yaro's office. She entered and saw Lola sitting at her desk, reading some papers. Lola could not believe her eyes as Janice walked in looking so cool and confident and beautiful.

"Hello, Lola; may I come in?"

Lola motioned to a chair in front of her desk and not taking her eyes off Janice; put the papers in a tray. Janice fiddled with her bag as the two women eyed each other, waiting for the other to speak.

"Why, Janice, what brings you to my office?"

Janice looked at Lola and saw that she was uncomfortable. Her girth was noticeable. Her stomach barely fit behind the desk, and the caftan, though loose, could not hide the nine-month pregnancy.

Janice pointed her finger at Lola's stomach. "That is what brings me here."

Lola looked in the direction of her finger and smiled nervously. She was not feeling her best this morning. The baby kicked all night, so she got little sleep. She also had begun having mild contractions. She dismissed them, but this morning they were becoming stronger.

"Oh, you mean the baby. We are doing just fine. How is your son, Charles? He should be a big boy now."

"Charles is fine, Lola; about your child ... You look uncomfortable. Are you all right?"

Lola's face grimaced with pain as a contraction came with full force. She leaned over on the desk, her eyes filled with fear, thinking, *No, not now — it's too soon!* She bit her lower lip, trying to mask the pain, but the pain filled her eyes. Just at that moment, Alhaji Yaro walked into the office. He was splendid looking, wearing a light blue *baba riga* of guinea brocade. He was hatless; his black, wavy hair was slicked back from his forehead. He was startled at the vision that met his eyes. At once he knew that this was Janice Adegoke, Lola's mate. His eyes raked her over from head to toe, taking in her light brown hair and eyes, her pink lips, and shapely body. *Beautiful woman* he thought; *no wonder Olufemi was caught. What man could resist this vision of beauty...?*

Janice, too, was in awe of Lola's boss. He was very distinguished looking and so handsome. How different the Hausa and Yoruba men were. She could see the royal bloodline in his aquiline features as he stared at her, wondering why she was here.

The pains had subsided, and Lola was able to introduce Janice to her boss. They shook hands in the American fashion. Alhaji looked with concern at Lola. She was trying to wipe the sweat from her face while Alhaji was greeting Janice.

"Lola, are you all right?" Alhaji asked.

But before she could answer, she doubled over again in pain. This time she cried out. Both Janice and Alhaji rushed to her side. Janice, holding her around her shoulders, looked at Alhaji; her eyes said what he feared ... *Lola was in labor*.

"Alhaji, we must get her to the hospital. She is in the early stages of labor."

"But it is too soon; she told me the child is not due for another month."

Lola was in so much pain that she was oblivious to their conversation. Alhaji looked at his secretary with more than a boss's concern; Janice was struck with admiration as he sprang into action. He gently gathered Lola into his arms and lifted her from the chair before she could protest, then he carried her down the stairs into the street. His driver was waiting, and he placed her into his Mercedes Benz. Janice closed the office door, following close behind. At that moment, Olufemi was arriving to take Lola to lunch and saw his wife and Alhaji putting Lola into the Benz. He parked his car and rushed over to them. He was startled, seeing Janice assisting Alhaji with Lola. He wondered what in hell she was doing there. Janice looked at him, embarrassed, and said quickly,

"Femi, Lola is in labor. I will explain why I am here later. First, we have to get her to the hospital."

Femi and Alhaji got in the front seat with the driver and Janice rode in the back with Lola. Lola was writhing in pain with each contraction. Janice kept wiping her forehead with her handkerchief.

"It's too soon," Alhaji kept repeating. "The child is not due yet."

Even Femi was touched by the worry in Alhaji's voice as he spoke to his driver, Haruna, in Hausa, asking him to hurry along. Olufemi looked at him closely. He saw genuine concern on his face. It was a crazy afternoon.

Lola squeezed Janice's hand, crying in pain, as the contractions got closer together. Lola held her hand so tightly, causing her to wince in pain as well. They arrived at the maternity hospital, where the nurses took over. The three were escorted into the waiting room while Lola was prepared for delivery. Femi pulled Janice aside to ask her why she was there. She told him about her suspicions, and he shook his head in disbelief.

"I have proof, Femi. This is the proof. Lola's pregnancy is *full term*. If you don't believe me, then ask the doctor."

This was all happening too fast for Femi. How? Why? Why would Lola stoop to this? But he knew the answer to that, because she loved him. Again he could blame no one but himself. Femi rushed down the hall to find the doctor to confirm what Janice said. Alhaji Yaro was pacing the floor as if he were the father awaiting the birth of his child. He saw Janice watching him curiously and suddenly gathered his robes and sat down next to her.

"Mrs. Adegoke, do you think Lola will be all right? I mean, the child is too young. Will it survive?"

"I think so, Alhaji. I suspect that Lola is farther along than she told us."

Alhaji looked with curiosity at Janice. "Why do you say that, Mrs. Adegoke? Do you know something that I do not?"

Before Janice could say anything, Femi returned to the room wearing a big wide grin on his face. His eyes told them both that Lola had given birth.

"How is she?" Alhaji asked. "How is Lola?"

Femi was just grinning, "Lola is fine and so are the babies."

Janice heard the words 'babies,' but was sure that Femi had made a mistake. "Femi, what do you mean 'babies'?"

"Just what I said, Janice. The babies are fine. Lola has given birth to twins, a boy and a girl. I don't believe it — twins!"

Janice could not believe her ears. Her mind began to race with his words, "Babies, babies, twins!" *Oh my God, she had twins! Jesus, why, why?* Janice felt the hot tears sting her eyes and brushed them away quickly. She looked at her husband, beaming with pride at the birth of his children. He was oblivious to her feelings. She felt as though her whole world had ended. She noticed that Alhaji had walked over to the window. He looked defeated, and she wondered why. Janice shook herself to clear her thoughts and hugged her husband and congratulated him half-heartedly. But all she wanted to do was to escape from this place and run, keep running until she was free from this hell. Oh God, why? One child would have been enough, but twins? How could she ever compete with this tragedy?

The doctor came into the room and asked who the father was. Alhaji turned to look at Olufemi with hatred, and that look was not lost on Janice, who, though she was in shock, could not help but feel that there was more to Alhaji Yaro than he let anyone know.

Olufemi proudly shouted, "I am," and followed the doctor, leaving Janice and Alhaji alone.

"It's Allah's blessing that Omolola has twins. Praise be to Allah!"

Janice looked at Alhaji, who looked like he just lost his best friend. And once Janice's curiosity was aroused, there was no stopping her. So for the moment, she forgot about her own pain and delved into this man, who she met just a few hours ago.

"Alhaji, why do you sound so happy, yet look so unhappy?"

The handsome man turned his sensuous, brown eyes to look into Janice's own. His eyes told their own story.

"Yes, I am. I cannot lie. I love Omolola Adegoke."

"Does she know this, Alhaji? Does Lola know how you feel?"

"Yes, I believe that she does, but she is in love with her husband and I cannot come between that, especially now that they have twins. I know that I have lost her forever..."

Janice now saw this proud, handsome, Hausa man in a different light with his robes sagging and his shoulders hanging in defeat. He sat down next to Janice in a chair, turning his face away so she could not see his despair.

"Well, think about me, Alhaji. Now I will have to accept being the second wife again and share my husband with Lola. I don't want to do that. I don't want her back in my life again." Janice could no longer hide the tears of disappointment. She sobbed into her hands. Alhaji moved closer, offering her his handkerchief while attempting to console her. She wiped her eyes and thanked him, then sat quietly, waiting for her husband to return.

Olufemi and the doctor entered Lola's room. She was sitting up in bed holding one of the twins. A nurse held the other and passed it to Olufemi, who sat down in a chair with his son. He looked at the child with his fair skin with curly, black hair. So different from Charles, who looked more and more like him every day. Lola looked with love at her husband.

"Baba be ji, Father of twins."

Olufemi smiled at Lola and completely forgot Janice and Alhaji waiting. He kissed his son and walked over to the bed to kiss his daughter. Lola held her face up to him. He looked at her beautiful eyes and bronze cheeks and kissed her on the cheek. Then he returned to the waiting room and found Alhaji had already left.

"He took a taxi and left his car and driver for us."

"That was nice of him. Would you like to see Lola, Janice?"

"No, Femi. I want to go home."

They left the hospital in the Mercedes Benz .The first thing Femi did was to call Titiloye and tell her the good news. Her shouting could be heard through the telephone. Then Olufemi called his parents and sister. Janice phoned Sharon, who could not believe the news.

"Oh, Janice, twins. That is devastating. So that is why she was so big. Her doctor was wrong. How much did they weigh?"

"Femi said they weighed five pounds each."

"Still, I think they were full-term twins, Janice."

"Well, no one will know that except Lola and God. But Sharon, get this — her boss, Alhaji Yaro, told me he was in love with Lola. Now isn't that strange? A man like him. He can have any woman he wants; yet he chooses a woman who is married. Life forever amazes me."

"So, Janice, what will you do now? Are you prepared to go back living the way you were before you returned to America, or are you going to fight for your marriage to Femi, even though you may lose?"

"Sharon, I'm a fighter. I ran away before, but I fully intend to see this through. Femi promised me that I would not have to live in polygamy again. I am going to hold him to it!"

Olufemi and his parents met with Titiloye to choose a name for the twins. They would name the babies on the seventh day. It would be celebrated with pomp and ceremony. The ceremony was to be held at Taju and Bisola's home on Victoria Island. Emmanuel and Olufemi arranged for chairs and musicians to be at the party, and his mother sent out invitations to all the family and friends. It was not everyday that their son had twins. Lola was enjoying all the attention she was receiving. Gifts for the twins poured in from all parts of the world. The Adegoke family was well known and had lots of connections. Lola's brother, Segun, and Aduke were to fly in from Chicago in time for the ceremony. Abimbola had a special *Ashoke* outfits tailored for her family. They spared no expense.

A few days before the naming ceremony, Femi took Janice aside to tell her about all the preparations and what part she would play in the ceremony. He showered her with praises, for she had been very patient throughout this. Femi had not been home lately, busy with the arrangements.

"Janice, I want you and Charles to be by my side when they name the twins. You and Lola will be wearing matching outfits. I need you, Janice, to get through this."

Janice had held her anger for as long as she could. She did not want to say anything that would drive Olufemi into Lola's arms, but he had promised her he would not ask her to live in polygamy again. He had told her he was going to divorce Lola.

"Femi, I will not be a part of a ceremony that will show the world that you have two wives. You promised me, Femi, promised that you were through with her. Now, just because she has twins, all of a sudden you have gone back on your word!"

"Janice, I don't want to fight with you. I need you to be there. If you are not, it could send the wrong message to people. I told you that I have an obligation to my children."

Janice interrupted abruptly, "No, you mean to Lola and your children. You know that you cannot separate the two. I cannot participate, Femi. To do so would mean my acceptance of you're having two wives. I refuse to do that. I have to think about Charles."

"But, Janice, this is about him. The twins are his brother and sister. You cannot separate them forever. I will not pressure you, but think about it, and then let me know your decision. I will respect that." So that was where he left things.

Abimbola came over to talk to Janice to try to convince her to attend, but she failed, as did Bisi. Lola was home from the hospital. Olufemi had hired a nurse to assist her with the twins. They were so precious. Olufemi would spend as much time with them as he could. He would hold them and caress them while Lola looked on. He was a devoted father to all his children.

The day before the naming ceremony, Femi tried one more time. When Janice refused, he told her he was taking Charles to the ceremony without her. Janice was livid, but she could not refuse him. Abimbola would come and take Charles to go with his grandparents. Janice flashed an angry look at her husband, knowing full well that she could change her mind and go. But she stood her ground, refusing to be in the same room with Lola.

Alhaji Mohammed Yaro received the invitation to the naming ceremony with mixed feelings. A part of him wanted to go, while the other wanted to stay away. He missed his secretary and realized how much he wished that the twins she bore were his. He envied Olufemi and his beautiful, educated, sophisticated wives. None of his wives measured up to Lola. She would make a wonderful inclusion into his family. All he could think of was her long, slender legs wrapped around him in their one moment of passion. *Oh, Lola, I miss you. I want you to be mine. I will attend your naming ceremony just to be near you again.* Alhaji would go to the ceremony and take with him all three of his wives to show Lola who he really was. She always told him that she would not live in polygamy, especially becoming a part of his harem. He knew that, but he could not attend a large gathering like that without his wives. He had spoken to his wives, Aisha, Hanna, and Fatima about taking another wife. They had not given their permission yet. They wanted to meet Lola. But when he told them she was still married, they were horrified that their husband would dare to approach them about a woman who was not free to marry and who was not a Hausa and not a Muslim and not a virgin! They thought their husband was not himself. But Alhaji was adamant that they all should attend her naming ceremony and see her in person. Finally, the Yaro family agreed to accompany him to naming ceremony.

The day finally arrived for the naming ceremony. Femi was at Taju's home early with his son, Charles, in tow. Abimbola was happy to take care of him, but she was sad that Janice had refused to take part in the christening. Secretly, Lola was rejoicing at Janice's refusal. Taju sent a car to the airport several times to pick up out of town guests and put them up in the hotel. Segun and Aduke were the last to arrive via London. Everyone welcomed them happily, and Segun was overwhelmed with joy and bearing gifts for his first niece and nephew. He and Lola spent nearly an hour closeted up together, catching up. Aduke was disappointed when she heard that Janice would not be there.

"What happened, Femi? Why isn't Janice coming?"

"Well, Aduke, you know Janice. She refuses to be seen in public with Lola. She does not want anyone to suspect that she agrees with polygamy."

"You know that she doesn't, Femi, so why push her?" Aduke asked, placing her hands on her hips defiantly. "Since she is not coming to keep an eye on you, I guess I will have to."

"That will not be necessary, Aduke. I love Janice and I love my son. My feelings have become stronger for her. I did not reconcile with Lola. I only accepted my children. After all, I am their father."

"That is all good, Femi, and I am sure that everyone believes that except your two wives. Lola will not rest until you and she are back together again. Segun and I have discussed this at length. She will just use the children, Femi. Can't you see that?"

"Now you sound like Janice. Aduke, give Lola some credit, will you? She just gave birth to twins. Can't we just rejoice on this occasion and let all the negative thoughts rest for a day?"

Aduke decided to keep her piece until she saw Janice and heard her side.

Segun entered the room that Bisola gave Lola and the children to rest in and prepare for the ceremony. Lola was nursing the girl child. He picked up his nephew and looked closely at him. He saw no resemblance in the child to the father and was concerned.

He looked at his sister, who appeared angelic, holding the baby to her breast.

"Lola, they are beautiful. The boy looks like our father."

Lola blanched at Segun's assumption, but did not answer. Last night, Abimbola had said that the girl looked just like Lola, but that neither of the children had their father's hair or eyes. Again, Lola did not say anything.

"Segun, when are you and Aduke starting a family?"

"Not for a few years. At least until she finishes her Masters degree and I have my first degree. We cannot afford one now, especially after all the expense of the wedding. Lola, is everything all right between you and your husband? Mama told me that Olufemi does not live with you, that he is only your husband in name. Is that true?"

Lola looked away from her brother, trying to find the words to explain why she accepted her situation.

"I wanted to have Olu any way I could. He was very angry when I came to America. He said he would take care of the children, but he would not live with me. I am trying to get him to change his mind, Segun."

"Kemi and Jide sent gifts and letters for you. Kemi wanted me to hand deliver this one."

Lola burped her sleeping daughter and lay her down before taking the letter. She opened it and began reading,

> Dear Omolola,
>
> I hope this letter finds you well and happy. Congratulations on the birth of your twins. I am sorry that Jide and I cannot come to the naming ceremony,

but I hope that you will still make us the godparents. We do not have our green card yet and cannot travel until we become permanent residents. If we leave, we cannot return. I know that you will understand.

Lola, I worry about you. I have not heard from you for many months. But Yinka wrote me and told me of how you are obsessed with Olufemi. I am aware of his decision to live apart from you. Lola, I am sorry, but I warned you that he is not the kind of man you can deceive. Does anyone know about you and Alhaji? How do the babies look? Do they bear any resemblance to him? I hope and pray that you will not be discovered. For I know it will mean the end of your marriage to Olu. I pray that the children will be strong and look like you. Please, write me and let me know what is happening. Until I hear from you,

Yours, Kemi

Lola sighed and refolded the letter, wiping a tear from the corner of her eye.

"What did she say, Lola? I hope that it was not upsetting."

She looked at her brother and smiled. "No, Segun, she just wanted to remind me that she and her husband would be the godparents."

Segun was not satisfied by her answer, but decided to let it go. He knew that all was not right with Lola and that for now; she was not talking to anyone. Not even him...

19

*J*anice paced her bedroom floor until she made tracks in the plush carpet. Peter stopped in and asked if she was all right, and if he could do anything for her. She told him no; in fact, she offered him the rest of the day off. *I must be crazy to not be there,* Janice thought. *I am playing right into her hands. This is what she wants. She wants Femi all to herself and I, like a fool, am allowing her to get away with it.* She continued to pace, trying to decide what to do when suddenly the doorbell rang. She rushed to answer it since she had let Peter have the day off, and to her delight was her friend, Aduke.

"Aduke, how are you, my friend? Come in, come in, and sit down! You look wonderful! Married life seems to agree with you."

Aduke embraced Janice. Immediately, Janice noticed that Aduke was not very talkative like she usually was. They both sat on the sofa and waited for the other to speak.

Janice complimented Aduke on her outfit.

"You have one, too. It is the same one that you should have on now, Janice. Why are you not coming to the naming ceremony?" Aduke finally said.

"You know why — I cannot be at the same place with Lola. It would be the same as saying that I agree with the situation. I sent my son, Charles, to stand in for me."

"But, Janice, you are letting Lola win. How can you, after all you went through? You should fight. By not coming, you are letting everyone believe that she and Femi are happily married. Please go and put on your *iro* and *buba*. I will tie your head tie for you."

Janice took a deep breath to steady her nerves before telling Aduke how she felt. She was surprised at her friend, who was now the sister-in-law to Lola.

"Shouldn't you be more loyal to Lola, Aduke? What does your husband think about you coming here to convince me to go?"

"No one saw me leave. You must come, Janice. Your family is behind you 100 percent. Everyone understands."

"Not everyone. Femi had told me I would not have to do this again. He promised."

Aduke walked over to Janice and put her arms around her shoulders in support.

"If you don't come, then you cannot make him go through with his promise. It is a special day when a family has twins. It is a good omen. Femi and Lola are the center of attention. If you are there, it will take away some of her glory. She is gloating that she has Femi all to herself!"

That was all it took for Janice to get off her behind and go and put on her African dress. Aduke stood back to admire her handiwork as she tied Janice's head tie to perfection. The family had chosen the colors of white and blue lace, with white, silver and blue head ties to match. Janice took out her diamond necklace that Femi had given her for their anniversary. It had a matching tennis bracelet and drop earrings. Aduke "oohed" and "ahhed" over the gems as Janice stood back to admire herself in the long mirror. Satisfied with her appearance, she slipped her feet into her white-heeled sandals and grabbed a matching handbag. She knew that her husband would be surprised to see her; she would take her place next to him and Lola for the festivities.

Suddenly, she was reminded of the last time she went to a party with them. What a disaster it had been. That and subsequently finding Lola and Femi together in bed were the reasons that she left Nigeria. Now here she was again, acting as a second wife. The very thought filled her with nausea.

"Are you all right, Janice? You suddenly look pale."

Janice took a deep breath before answering her friend. "I will be fine, Aduke. Just drive. We don't want to miss any of the ceremony."

All the guests had gathered in the large recreation room at Taju and Bisola's home. The caterers had provided extra help to seat everyone. Taju and Bisola took their place, with their children sitting behind them. Abimbola and Emmanuel, along with Titiloye and Segun, sat in the front row. Abimbola held Charles, who was sitting quietly, playing with a toy, and the twins were sleeping, each in a carry chair on the table. The preacher was at a special table where Lola and Femi sat on either side of the altar.

They were about to begin the ceremony when all eyes turned towards the door. In walked Aduke followed closely by Janice. The room began to buzz with excitement as the two beautiful women walked over to their husbands. Olufemi was amazed that Janice had decided to come. He stood up and pointed to the chair next to him. As Janice passed by Abimbola, Charles began to reach for his mother. She curtsied before her mother- and father-in-law and did the same for Titiloye, who nodded, her eyes holding a look of defeat. She smiled at Taju and Bisi, while taking her son from his grandmother and turning to walk to her seat. She did not look at Lola, who tried unsuccessfully to look nonchalant. Janice then gave Charles to Femi, walked over to Lola, and curtsied, then looked her straight in her eyes, daring her to make a scene. She then greeted the preacher and looked at the two perfect children who lay side by side sleeping. If she was surprised by the appearance of the babies, she did not show it. She then took her seat and waited for the remaining guests to be seated.

Lola called her brother to come to the table. "Segun, you need to control your wife! Who gave her permission to bring Janice here?"

Segun was taken aback by the tone in his sister's voice. He was about to respond when Aduke came to the table.

She smiled sweetly at her sister-in-law. "Isn't it nice that Janice decided to come, Lola?"

Lola could barely contain her anger at Aduke.

Segun patted her gently on the arm. *"E' jo* sister-*mi, e'jo.* Just be cool. She is here now, so do not make a scene."

"I will not, Brother, but I refuse to let her steal my show."

That old green-eyed monster of jealousy reared its ugly head in Lola, especially when Janice took her place next to Olufemi, holding Charles. Lola hoped that nothing else would go wrong, when another group of guests entered the room. Lola stood up in shock as Alhaji Mohammed Yaro, her boss, followed by three beautiful women; each dressed in the same outfit, and was shown to some seats in the rear of the room. Lola's eyes locked onto his, and he nodded his head to her. She sat down hard, wondering why all this was happening on such a special day. But no one thought it irregular that her boss was there.

The preacher began by giving praise to all the participants at the gathering. Then he blessed the parents of the new babies, after which he gestured for them to pick up one twin each and stand next to him. He asked for the names that Olufemi had written on a piece of paper. First, he whispered the name of the boy into the child's ear, "Taiwo Adedeji Sampson Adegoke." Then he whispered the name of the girl twin into her ear, "Khendi Adedayo Sarah Adegoke." He finally said the names out loud to all the people in the room, who then cheered and clapped with joy. Lola and Olufemi stood together proudly as Janice watched them, feeling a bit uncomfortable. When the preacher asked for the names of the godparents, Lola told him they were Kemi and Jide, who were not present but living in America. They said more prayers for the people who brought gifts of money to the altar.

Then Alhaji got up from his seat and walked to the altar to ask the preacher to pray for the twins and their mother. His eyes caught Lola's and held them as he gave the preacher a huge amount of *Naira* to pray for the twins. Even Janice was impressed by his generosity. Then he went to Lola's chair and whispered into her ear, "Congratulations, Omolola. They are fine children. You have made your husband a proud man."

"Thank you, Alhaji, for coming and bringing your family to celebrate the birth of my children. I hope that you will introduce me to your family."

"Of course, I will. As soon as they complete the prayer."

Alhaji nodded to Olufemi and Janice, and then returned to his seat.

His senior wife, Aisha, was watching the exchange between her husband and his secretary. She confided her suspicions to the other wives. "Fatima and Hanna that must be the woman who has won our husband's affections."

The two women turned towards Aisha's stare.

"She is lovely. No wonder he cannot think straight and has been coming home late every night."

Fatima, the youngest wife, added, "But she is married to a very handsome man and only has to share him with one woman. She should be grateful, especially since God has blessed her with twins."

The three women all agreed, then sat back and waited for the food to be served and the dancing to begin.

Lola and Olufemi stood side by side to greet all the well-wishers who had come to the ceremony. The band started to play, and refreshments were being served. Lola took the children back to the room, where she changed into another outfit. Femi and Janice mingled among the crowd.

Abimbola told Janice how proud she was that she decided to show up.

"You are becoming a true Nigerian, Janice. I had expected you to stay at home. Your coming today has made your husband very happy. You look marvelous in the outfit we had made for you. Let me take the baby, and you go and join your husband on the dance floor."

Janice handed her mother-in-law the baby and looked around the room until she saw Femi in the corner talking to Alhaji. She joined them, and he introduced his wives to them.

"Olufemi and Janice, I want you to meet my wives. My first wife, Aisha; second, Hanna; and third wife, Fatima."

Olufemi bowed eloquently to them and Janice shook hands with them. Fatima was very shy and lowered her beautiful eyes, revealing the longest eyelashes Janice had ever seen. *Yes*, she thought, *Alhaji is a very lucky man to have three women who agree with polygamy and who are willing to live in it.*

It was then that Lola entered the room. She was dressed in a gold Austrian lace gown with a matching head tie and sandals. She looked refreshed and absolutely gorgeous. The eyes of every man and woman were on her as she boldly walked over to Olufemi and claimed the first dance. Janice stood back in shock as Lola pulled him onto the dance floor. The musicians began to play the latest Fuji music and Lola and Olufemi danced as if it were choreographed just for them. All Janice could do was watch. She even forgot that she was standing with Alhaji and his family. Alhaji escorted his wives to the refreshments, and then came back to Janice. He threw his robes over his shoulder and bowed to Janice before asking her to dance.

Startled, she responded, "Alhaji, do you know how to dance the Yoruba dances?"

He smiled, taking her hand in his and kissing it gently. She felt a thrill go through her, thinking; *this man knows how to romance a woman. I wonder if he ever did this to Lola. After all, he has captured the hearts of not one, not two, but three beautiful women.*

Janice took one look at the couple on the dance floor and decided to dance with Lola's handsome boss.

"I would love to dance, Alhaji ... that is, if your wives don't mind."

"They are content to eat and sit and watch. Normally, my wives are in purdah and do not accompany me to these types of occasions. But I wanted them to meet my secretary and see her newborn children."

Then holding her hand, Alhaji escorted Janice onto the floor. They made a handsome sight. Janice could see Alhaji had no trouble following the music and soon he was spraying money on the other dancers. They made their way over to where Lola and Olufemi were dancing, and Alhaji began to spray Lola. You had to be a fool or blind not to see the love and admiration in his dark, sensuous eyes. Each 1000 *Naira* bill was laid on her head with such tenderness. Lola thanked Alhaji, wishing he would go away. He had a way with women, and that effect was not lost on her. When he saw he was neglecting Janice, he put his arm around her and joined her dancing. He did not spray Olufemi, an intentional slight on his part. When the music ended, he smiled a wicked smile at Lola, who was standing there; humiliated at his slight to her husband, then he led Janice to a seat.

Titiloye was in the bedroom with Ajoke and T.J., watching the twins when several guests came in to see the babies. Among the visitors were Alhaji's wives. They greeted Lola's mother and walked over to the crib. Aisha picked up Taiwo gently, cradling him in her arms. She was startled at the resemblance he had to her son Abu Bakar when he was born. The same nose and hair and those long lashes that was the trademark of all Alhaji's children. *No, no. It cannot be*, she thought, as she shook her head. *This would be a real tragedy*. Then she called to Hanna, who was holding Khendi, to bring her closer. Again she could see the resemblance to Hanna's daughter, Halima. *Allahukbar!! These children must be Alhaji's*. She kept her thoughts to herself. She would speak to Alhaji as soon as they got home. Aisha spoke to Titiloye, complimenting her on their good looks. Titiloye just beamed proudly and thanked them gracefully.

Alhaji took the seat next to Janice.

"Madame, I wish to talk to you in private. Maybe we can meet for lunch one day next week. I wish you to be very discreet. I want to continue the discussion with you that we started at the hospital. It was such a hectic time. Now that things have settled down, I think I need to clarify my position."

"Yes, Alhaji. I would like to know where you stand. A man like you is lucky to have such beautiful women, and yet you profess to love another. Yes, let's meet at 12 noon on Friday, say at Tinubu Square?"

He did not answer, just nodded and stood up, his robes sweeping and smelling of expensive cologne. The man was so cool that he did not even break a sweat on the dance floor. He gathered his harem, and they went to say good-bye to Olufemi and Omolola.

He walked up on Lola and she turned around, startled. "Ah, Alhaji, leaving so soon?"

He took her hand and led her towards the door with his wives close behind, trying to hear every word.

"Yes, we must go now. I am going to miss you, Lola. Will you be returning to work?"

"I don't think so, sir. It will be too hard with the twins. I want to be home to raise them properly. Did you get a chance to see them?" she said nervously.

He stood close to her, his eyes looking deeply into hers. She blushed.

"No, but I think my wives visited with them. I am sure they are beautiful, but I could not stand to see the one thing that has come permanently between us, Lola."

"Oh, do you mean my husband Olufemi?"

"No. I mean the children who will take you away from me. Good-bye, Omolola. Come by the office and visit me sometime."

His look was not lost on his wives, who could not wait to get home to ask Abu Bakar to intercede for them. They saw the woman that their husband was in love with return his look. They knew that they had a problem ... a real problem. For each woman was thinking that Lola was not one of them. She was a Yoruba woman, and a beautiful and educated one at that.

We truly have a problem. Aisha took a deep breath thinking, *What if these children are Alhaji's?*

Janice was dancing with Taju, and Bisola was dancing with Segun. Aduke and Olufemi were sharing a drink with his father while his mother was taking care of Charles. The party was in full swing.

Lola went to feed the babies. Her mother handed her Khendi first, for she was crying. Lola placed the baby girl with the curly, black hair to her breast, allowing her to feed until she drifted back to sleep. Then she took Taiwo and fed him. Her mother watched with joy.

"Omolola, those Hausa women came in to see the babies. They were amazed. One of them said they looked like Hausa children," her mother said.

"Oh, Mother, you know that it is too early to tell who they look like."

But Lola was not convinced herself. She wondered how she could pull this off. She almost had Olufemi where she wanted him, and with a little more pressure, she would have him in the house again and in her bed where she wanted him. If only Alhaji would just leave her alone. Again, she remembered his arms on her body and looked down at her son who suckled at her breast. She saw Alhaji's nose and mouth, and she cringed at the thought that one of his wives may have noticed the slight resemblance as well. She held his small head against her breast and touched his tiny cheek. His skin color was of a fair tan, almost peach in color. His hair was thick and curly, his nose straight and pointed like aristocracy, his top lip was thin and his lower lip full and he had a cleft in his chin — a dead giveaway because Alhaji's dark, masculine, good looks were accentuated by a deep cleft in his chin. *Oh God,* she thought, *Taiwo does look like him. What shall I do? What shall I do?*

20

Alhaji and his wives left the party well after the midnight hour. They were all tired, but the women could not stop chattering about the party and his beautiful secretary.

"Alhaji, I know that you are sorry to see her go," Fatima remarked.

"Yes, I am. She was a very good employee. She was more than a secretary."

His eyes took on a wistful look as he remembered the one afternoon he tasted the sweetness of Lola. He knew now that since he had tasted her forbidden fruit, he would always want more and more until he made her one of his wives.

The driver reached their exquisite mansion near the ocean. The junior wives went inside to see to their children, while Aisha stayed with their husband. It was her week to be with him. He told her he would join her in a few minutes. Aisha was anxious to speak to Abu Bakar and enlist his help in finding out more about Lola.

She retired to her apartment and prepared to be with her husband. It was during this time that she saw to his every need, including lovemaking. But since she was the eldest wife, a mere 32 years old, she found that Alhaji saved the best of himself for Fatima, his third and youngest wife, who was only 23.

She chose a blue silk nightgown and robe, and lay down on her bed, waiting for her husband to come to her. Alhaji entered the room, refreshed from his shower and laid next to his wife. She wanted to tell him of her suspicions about Lola's babies, but knew that she should not. How could she accuse her husband when he had approached her for her consent to take another wife? It was their culture to get permission from the other wives before taking a new one because a new wife needed to be accepted by the other women. But Aisha already did not like Lola. She knew that Lola would never accept living in the house with them.

They made love as usual, Aisha knowing full well that Alhaji only pretended to be interested in her. She could always feel that he was just performing his duty as a husband, which frustrated her, for, as she grew older, she began to enjoy the sexual act more, now that the threat of pregnancy no longer existed. Aisha had given her husband three children, and then was told she could have no more. That was when Alhaji took Hanna as his second wife and she presented him with two children. Fatima had given Alhaji one daughter last year, a total of six children for Alhaji from his three wives.

Aisha and Alhaji were betrothed as children. Her mother told her of the honor that had been bestowed on her from birth. She was groomed to take her place beside her husband, and she did not see him for the first time until their wedding day, sitting tall on his horse, wearing a traditional dress while carrying a long sword designating his rank. She was afraid of the unknown, and he showed her that he, too, was afraid. Though he was not a virgin, he was but a young man of only 18; Aisha was 15.

Over the years and after having three children, she grew to love him and thought he would be satisfied with having only one wife until the day he told her about Hanna. Her heart became stone. She knew that she was doomed to a life of sharing her husband with other women. Her mother had warned her not to expect anything else, but to be thankful that she was the senior wife and in control of the household. But Lola was different. Aisha was afraid of Lola. She knew that she could never control that one, especially if she chose to live outside the home.

Yet, Aisha sensed the restlessness in her husband and knew that no matter what, he would have this Yoruba woman. She knew that Alhaji would always be fair to his wives. They lived a life of luxury, had homes in Kano, Lagos, London, Paris, and a condo in Saudi Arabia. They had a team of servants and lived in a mansion. What more could they want? But even those things really didn't matter, because since her firstborn son, Abu Bakar, would be Alhaji's heir, the luxury they had all became accustomed to still would not belong to them.

*****

Janice reached Sharon's home early. She wanted to tell her all the details of the party, especially the part about Alhaji and Lola. Sharon joined Janice in the living room. She knew that Janice had a lot to talk about, so she called her nanny to come and take the children so they could relax. They went outside and sat under a palm tree on the patio.

"Janice, how did the naming ceremony go? Did you see the babies?"

"It was okay. I wasn't going at first, but Aduke came over and convinced me to go. And I am glad I did. You should have seen Lola. She was all over Femi."

"That Lola really has a lot of nerve," Sharon replied, in full support of Janice.

"The babies are beautiful. But they don't look at all like Femi."

Sharon shook her head before speaking. She knew that her friend would not like to hear what she was about to say.

"Janice, it may be just wishful thinking on your part. I know that you don't want these children to be his. You must have absolute proof before you can accuse her of anything."

"I know, Sharon. But you should have seen her boss. He came with his three wives, but he was panting for Lola. He really has the hot's for her and showed his desire in front of his wives! I don't see how they took it."

Sharon sat back amazed at what Janice was saying.

Janice continued. "And get this — he wants to meet with me on Friday. We are meeting at Tinubu Square. He doesn't want anyone to know and asked me to be discreet."

"Really, girl, this is deep. I wonder why he's confiding in you," Sharon said.

"Probably because he wants her and knows that I want Femi. We are sort of allies, both working for the same cause."

They spent the rest of the afternoon talking about their babies and the next club meeting. It was times like these that Janice missed her cousin, Mindy. She gathered her son and drove back home in time for dinner. Femi was not home yet, so she ate a quiet dinner alone after putting Charles to bed.

Taju and Femi sat in the club drinking their beers. Taju watched his brother-in-law with curiosity. He was dying to ask about Lola, but wanted him to initiate the topic.

"Taju, what am I to do? This dilemma I find myself in is terrible. How can I just turn my back on Lola and the twins?"

"Olu, you have already done that. You refuse to sleep in the same house with her. You are separated in my eyes. It is just a matter of time before she tires of being alone and lets you go."

"Ha, ha, ha!" Olu laughed. "She will never let me go. She is obsessed with me. Only an act of God will release her from me."

"Then you had better pray, brother ... that may be just what you need."

*****

Friday came and Janice left home for her rendezvous with Alhaji. Femi had sent the driver home for Janice to use, but she dismissed him saying she was not going to the market and did not need him today. She gave Charles to his nanny and went to her dressing room to prepare for her meeting with Alhaji. She took great care with her appearance and could not understand why. Had Alhaji mesmerized her too? She blushed while sitting in front of her vanity mirror brushing her long, brown hair until it gleamed. Her eyes sparkled as she applied her lipstick with care. She chose a beige two-piece outfit, a skirt and blouse and wore her white roman sandals. Then she put on her sunglasses, giving her a mysterious air, and she left the house for her appointment. The traffic was light for a change, and Janice arrived at Tinubu Square in less than 30 minutes.

She spied Alhaji sitting near the fountain and walked over to meet him. He motioned to her to enter his chauffeur-driven Mercedes. Once inside the car, Alhaji spoke to the driver in Hausa.

"Where are we going, Alhaji?" Janice asked, trying to appear confident.

"I am taking you to a nice, secluded restaurant where we can talk and not be disturbed. You are looking beautiful as usual, Mrs. Adegoke. How is your husband?"

"He is fine, Alhaji. And your family?"

"They are all well." They chatted that way for almost 45 minutes while the driver took them outside Lagos to a nearby town.

"We are here now. Come inside the chateau," said Alhaji.

The restaurant was in a secluded place near Badagary Beach. It was the kind of hideaway that only a millionaire could afford. It was beautiful and peaceful there. The location consisted of several hidden chalets, each surrounded by tropical foliage and exotic birds. Janice was in awe as they entered one of the chalets. It was decorated in the latest fashions, no expense spared, and it consisted of two bedrooms with separate baths, a living/dining room, and kitchen. There was a patio outside in the rear and a swimming pool. It was enchanting. Alhaji led Janice into the living room, where she sat down on a sofa covered in green brocade. He ordered drinks and lunch. He was wearing a light blue leisure suit instead of his usual *baba riga*, making him look cosmopolitan.

"Janice, I wanted to speak to you about what I said to you at the hospital and enlist your help."

"But how can I be of help to you, Alhaji?"

"Remember I told you how I felt about Omolola? I still feel the same; in fact, my feelings have grown stronger. Now she told me she would not be returning to work. I fear that I will not see her anymore. How will I convince her to marry me?"

"But, Alhaji, she is still married to Femi. And did your forget about the twins?"

"No, let me tell you something. When you were in America and Olufemi traveled to be with you, Lola was very distraught. She turned to me for what I thought was comfort, but in fact, she was just using me to give her more time off. We had an affair. Then she left for America, and the rest is history. I knew after making love to her that I loved her beyond love. I want her to be my wife. I know that your husband does not want her. Why would he, with a woman like you? I have already spoken to my wives and they have agreed that I can take a fourth and final wife. They are all secure in their lives and have their own children to look after. Janice, I love her as I have never loved a woman before. I cannot eat or sleep. I lay awake at night wishing she were next to me."

Janice listened to Alhaji speak passionately about his love affair with Lola and was amazed that he was so frank with her.

"Alhaji, why are you telling me all this? What can I possibly do to help you?"

He stood up, pacing the floor, his long, slender fingers entwined, turning as his mind was turning; trying to think of a way that he could make his wish come true. He looked into Janice's eyes, appealing to her for support.

While Janice sat there astounded, she thought about how cunning Lola was to fool everyone and how she deserved Alhaji, as they were both unfaithful in their marriages. This was exactly the ammunition Janice needed to convince Femi that Lola was up to no good. It was then that she began to realize that those children might not be her husband's.

"Alhaji, I will help you, but you must agree to help me too. You see, for some time, I have suspected that the twins are not my husband's."

Alhaji stopped pacing the floor to stare at Janice incredulously. He dropped down on the sofa next to her.

"Haba, Mrs. Adegoke, why do you say such a thing? I mean, surely they must be his children."

"Alhaji, when did you and Lola make love?"

Alhaji's eyes took on a mystical air as he remembered that afternoon in his office that they had made passionate love.

"It was around the time that your husband was in America. He had been gone at least a month already. But that proves nothing."

"I think it does, Alhaji. She was with you long after Femi had come to America to be with me when I had my baby. Have you seen them yet? They strongly resemble you. Actually, they don't look anything like my husband or his family."

Alhaji released a deep sigh, and then turned to look at the beautiful woman at his side. Wanting to, yet not wanting to believe her, he tried to clarify it in his own mind.

"Janice, if this is true, then Lola needs to be taught a lesson. I'm sure that your husband will divorce her if he finds out that she made a fool of him."

"And what about you, Alhaji?" Janice asked.

It was a few minutes before he answered her. He turned away and took a deep breath, his dark brows knitted together into a frown. He walked over to Janice and took her hands into his own, caressing them gently. She shivered in anticipation of his answer, sensing his emotions rising as he kneaded her hands gently. He looked deeply into her eyes, his own shimmering with tears as he fought to control his emotions, and his voice quivered as he made his declaration of love to Janice.

"I will love her until time is no more. If those children are mine, I will love them as I love and worship their mother. Janice, help me. Please, help me find a way to get Lola into my arms again."

He then dropped her hands and walked away to the window, looking out into the courtyard. Janice suddenly felt cold inside as she prayed that she was right and those children were not Femi's. But if she were wrong, she might be the one left on the outside. Femi would never forgive her, so she must be sure. She knew that she must go to Lola and confront her with her suspicions. It would be a chance, a slim one, but it was her only hope. She could already see signs of Femi weakening. Those children would make him be a father to them; after all, how can a Nigerian man turn his back on his children? But what is worse, how much longer would it be before he put Janice and Lola both back on a schedule. The very thought of sharing Femi again made Janice quiver with nausea. She looked at Alhaji's back and wondered what he was thinking.

"All right, Alhaji. I will help," Janice said, knowing that she had to act now and act fast. "But Femi must never find out that I was here, and that we had this conversation. Lola is a lucky woman to have a man like you waiting in the wings."

But Alhaji was no longer listening. His eyes were almost closed as he looked out into the courtyard, seeing nothing but Lola and the twins at the naming ceremony. *Their names should have been Hassan and Hassanatu,* he thought to himself. *Oh, Allah, what if they are my children? Could it be only after one time together? If it is so, then we are truly meant to be together.*

Alhaji and Janice ate their lunch and spoke no more of Lola or Olufemi. They each found they had a lot of interests in common like politics, sports, and music and they both were avid fans of *Fuji* music.

After lunch, they entered the Mercedes and the driver took them back to Janice's car at Tinubu Square. Before she got out of the car, Alhaji looked at her with his sensuous eyes and said, "If things had been different, you would have been the one I would be chasing. Your husband is very lucky to have a wife that loves him like you do, Janice. You take care, and I will be in touch with you. S*alaam-a-laikum."*

"I will, Alhaji, I promise..."

Janice pushed through the crowd to her car and stood for a few moments watching the black Mercedes Benz maneuver through the traffic. Then she got into her car and hurried home because Femi would soon be returning from work for dinner. Peter had already prepared her meal and had set the table by the time she got home. She found a message from Femi waiting for her.

> *Sorry, Darling,*
>
> *Having a late meeting with Taju. Don't wait up for me.*
>
> *Love, Femi*

Strange, she thought as she went into the nursery to check on Charles. Then she sat down and ate the dinner Peter had prepared.

After waiting several hours for her husband, she decided to go to bed. Femi came in well after midnight, creeping silently into the bedroom and changing into his pajamas. Sliding between the sheets trying not to wake Janice, he lay back on his pillow with his hands folded behind his head, thinking of the evening he had had. *Oh, what a mess this is turning out to be*, he thought. *Lola had no right to involve my father in this.*

Olufemi's parents were at Taju's house when he and Taju returned from their dinner meeting. Emmanuel was furious that Olufemi would not spend any time with Lola and his newborn children.

"Father, you just don't understand. I told you I would not jeopardize my relationship with Janice. She only came back to me on condition that I give up Lola."

"But Son, Lola was not pregnant then. Janice has been here long enough to understand our culture. She cannot expect you to give up your children."

Olufemi's mother kept quiet until she could take it no longer. Watching her son's dilemma was making her suffer for him. He had a very difficult decision to make and she wondered if he could find a solution that would satisfy the two beautiful women he was married to.

"Son," his mother spoke softly in contrast to her husband's harsh demanding tone, "I want you to think about this. Janice loves you and has given you a son. She had a very rough time finding out about Lola, and I think that it would be very unfair to her if you betrayed her now. Lola knew about the situation between you. She did everything possible to come between you and Janice. She is the one who coerced you to break your first agreement, and she is the one who followed you against your wishes to America and caused trouble there. Olu, my son, you need to be very careful how you handle this delicate situation. The choices you make today may change the very course of your life."

"Oh, Mother, why do you talk in riddles? You know I have made Janice and Charles my first priority. But I owe Lola so much. Anyway, it's late. We will talk again soon. I am going home."

"Which home, Son?" his father asked.

"Home in Ikeja, to Janice, where I belong."

The weeks flew by and Lola lay alone in bed feeling like she was the loneliest woman on the planet. Even though the babies kept her busy, she still found time to dwell on her situation. Titiloye got up early everyday to help the nanny bathe the children, who then took them to their mother to be fed. Lola fed each of the twins and rocked them back to sleep. Then she got up to take a shower and dress. She had just gotten out of the shower when she heard Olufemi's voice in the bedroom talking to the children. She walked out of the bathroom naked except for a towel that she had wrapped around her head. Femi stood up, taking in her full breasts and long slender legs before turning away embarrassed that she still had the power to arouse him.

"*Oko mi, bayoni!* What a surprise! I am glad that you came to visit us," said Lola.

Before he could answer, she rushed across the room throwing herself at him and losing her towel in the process. He tried to hold her off, but felt himself becoming aroused being close to her freshly bathed body. Lola was a beautiful woman. Her smooth, shapely curves were ready for lovemaking. She looked into his eyes and took his hand and placed it on her hard nipple, daring him to remove it. Her breasts, full with milk, were firm and round, ready to be kissed. It was impossible for Olufemi to resist her. She pulled him over to the bed and on top of her. They struggled with his pants as she moaned with pleasure when he placed his mouth around her nipple and helped himself. She arched her back as his fingers explored her moistness while she guided him into her depths. Together they plunged into the waves of passion, struggling to stay afloat while being tossed on a rough sea. Lola felt him deep inside her, strong with his movements, not at all like in the past when they both would take more time teasing each other. Olu was different now, and she could feel it. It was almost as if he were doing her a favor, while he enjoyed it. His hands cupped her buttocks as he pushed her up into the sky, and they came, tumbling down together breathlessly. She held him in a viselike grip, her legs wrapped tight around his waist while ecstasy claimed them both. When their passion was spent, he sat up on the bed thinking, *Could he have been wrong? Was he being unfair to her? Was he abandoning his culture for Janice?* He shook his head as if trying to clear it, and then went into the bathroom to wash.

"Lola, that was wonderful. Almost like old times," Olu said when he came out of the bathroom.

"No, Olu, it can never be like 'old times' again. I can only wait for you to come once a week to see me. You made your decision to keep me out of your life, didn't you Olu?"

Olufemi put his hands over his face. He was tired of all this *wahalla.* He just wanted a normal life with one wife and child, not two wives. *You never have any peace. Always trying to be fair to the other. Trying to schedule your life around theirs. It just doesn't work for me. Not for me,* he thought.

Olufemi picked up his son and cradled his small head in his arms.

"Their color is so like Charles. So pink. I am surprised. We are both brown skin in color. I wonder who they inherited this from."

"Look at their ears, Olu, if you want to know what color a baby will be in a few months," Lola said, her voice a bit edgy.

He did look at their ears, and they, too, were a tan color, only slightly darker than their faces. He shook his head, and then placed the sleeping child back into his crib.

"I must be going now, Lola, but I will visit you again in a few days."

He left and returned to his office, feeling guilty about making love to Lola. He did not want to lead her on, but he knew she had her needs too. *It was not like it used to be between us,* he thought, looking out at the busy traffic on the street. *My life is a lot like you, Lagos, always a hustle. I am tired and just want a rest.*

*****

Alhaji sat in his living room with his eldest son, Abu Bakar, and was startled when his son asked about Lola and their relationship.

"Please do not be offended, Father, but Mother is worried about your relationship with the woman called Lola. She is afraid that you will move away and abandon us."

Alhaji was startled by his son's frankness. Questioning him about his personal affairs took a lot of courage.

"Abu Bakar, I intend to make Omolola my fourth and final wife. So you can tell your mother not to worry anymore. Her position in this household was secured a long time ago when you were born."

"That is another thing, Father. Mother seems to think that the children this woman bore are yours. Is this true? Did you father these children?"

Alhaji was becoming perturbed at his son's line of questioning. *What right had Aisha to even question the paternity of another woman's children?* He thought.

Before he answered his son, he wanted Aisha to be present, since she was the one spreading rumors.

"Abu Bakar, call your mother. I wish her to be here before I speak any further."

Abu Bakar asked the steward to go to his mother's apartment on the other side of the mansion. It was a full ten minutes before Aisha appeared.

"*Sannu*, Alhaji. You called me to you. It is not my week, my husband. Hanna will be angry," she said.

"No, Aisha, I called you so that you can hear what I have to say on the subject of Omolola Adegoke and her children. But first, I want to hear your feelings on the subject, if you don't mind."

Alhaji leaned forward on the sofa, waiting for his wife to speak. Aisha looked nervously at her son, who would not meet her eyes. She knew that she had put him in a bad position.

"Alhaji, I suspect that the twin babies that your former secretary had are your own children."

He raised his eyebrows and looked at his first wife. Then he asked, "And what makes you think so, woman?"

Aisha adjusted her veil to cover her head before continuing.

"When I saw them at the naming ceremony, the boy looked just like Abu Bakar when he was a baby. Taiwo even has a cleft in his chin like you, Alhaji. Even Hanna remarked about their fair skin. *Wa-Allah*, I would not lie. Ask Hanna if you do not believe me."

Alhaji raised his hands up and down attempting to calm Aisha.

"That will not be necessary. I believe you, for you are not the only one who has suspicions about the parentage of the twins. Olufemi's other wife, the *bature,* Janice, has voiced the same suspicions to me."

Now it was Aisha's turn to be surprised. *When did her husband see the foreign woman and get this information?* She thought, but she dare not ask him directly.

"I hope I have satisfied all of your curiosity, Son. Believe me, I am looking into this matter, and I will keep you informed of all developments."

The father and son shook hands, and then he motioned for Aisha to return to her apartment. Hanna entered the room, followed by one of her children, and prepared her husband's dinner. Alhaji was quiet for the rest of the evening, deep in thought. He was wondering what Janice was doing in finding out the truth about Lola.

*****

Janice and Femi sat outside by the pool, relaxing while Charles took a nap. She was wearing a new bikini, which showed off her figure to perfection. Childbearing had a good effect on Janice. Her once slender hips were now shaped into curves, accentuated by her small waist. The bikini left nothing to the imagination. She stood up, stretched like a feline, and walked over to the diving board, preparing to jump. Her husband watched her gracefully climb on to the ladder and dive into the deep end. She came up quickly and with professional agility, swam to the other end of the pool, then turned on her back to float.

Olufemi, who could no longer resist being away from her, dived in next to her, pulling her back under the water. They played for a few minutes underwater until their lips touched. His hands grabbed her hair, pulling her to the surface for air. They broke apart out of breath, laughing at each other as he took her again by her hair and pulled her mouth to his. His strong body gleamed in the shimmering water that rippled like the muscles in his chest. Janice ran her fingers around his face as their legs tread water to keep them afloat. They swam to the shallow end, where he pulled himself up on the edge, then grabbed her by the waist and pulled her up to him. He was aroused, and she rubbed against him, feeling his hardness inside the thin swim trunks. He wrapped his long arms around her body, crushing her to his chest as his tongue explored her soft mouth. They played this game with each other until deciding to go inside their air-conditioned master suite, and there they made exquisite love until Charles awoke for his dinner.

The days flew by quickly. Janice began to feel that something was going on with Femi because his lovemaking was too frequent. He seemed insatiable and that is when Janice remembered the last time he was like that. It was when he was sharing himself between her and Lola.

No, he wouldn't, she thought to herself while cooking dinner.

Her friend, Aduke, came over to say good-bye. She and Segun had to return to school in Chicago. Janice did not want Aduke to leave until she knew the truth about Lola; in fact, she wanted to enlist her help in getting the truth.

"Aduke, how is your sister-in-law these days? Is she able to handle the twins?"

"You know she has a nanny and her mother to help her, Janice. She is fine, and so are they."

Aduke knew Janice too well not to wonder where her line of questions was leading.

"Janice, how are you and Femi doing?"

"We are fine, but I suspect that he is sneaking off to see Lola and the twins and is too much of a coward to tell me."

"Well, Janice, it is our culture. He must take an interest in his other children. Change places with Lola. Would you like him to neglect Charles?"

Janice was surprised at her attitude.

"No, I wouldn't, but does he have to sleep with her, Aduke?"

Now it was Aduke's turn to be surprised. "Who told you that he was?"

Janice turned a cool eye on her friend. "He is, isn't he, Aduke? Don't lie to me."

Aduke looked with sadness at her friend. "I'm sorry, Janice. I wanted to tell you, but Bisola and Segun forbade me to. I am truly sorry."

Even though Janice was shook up hearing what she suspected all this time, she held back her emotions. She needed Aduke to help her discover the truth about the children. That was her only weapon against Lola. She knew that sooner or later, as her friend, Linda Hassan had warned her, that the other wife always wanted to live in the house with you. Lola would eventually demand that, and it would spell doom for her marriage to Femi. Janice was determined to stay in Nigeria and make her marriage work, even though her mother forbade her to live in the same type of situation she left, or worse. Edna had told Janice to come home immediately if Femi should try to have two wives again. But Janice knew she would not leave because of Charles and the fact that she was deeply in love with Femi, even more now, than before. She would not, and could not, lose her husband to Lola the way Lola lost Femi to her.

She held onto the table for support as she told her friend of her suspicions and the flimsy proof that she had. Aduke told her it was not enough. She had to get more.

"How can I unless I confront her myself?" asked Janice.

"You just answered your own question, Janice. You must go to Lola and tell her that you know about her affair with Alhaji. Then you must throw it into her face about the children. She can only deny it."

"But what if she goes to Femi and tries to use what I did against me. I could lose him, Aduke," Janice said helplessly as a tear rolled down her cheek. "Oh God, I cannot let him go. I love him so. He is inside me, Aduke. If I fail, I may..." Her voice trailed off into a sob as Aduke handed her a tissue.

"Janice, stop this. This is not the woman I know. You are very strong to come this far, girl. Believe me; if those children are not Olufemi's, then God will not let this tragedy continue. I cannot blame Lola for trying, though. But it is time for her to realize that she lost him when he went to America. Come on, my friend, dry your eyes and let's plan how we will burst this bubble that Lola has been floating on. Even my husband is suspicious of his little sister. He also mentioned the children's coloring. The only one who is not affected by anything is Titiloye. She is so happy that her daughter has a husband and children that she cannot see the trap that her daughter set for herself."

The two women spent the rest of the afternoon planning what they were going to do. Femi came home from work and joined them in the living room. They quickly changed the subject, and Aduke left a short time later, winking her eye at Janice and giving her a supporting hug.

Femi sat with Janice and told her the events of his day, asking how her day went. She smiled and said it was a whole lot better now that she had seen Aduke. Then she looked at her handsome husband, wondering if he had just come from being with his other family and his other wife...

21

*7*itiloye was surprised when she saw the shiny Mercedes
Benz drive into the yard. She was not expecting any visitors this
morning, so she rushed to the door, curious as to whom it was. She
opened the door to find Lola's former boss, Alhaji Mohammed
Yaro. He looked handsome, wearing a light green *baba riga* with a
matching cap. He bowed slightly, and greeted Titiloye with flawless
Yoruba.

"Ekaro, Madame. Se' da da ni?" he asked.

"Adupe, sir. E'kabo, ewole, come in."

Titiloye led her distinguished guest into the parlor, and then
asked if she could get him something to drink.

He thanked her, but refused and asked to see her daughter,
Omolola.

Titiloye nodded and went upstairs to call her.

Lola was just finishing dressing when her mother knocked at the door.

"Tani."

"Emi, your mother. You have a visitor."

"Tani, kilo fe?" Lola asked, annoyed.

"It's Alhaji Yaro."

Lola almost dropped the hand mirror she was holding while putting the finishing touches to her hair. Her heart began to race as she tried to think of what reason he could possibly have to see her. She had asked him to stay away from her.

Adjusting her dress, Lola went downstairs to the parlor. Alhaji was standing by the bookcase, waiting. She saw him looking extremely handsome in his attire. The green color in his outfit went well with his tan complexion and set off his dark, sensuous eyes.

She cleared her throat, letting him know that she was in the room.

"Omolola, how are you?" he greeted her effusively, extending his hand.

She refused it and walked to the other side of the room before greeting him.

"You are welcome, sir. May I ask why the unexpected visit?"

Alhaji smiled slyly, sensing his presence was not desired.

"I just came to see how the new mother was doing and to see if you needed anything?"

"Well, thank you kindly, Alhaji, but my husband sees to all my needs."

Alhaji flinched at her tone of voice and what she was insinuating.

"I am glad he is, Lola, but I am training a new secretary and she has so many questions I do not know how to answer. I was wondering if you could spare a few hours to train someone to do your job. I would be very grateful."

Lola looked away from him, ashamed at the way she had spoken. It was then that the nanny came into the parlor with one of the twins and Titiloye followed closely behind with the other. Lola's face bore a look of surprise as her mother walked innocently into the parlor.

"Alhaji, come and see how the babies have grown," Lola's mother said.

The two women walked over to where he was standing, while Lola stood holding her breath in dismay. Alhaji looked at her, wondering why she had become so nervous.

"May I hold him?" he asked Titiloye, who was more than happy to let him hold Taiwo.

"Do be careful of your robes, sir. I wouldn't want him to soil them," she said.

Alhaji laughed with a happy sound that filled the room with merriment. Only the corner that Lola stood in was bleak.

"Madame, I am the proud father of six children. My eldest, Abu Bakar, is eighteen and my youngest is but two years. I am very familiar with the ways of babies."

Titiloye handed him the boy as he walked over to the sofa across from Lola and sat down. His face was a mask. Lola could not read it, for if she had, she probably would have died. In Taiwo's peach and cream face, Alhaji saw his pointed nose, the thin top lip, and the cleft in his chin. He smiled at the baby, not portraying his true feelings as he held the tiny hand and saw his long, slender fingers. *Aisha was right*, he thought. *Lola's son is the spitting image of Abu Bakar when he was an infant.* He then rose from the sofa and moved near to where Lola stood, who would not meet his eyes. Titiloye noticed the exchange between them and was baffled by her daughter's attitude. Khendi began to whimper since it was close to feeding time. Taiwo was content to lie in Alhaji's arms, staring up at him.

"Give me Khendi, Kumbi," Lola said to the nanny. "She is hungry and wants to be fed."

"Wait, Lola. Before you feed her, I want to see her, too," Alhaji said, giving her a look that held several messages.

Lola hesitated, but decided it was no use and she might as well let him see the other twin. Like an angel, Khendi lay in her arms, her eyes brimming with tears ready to be shed, her thin lips pouting and quivering, and her petite hand fingering her mother's dress searching for her food. The baby's dark, curly hair and pointed nose told Alhaji all he needed to know.

Lola stood face-to-face with Alhaji, not saying a word as he looked deeply into her eyes, daring her to lie to him about the twins. She stood there, holding her daughter; both their eyes brimming with unshed tears, both their lips quivering.

Alhaji whispered, *"Allah Akbar!"*

Lola then took her crying daughter to the sofa and opened the top of her dress.

"Alhaji, you must excuse me; I have to feed the baby," Lola said.

"Fine, Lola. I will take a walk with Taiwo, if that is all right," he said, looking at Titiloye, who nodded. He then walked into the garden outside in the light of the morning.

Lola placed her daughter to her breast, wiping tears from her eyes and sniffing. She knew she was trapped. *God! Why did he have to come now? I am so close to winning Olufemi back,* she thought. All this was not lost on her mother, who had been trying to figure out why her daughter was so hostile to Alhaji. Titiloye looked out the window watching Alhaji, so comfortable with Taiwo, talking to him as if he were his.

Iro, iro, O ti o o o o! Omolola, why? Why? Why you go and ruin your life? Why now? She thought to herself while watching her daughter nervously feeding Khendi. She would not say anything to Lola until Alhaji left, for she too had noticed the uncanny resemblance of Taiwo to Alhaji, especially while he was holding him. There was no mistaking the father of that baby!

Lola finished feeding Khendi and gave the sleeping girl to the nanny. Her mother sat across from her, looking with pity at her daughter. Lola noticed her mother's silence.

"Mama, are you all right?"

Titiloye smiled distractedly and replied, "Yes. No ... I don't know."

Alhaji returned from his walk in the garden with Taiwo, who was now sound asleep. He smiled as he gave him to his grandmother.

"Madame, please. I wish to speak to your daughter ... alone."

"Certainly I will take the baby upstairs."

He waited until Titiloye was out of the room before letting the dam of emotions burst. Then he rushed over to Lola's chair, towering over her and pinning her down by holding her arms.

"Kai! Haba! Omolola! How could you deceive your husband and me this way? How long did you think you could carry on with this charade?" he angrily questioned her.

Alhaji was breathing heavily, trying to control his anger. She was afraid he would hit her, so she just sat there in his power, his dark gaze fixed on her face. She was afraid to look at him, afraid that she would break down and what she had been holding back would come flying out at any time. So she remained silently stubborn, biting her lower lip.

His hands tightened on her arms, making them numb. He wanted to slap her, but how could he? She was the mother of his children. She sat there, tears streaming down her cheeks; sobbing silently for all the pain she caused him. She knew his culture and his position in society, and that this would be a disgrace to his family. He would have to explain this to his parents and his uncle, the Emir of Kano. His body began to shudder as he took a deep breath, trying to regain control of his emotions. He slowly released her and walked silently to the door.

"Alhaji," Lola cried to him, "please understand why!" she sobbed.

He stood there, his body shrouded with an air of defeat. "Understand. Lola, how? You have robbed me of my rights as a father." He turned to face her. "You have denied their sisters and brothers." Then he rushed over to her and pulled her from the chair and began shaking her.

"Wake up, woman, and face the man who loves you and tell him the truth!"

Sobbing uncontrollably, Lola cried, "All right, yes! Yes! You are the father of Taiwo and Khendi!"

The slap could be heard upstairs as Titiloye rushed down, hearing her daughter's cry. She ran to Lola, who was crumpled on the floor sobbing hysterically.

"Alhaji, *e' jo, e'jo,* please stop; you cannot. Stop! What is happening?" Titiloye screamed.

He gathered himself with as much dignity as he could muster and walked towards the door saying, "Ask your daughter, Madame." Then he left the house, slamming the door.

Hearing the door slam must have jarred her senses, for she leaped away from her mother's arms and rushed outside just as Alhaji's car was pulling away.

"Alhaji, wait! Please let me explain! Please!" she screamed, but he would not stop and drove into the traffic.

Lola dragged herself back inside and cried until she was almost unconscious. Her mother put ice on her cheek that still stung from Alhaji's slap.

"Now, daughter, tell me what is going on."

Lola began the story of how she wanted to keep Olufemi and what lengths she had to go to get to that point, and she told her mother about her affair with Alhaji.

"Mama, it was just one time. I knew he loved me, but I was not sure he would give me the time off to travel to America."

"Lola, how long did you think you could keep deceiving everyone? Those children are looking like their father more and more each day. Your husband is bound to be suspicious. And what about Janice? How long before she finds out now? You have really done it this time, Lola."

"Oh, Mom, what will I do? I don't want to lose Olufemi."

"I believe, my child, that you did that day you had sex with Alhaji. God done catch you!"

Several days passed after Alhaji's visit. He sent a message to Janice that he wanted to meet with her at the chalet in Badagary. He had some news. Janice again arranged for Charles to be kept by the nanny and dressed to go on her rendezvous. They met this time at Apapa Amusement Park, where she parked her car nearby. They reached Badagary Beach in less than an hour. Alhaji was again wearing casual attire, but he looked tired and drawn. He had already ordered lunch, and they talked very little while eating. When they were finished, he led her into the living room and sat in a chair across from her.

"I saw Omolola," he said, saying Lola's name with great difficulty.

"Is she well ... and how are the twins?" She saw how her question changed his expression.

"They are well, and I suppose she is okay, Janice. Your suspicions were correct. I am the father of the twins."

Janice sat there with her mouth agape, staring at him. She could see that he had been wrestling with the news in his own way.

"Alhaji, are you sure?"

He sat calmly in his chair. "Quite sure, Janice. She confessed to me under duress. I went to see her unexpectedly, and she could not lie. When I held Taiwo in my arms, he reminded me of my eldest son, Abu Bakar, when he was an infant. The boy has the same cleft in his chin, my lips, my coloring, and my nose. Janice, how could she do this to me? This is such a shame to my family. And with her still being married to Olufemi, I have no rights in this matter."

They both sat quietly, thinking.

Then Janice finally said, "Oh, poor Femi! He will be devastated when he finds out he is not the father to the twins, and that Lola was unfaithful to him!"

While Janice really did feel terrible for Alhaji and for the anguish Lola had put him through, secretly she was cheering. As far as she was concerned, she finally had a way to get Lola out of her life and, at last, put an end to all of her pain.

He looked at her with eyebrows raised. "So, Janice, do you have a plan? How will you expose this lie without hurting the children?"

"Leave that to me, Alhaji. When I'm finished, Lola will be running to you, begging for forgiveness."

"Ish Allah, Ish Allah," was his only reply.

After their meeting, Alhaji and Janice decided to remain in touch and keep each other informed on what was happening. Janice returned home and sat in her bedroom, trying to figure out how to tell her husband about Lola. Then she decided to pay Lola a visit. *I want her to tell Femi herself. I want her to admit she planned this to keep him,* she thought.

Leaving Charles with his nanny, Janice drove to Surulere. The traffic was unusually heavy; there were many delays. She sat in traffic while the hawkers came by her window, trying to sell her various goods. When she finally reached Lola's home, she drove into the driveway, entered the gate, and rang the bell. A young woman answered the door and showed Janice into the parlor. Lola was in her room with the twins when Kumbi came into the bedroom to announce the visitor.

"Tani, Kumbi, *kini-nwn-fe?"*

"Janice Adegoke is waiting to see you, Madame."

Lola turned and stared with disbelief at Kumbi, just as Olufemi came in from the nursery.

"Olu, Janice is here. Does she know that you are?"

Olufemi began to sweat nervously. He would often come by on his lunch hour to visit the twins. How could he explain this to Janice?

"I will go down and see what she wants," Lola said quietly.

She put on her slippers and walked quickly from the room downstairs to the parlor. She stood for a few moments outside the door, looking at Janice. Janice was sitting on the sofa, fiddling with her pink painted fingernails and turning her wedding ring around and around on her finger. She was dressed casually, wearing khaki-colored pants and a light blue short sleeve knit top. Her hair was tied neatly into a ponytail held by a blue barrette.

Janice turned as Lola entered the parlor.

"Well, well, well, Janice. What brings you to visit?" Lola said with a smile on her face, putting her hand on her hips with a challenge.

"I came to talk to you, Lola. I saw Alhaji Mohammed."

Lola's smile froze as her lips quivered. She instantly took a defensive stance.

"And?" she asked nervously.

Janice stood up and walked a few feet near where Lola stood.

"He told me everything, Lola. I know about the children. I know that Femi is not their father."

Lola stood staring at Janice as anger began to rise into her cheeks.

"Olufemi will never believe you. He is here right now, visiting the children."

Janice winced when Lola said that Olufemi was there. She had wondered why he had not said anything about the children to her lately. Now she knew why. He had been seeing them without her knowing. Still, she knew that when he heard the news that he was not the father, he would be devastated.

"Lola, I am going to tell Femi that he is not the father. Where is he?"

Lola laughed. "Janice, did you forget that this is my house? Tell him at your home. I will not let you ruin a perfectly pleasant afternoon."

The tone of voice that Lola used ran right through Janice, making her angry. "If you won't tell me where he is, then I will find him myself." Janice started walking towards the doorway where Lola was standing.

"Excuse me, Lola. I'm coming through."

But Lola stood her ground, refusing to be intimidated in her own home. The two women stood toe-to-toe, daring the other to make a move. Janice stood firm, her nostrils flaring, and her eyes flashing fire, while Lola shot Janice the fierce, angry look of a woman who had lost all options.

Janice was tired of waiting for Lola to move and began to shove her aside.

"Move, Lola; I want to see my husband!"

"What do you mean 'your' husband?"

Then the two women exchanged blows. Lola balled her fist and shot Janice a hook into her mouth, drawing blood. Janice screamed then began to hit Lola in the face, grabbing her long braids and pulling them. The two women were in a struggle to see who would be the victor. Their blows and screams could be heard throughout the house.

"Asewo," Lola screamed between blows as she kicked Janice's legs from under her, causing them both to fall on the floor. Upstairs with the nanny, Olufemi could hear the noise of the fight. He rushed onto the landing, staring in disbelief at his two wives beating each other up.

Lola was sitting on Janice, banging her head into the floor, while Janice was pulling Lola's hair and hitting her in the face. Olufemi ran down the stairs, two at a time, reaching the women at the same time as Titiloye rushed in from the kitchen.

"Stop it, stop this now!" Olufemi cried at the women. "Janice, what are you doing here?"

Janice screamed. "I came to tell you about..." she started just as Lola hit her in the mouth again. She cried out and began trying to kick Lola off her.

Olufemi pulled Lola off Janice, while Titiloye tried to restrain Janice, whose mouth was bleeding badly from the blow. As Olufemi dragged Lola, kicking, biting, and screaming, off Janice, Janice hit her hard in the face, knocking her into Olufemi. He then lost his balance, and the two of them tumbled into a heap on the carpet. Janice wiped the blood from her mouth as she looked at them on the floor.

"Femi, I came here to speak to Lola about something, and I find you here. How long has this been going on?"

Olufemi pulled away from Lola and stood up quickly while Lola sat on the floor, stunned by the fall. Her mother rushed to her aid. Femi pulled his handkerchief out of his pocket and began to apply pressure to Janice's bleeding lip. Her eyes were filled with tears and pain as she caught sight of Lola coming towards her menacingly.

"Femi, I must tell you the truth. Lola lied to us all. The twins are not ..."

Before she could finish, Lola pushed Olufemi aside, clawing at Janice's face. Olufemi had grown tired of the fighting and turned on Lola. He took her arms, held them together, and gave her a look that stopped her cold. Then he threw her onto the sofa.

"Now stay there! Don't you move!" he told her.

Janice had moved quickly to the other side of the room, her eyes darting from side to side, poised for danger.

"Olufemi, *kilode?"* Titiloye began in anger. "This is my daughter's house, and I refuse to let this *oyingbo* cause any more *wahalla!* Take her out of here."

Janice stood up, glaring at the older woman. "Olufemi," Janice addressed her husband by his full name, "Lola lied to you. Listen, my husband, to the truth!"

Lola began to shrink into the sofa, her face red and swollen, and her eyes holding the look of total defeat.

"Janice, what do you mean she lied?"

Even Titiloye was silent.

"Go on, Janice," Femi shouted, impatiently. "Tell me!"

Janice looked at the two women across the room. She saw the look of pure unadulterated hatred in Lola's eyes, while Titiloye looked at Janice, pleading with her eyes and ringing her hands as if in pain. Janice took a deep breath, preferring not to look at the women any longer and began her story from the beginning. She told him that he was not the father of the twins, and that Lola used them as a means to convince him to stay with her.

"She wanted you at any cost, Femi. She did not think about who would be hurt by this." She dabbed her cut lip with the handkerchief.

Everyone held their breath as Femi's face changed several times from confusion to anger as he attempted to digest the news. His whole body was filled with pain. His mind was racing. *How could this happen?* He looked over at Lola, who sat rigid on the sofa, her face wet with tears, for every word that Janice told Olufemi was like a blade cutting into her heart. She knew that she had lost him forever. Titiloye tried to console her daughter.

"Omolola, is this true?" Femi asked, his fists clenched at his side.

The room became so silent; you could hear everyone's breathing. Then Femi felt his anger begin to rise at the realization that he had been used and made a fool of.

"Omolola!" he shouted. *"Se'-oto-ni!?"*

Lola wiped her face with the back of her hand, pushing her mother away. She stood tall, proud, and unafraid of her husband. She knew that she had lost him. She had never seen him so hurt before. His handsome face sagged with anguish, his strong hands clenched into tight fists. She moaned, throwing herself at his feet. *"Oko mi, egbamio, ejo, ejo,* I am sorry, but I loved you so much. I had to do something!"

Lola was sobbing and clinging to his legs. Olufemi stood there for a moment, looking at her body at his feet. He bent down, lifting her face to look into her almond-shaped eyes running with a river of tears. A look of pure disgust came over his face as he pushed her away with such force that she slid across the floor.

"Asewo! O-lo shi!" Femi shouted at Lola, pointing his finger with anger. He was about to strike her when Janice screamed.

"No, Femi, no. It will not change anything!" She rushed to his side, pleading with him. "Come on, let's go home. Let's go."

Janice grabbed his hands and held them before he could inflict any blows on Lola. Lola lay on the floor sobbing with her mother trying to console her. Janice pushed Femi out of the house and into her car. She rushed to the driver's side and drove him home in silence. She could see how hard he was fighting to control himself, not wanting to break down in front of Lola and show how truly hurt he was.

When they reached home, he ran into their bedroom. Janice could hear the sound of breaking glass as she rushed into the room to find him standing in front of their dresser, the mirror shattered and his hand bleeding profusely. She went into the bathroom and got a wet towel and wrapped it around his hand. Then she led him to the bed, cradling his head in her arms. She held him like a mother holds a baby. His body was shaking with emotion as he let go of all the frustration and anguish that he held inside. He was devastated at his loss. Femi lay there in the comfort of his wife's arms and turned his face towards hers. He looked with confusion into eyes, and then bolted up from her arms, pacing the floor in anger.

"Who is the father, Janice? Do you know?"

Janice was not sure if this was the time for her to reveal Alhaji. She was not sure how Femi would react to this. But then again, he needed to know, so she decided to tell him.

"Darling, it is Alhaji Mohammed Yaro."

"What? Who? I don't believe it!" Femi shouted, hitting his hand, making it bleed again.

"Janice, who else knows about this, I mean, how did you find out Lola was lying to me?"

Janice's mind was racing. She did not want to reveal her cooperation with Alhaji. She was not sure that Femi would appreciate her duplicity. So she told him about the time that she and Sharon saw Lola at the obstetrician's office, and how Sharon asked the doctor to tell her how far along Lola was.

"It was then that I became suspicious, darling. I thought that she was too large to be only seven months pregnant. Then I, too, was confused when she gave birth two months early."

Femi began to pace the floor agitated.

"I wonder if Alhaji knows that he is the father of those beautiful children. Oh, God! Why? How will I break this to my mother?"

"Don't worry, Femi. We will tell everyone together. I will not let you go through this alone. I am just glad that you know the truth."

"I hope that I do know all of the truth. There will be hell to pay if I find out that I have been deceived again."

Janice took a deep breath. Then she prayed to God that nothing else would happen to wreck her chances for a happy marriage.

22

*L*ola lay on the floor crying hysterically. She was unable to fathom the loss of Olufemi and possibly Alhaji, as well. She had been very stupid, and she cursed herself over and over for allowing things to go as far as they had. Her mother and Kumbi tried to calm her, but when they did not succeed, they carried her upstairs to her room and undressed her. Titiloye gave her a cup of herbal tea laced with a sleeping potion, and soon Lola was asleep.

Titiloye and Kumbi fed the twins formula, since their mother was in no condition to nurse them. Then she was forced to confide in Kumbi about what had happened to cause the catastrophe.

"I am so sorry for Madame Lola. I will pray for her recovery," she said softly.

Titiloye sat back in the rocking chair, holding Taiwo thinking, *what will my daughter do now? She will have to leave this house. Olufemi will surely divorce her and turn her out and she will return to Ileshia in disgrace. Lola has done the worst thing to a husband. Not only was she unfaithful, but also she had children by her lover. What a shame ... oh, what a shame!*

Lola was in a deep sleep. The herbs her mother laced her tea with gave her strange dreams. She dreamed that she was in a large, white room standing with Femi when Alhaji Mohammed entered with Janice. Janice was pointing an accusing finger at her, shouting "Liar, liar; you are a liar." Then she took Olufemi's arm and walked away from her and Alhaji, leaving Lola begging for Olufemi's forgiveness. Janice and Olufemi did not listen to this, but instead, left the room. Alhaji was standing by the window with his back to Lola. She hesitated, and then walked over to him, tapping him on the shoulder. No words were spoken. He only took her hand and kissed it. His handsome face and sensuous eyes shot bolts of fire at her. She was frightened, but he reassured her that he loved her over and over again. "I love you, Omolola, and I want you and the children."

It was nearly evening the next day when Lola awakened from her drug-induced sleep. She looked around her dark bedroom and, upon seeing no one, lay still, remembering her dream. She saw Alhaji as her only salvation, and she knew that she would have to face all of the Adegoke family and tell them that Taiwo and Khendi were not Olufemi's children. She felt drained of all emotion; her body was cold and stiff. She shivered in the heat of the Lagos afternoon, unable to bring herself to rise from her bed.

Lola stayed that way for several days, causing her mother to worry that she had lost her mind. When she and Kumbi brought Lola the children to feed, she would turn her back on them and refuse them, which made Titiloye very angry. Her daughter had done enough damage to everyone, but Titiloye would not allow her to abandon her own children.

Titiloye opened the door to Lola's bedroom. It was musty from being closed up for several days. She proceeded to open the closed drapes and let the fresh air into the room. There her daughter lay, her hair unkempt, her body unwashed. The normally beautiful, expressive, almond-shaped eyes stared into space, red-rimmed and swollen from crying.

Titiloye pulled back the sheet and lifted her daughter's head.

"Tisk, tisk, tisk, my daughter. You cannot do this. You caused all this trouble, now you lay here as if that will change anything. You must get up and take care of your children. Olufemi called and told me his mother and father are coming to Lagos. They will be at Ikoyi and want to meet with you today. You have to go and face your in-laws and beg for forgiveness for all the lies and damages that you have done. I will be with you, daughter. You will not be alone."

The mention of Olufemi's name had a tremendous effect on Lola. Her eyes began to shine, and she looked at her mother.

"Mama, I know that I have lost him. I know. Please bring me my children after I bathe."

The telephone rang and Kumbi rushed upstairs to tell her mistress that she had a long distance call. Lola thought it was Segun, but instead it was her friend, Kemi.

"Kini nkan, Kemi, is that you? I am so happy to hear from you."

"Omolola, my friend. How are things? We haven't spoken since the twins' birth."

"Kemi, my life is finished. Olu found out the truth about the twins. Janice told him."

"Oh, my *shewu*, Lola," she said with dismay. "How did she discover the truth?"

Lola went on to tell her friend about the events of the last few days, including her confrontation with Alhaji.

"Lola, remember I warned you. I told you not to try to deceive Olu. He is not a fool, you know. You have probably destroyed any chance of reconciliation now."

"I know," Lola said tearfully. "They have called a family meeting to discuss it. I know that they are going to cast me out of the family, and my children will not have a father. What am I to do, Kemi?"

Kemi thought for a moment. She wished she were in Nigeria to be of more comfort and support to her friend, but for now, the advice she gave her would just have to do.

"Lola, listen carefully. I want you to stop crying. You have to be strong for your children's sake. I want you to wear your best gown and make yourself pretty. Then you go with your mother to the Adegoke house and greet Olufemi's family well. Take all the chastisement they give you, for you have deceived them all and caused them tremendous pain. They have lost two beautiful grandchildren, so do not think Abimbola will take kindly to this. You will be cast out of the family, but they will give you time to make provisions for your children."

"I know all that, Kemi. I am prepared to accept my punishment. It is only fair, but I still love Olu. My God, how can I live without him?"

"My friend, listen to you. You slept with your boss and had his children. You lost Olu when you lied to him. You caused a lot of trouble in America, too, remember? I am your friend, so please listen to what I say. After they cast you out, then you reveal the father of the children to them."

"Why to them? What difference will it make then?"

"Oh, my naive friend. I really miss you, Lola. Then Olufemi will go after Alhaji and make him take care of you and the twins. I always thought you should have been with him in the first place. I remember how he used to look at you."

"But Kemi, Alhaji already has three wives. I don't want to be a part of his harem."

"You won't. Once Alhaji has agreed to take care of you and the twins, then he will have to give you accommodation. Tell him you want your own house in Lagos. He will agree to take care of you until your marriage to Olu is dissolved, then he can marry you and give your children his name, but you will already be established outside his polygamous house."

Lola scratched her head, trying to understand what Kemi was telling her. It may be her only hope to avoid returning to the village with her mother. She liked Lagos life and wanted to stay.

"All right, Kemi. I will do as you say. Thank you for caring enough to call, my friend. Say hello to Jide. By the way, how are things in America?"

"Well, that was the next thing I was going to suggest. If Alhaji won't marry you, then come to America to live with us. We are doing well here, and have plenty of room for you and the babies. I know that you will find a husband here even with children. American men don't care if you have children, especially if they love you. My cousin Yetunde just got married to an African-American man, and they are very happy. He treats her with so much respect. Sometimes I wish Jide would do some of the things for me that Yetunde's husband does."

The two women continued to chat until Titiloye came into the room to ask Lola to hurry and get dressed for the meeting. She did not want them to be late. As Lola prepared herself, she told her mother what Kemi suggested.

"Omolola, I did not know that such a rich and handsome man as Alhaji wanted you. Why didn't you tell me? I would have told you to let Olufemi have his *oyingbo*. Maybe you still have a chance for happiness yet. I will invite Alhaji to come over and talk after the meeting. You two need to talk to decide how you will raise your children. He has the right to his children, and they have the right to his name and fortune," her mother said, happier than she had been in days.

Janice carried Charles to the car and put him in his car seat. He squirmed and protested at being strapped in. Femi took the wheel and drove through the light afternoon traffic to his sister's house in Ikoyi. They were both quiet, thinking about what lay before them. His parents had arrived this morning, and they were very unhappy about the situation. Olufemi thought to himself, *It appears that my difficult choices have been taken from my hands. They were made for me. Lola saw to that.*

They arrived early. Lola and her mother were not there yet. Abimbola took Charles into her arms and proceeded to plant kisses on his round cheeks. Ajoke and T.J. fought their grandmother for the baby. Janice and Femi joined Taju and Bisola in the den, while Emmanuel sat silently with a frown on his face, not speaking.

"Father, come on. Be nice. This is not the end of the world," Bisola teased her father, who scowled at her.

"Bisi, do not take this lightly. This is the first time an Adegoke has had this problem. Your situation with Abbe, Taju's first wife, did not involve any children. I thought those children were Adegoke. I am very disappointed that our youth today seem to have no morals or conscience."

"Now, now *oko-mi,"* Abimbola interrupted, walking into the room carrying her active grandson. "You must understand it from a woman's point of view. Lola was in love with our son. He married another woman, and she never recovered. Do not be too hard on her. She must be very unhappy now."

Janice stood near the bookcase, sipping her coke while trying to understand their Yoruba. Femi came and stood by her, touching her cheek and smiling.

"This must be very hard for you, Janice. I am sorry that I put you through this."

She touched his bandaged hand reassuringly.

"Everyone have a seat. Mrs. Shodeye and Omolola have arrived," announced Taju.

Janice and Bisola sat next to each other while Abimbola and Emmanuel sat in the center of the room. Taju and Olufemi took seats on either side of them. Into the room came Lola and her mother. Lola was dressed in a light blue satin lace *iro* and *buba*. Her silver-blue head wrap shimmered and was tied to perfection. Her long braids hung down her back, and her nails were painted a deep ruby-red to match her lipstick. As her eyes lowered, revealing her long lashes, she walked in with the dignity of a queen who was being dethroned and facing her final triumph. Titiloye was also dressed splendidly in gold and white lace with matching accessories. The twins followed, in a carriage pushed by Kumbi.

Omolola prostrated in front of her in-laws while her mother knelt next to her daughter.

After the traditional greetings, Taju led the women to the chairs placed in front of the family.

Emmanuel began. "This is a sad time for the Adegoke family. It is always sad when a marriage is ending. We, the parents, do everything in our power to ensure our children's happiness. But once they leave the home, it is then up to them to seek and find their own happiness. It is unfortunate that our children cannot come to terms with their problems, and this marriage must be dissolved according to native law and custom in Nigeria. Do either of you have anything to say before we proceed with this?"

From across the room their eyes met. Olufemi and Omolola struggled with their emotions. Their love had been filled with happiness and joy until he left to study overseas. He looked at her and remembered the young girl in the village that hung around the store when he came to Ileshia with his father. Her long, slender, bronze legs and expressive, almond-shaped eyes held him mesmerized today, as they did back then. Lola's heart skipped a beat and her breath caught in her throat at the thought of feeling his hands hot on her body or feeling him deep inside her giving her pleasure beyond her wildest dreams. Her hand flew to her throat as Olufemi began to speak of her in apologetic terms.

"I gave Omolola all the love and trust that a man can give to a woman. I am to blame for this tragedy as much as she is, and I even more. I betrayed our love by marrying another woman without her permission. I thought she would understand, but all I did was to drive her to do what she did."

He turned to Lola, his eyes pleading for forgiveness. "I am sorry, Lola. I am sorry for all the pain and suffering I caused. I think you need to tell my family who the real father of the twins is."

Lola shifted uncomfortably in her seat. She looked at her mother for support, and Titiloye nodded, giving her consent for her daughter to tell it all.

"Their father is Alhaji Mohammed Yaro. We were together only once while Olufemi was in America with Janice."

Everyone was stunned by her revelation except Janice, the only one to know the love that Alhaji held for Lola.

"Does Alhaji Yaro know of this?" Emmanuel asked, stunned.

"Yes, he knows. So you see, my children will lose one name only to gain another."

The room was hushed while they all took time to digest this earthshaking news. Janice was horrified at her husband's revelation, taking all the blame for their breakup himself. *This is crap*, she thought, but kept silent because she knew that to speak would damage her own position. When everyone regained their composure, Olufemi then kneeled in front of Titiloye and begged for forgiveness, and prayed that her daughter would find happiness. Then he offered the return of her dowry.

Lola stood up and walked to the center of the room. She was magnificent, so beautiful and graceful that Janice felt a twinge of jealousy.

"Baba mi and Mama mi," she said eloquently to her soon-to-be former in-laws. "This is truly a sad time for us all, especially the children — the two innocent babies whom you claimed as your own. Only I will know what they will miss not having a father like Olufemi." Her voice began to quiver with emotion. "I have always loved you all, and now must beg forgiveness for my deception. I did it for love. My only regret is that it has hurt you all and will take me away from you. Bisola, my dear, dear sister-in-law, you stood by me

from the beginning, and now we must part. You will always be my sister."

Then she walked over to Janice and stood towering over her. The scent of her perfume assailed Janice's nostrils. She flared them in deference.

"Janice, Olufemi is all yours now. Take care of him and make sure that he does not do to you what he did to me."

Janice looked at Lola and felt a twinge of pity. Then she turned to her handsome husband and smiled, "No that will never happen to me. I assure you." Olufemi returned her smile.

Seeing the look of love that passed between them, it was then that Lola truly conceded defeat.

"Then so be it," Emmanuel said. "Let the marriage between my son, Olufemi Augustus Adegoke, and Omolola Afolake Shodeye-Adegoke is formally dissolved according to native laws and customs of Nigeria."

They would have to go to the court to have the divorce registered, but for all intents and purposes, Lola and Olu were no longer husband and wife. *Strange,* Janice thought. *This was too easy, all too easy.* It made her afraid inside.

Abimbola took Lola into her arms and held her.

Then Emmanuel said, "My only quarrel with you, daughter, is that you lied about the children. I am unhappy to lose not only you, but two grandchildren." Then he walked away, his shoulders slumped.

Abimbola thanked Titiloye and told her she could collect the dowry from Taju, and that Lola should vacate the house in two weeks. Titiloye nodded and thanked Abimbola. They had been friends for many years, and she did not like losing a friend.

Janice and Femi stood together. He put his arm around her shoulders possessively as Lola walked into the courtyard, hoping that Janice could not feel his heart thumping because he was giving up his first wife. But Janice did feel his pain; she just did not let him know.

Lola and her mother walked away with as much dignity as they could muster. Lola entered the car, feeling desolate. She had no more tears to shed. Her marriage to Olufemi was over, and now she was soon to be homeless. She knew that she had to take action to stave off having to return to the village with her mother.

Taju walked them to the car and gave Titiloye the envelope that contained Lola's dowry. He also told her she could take whatever she wanted from the house in Surulere.

"My father-in-law did not mean two weeks literally. You can take all the time you need to vacate. They are returning to Ekiti tomorrow."

Lola kept her eyes averted while thanking him. Titiloye nodded and took the envelope while the driver started the car. Lola took one last look before the car moved into traffic.

When Taju came back into the den, he and Olufemi gave each other a knowing look while Bisola and Janice held onto one another.

"Welcome, my sister, welcome. I can now shout it out! You are the best wife for my brother and always have been!" She laughed, holding Janice and smothering her face with kisses. That is when Janice let out a deep breath and relaxed, for she now felt that she was truly accepted into the Adegoke family.

After Lola and her family were dropped off at the house, she took her children up to the nursery, and then she changed into something comfortable and sat in the garden reading and trying to forget what had happened earlier. She had decided to return to work, for the money from her dowry would not last long in these times, and she had two mouths to feed. Her mother had decided to stay with her in Lagos. They would have to find a flat to live in unless she took Kemi's advice and talked to Alhaji. *I am just not ready to do that now*, Lola thought.

Life became so simple for Janice and Femi. They were now a family without another wife. Janice wrote her mother and invited her and James to visit. Her mother was thrilled that Lola and Femi were divorced and that Janice was free of the other wife. Janice called Melinda and told her the good news, and her cousin wished her well and much success in her *new* marriage.

Janice attended her women's club meeting and made the announcement. All the women were happy for her, especially Linda Hassan, who was still fighting with her husband about Leti, the Indian woman he took as his third wife.

Sharon gave birth to a boy, and this made her husband ecstatic for a son completed their family. Ngozi now had a baby brother to keep her busy.

But Janice's biggest surprise was yet to come. Segun sent her a letter thanking her for forgiving his sister and offered his friendship. He knew that she and Aduke were best friends and did not want what happened with Lola to come between them. Even Femi was shocked at this.

Lola and Titiloye found a small two-bedroom flat in Agege. They moved there with the twins and Kumbi. Titiloye sold *eko* and *moyin-moyin* to make ends meet, while Lola found a job as a secretary. The pay was lousy, but at least it put food on the table for them.

One day Lola was at work when she saw a familiar face come from the minister's office. He was handsome, dressed in a white guinea brocade *baba riga* with a white hat trimmed in blue. His eyes shone with excitement when he caught sight of Lola. Alhaji Mohammed Yaro was on his way to the mosque-jid for the Jumat prayer. He was finishing a meeting with the director of the Ministry of Housing, and they were walking out of his office when he saw Lola standing by the copy machine. He asked the director who she was, and he told Alhaji she was one of the new secretaries that they had just hired.

"She is a beauty that one. I want to ask her out, but I am afraid of my wife."

Alhaji chuckled. "Stay away from that one. She is already taken."

Then he said good-bye to the minister and started walking over in Lola's direction.

"Mrs. Adegoke; hello. Lola, Omolola," he called, as she tried to turn away.

"Ah ... Alhaji Yaro. *Sannu. Lafiya,"* she said, lowering her eyes and fluttering her lashes.

"Lola, what are you doing here? Why did you come here to work? Why didn't you call?"

"Call you? Did you forget the last time we met? You were so angry, you slapped me. Why would I call you?"

Alhaji was taken aback by her tone.

"But Lola, I was hurt. What has happened to you since we last met? How are the children?"

Lola frowned and prepared to shout at him, but then she thought better of herself and remembered what her friend Kemi told her: "Be nice to him. He may be all you have." After all, he was the children's father.

"Come, have lunch with me after the Jumat prayer at the Central Mosque. You can wait in the car while I pray. We have lots to talk about Lola."

She grabbed her purse and followed Alhaji's flowing robes to his Mercedes Benz, waiting outside. The driver, surprised, rushed to open the door for Lola. She and Alhaji sat together on the back seat. He was silent, only speaking in Hausa to his driver to take care of Lola while he said his prayers.

They parked near the fountain a few blocks from the mosque and waited. Lola stood outside, throwing coins and making wishes into the water. It must have been a good omen for her to see Alhaji this way. At least she maintained some pride by not running after him.

They drove back to the mosque to pick up Alhaji, who was standing outside, conversing with the governor and other dignitaries. He waved good-bye to them while rushing towards the car. The driver opened the door, and he lost his serious look just sitting close to the woman of his dreams. He loved her, and it showed on his face. His mouth opened up into a smile that lit up the car as he took her hand.

"Omolola, my love. I have wished for this day for a long ... a very long time. I love you, Omolola, and I want to take care of my children. Most of all, I want to take care of you."

Lola stared straight in front of her, afraid to look at Alhaji. She caught sight of the driver's eyes in the rear view mirror. He was nodding his head "yes, yes," for he knew that his employer had been filled with sadness for some time and now he saw the glow of happiness in his eyes. He liked his boss this way.

Lola turned slowly, raising her eyes to look into Alhaji's. Her full lips formed the words he longed to hear for so long.

"Yes, Alhaji. You can take care of our children and me. I am free now. Olufemi has divorced me. I know that in time I will learn to love you. For how can any woman resist such a handsome and dashing man such as you?"

She took her free hand and placed it behind his head, rubbing his soft, curly hair through her fingers, knocking off his hat. He began to breathe heavily as he took her into his arms, crushing her into his chest, his lips hot and hungry as the fire in his loins kissed her neck. They caressed each other with passionate abandon, forgetting that they were in the car. When they came apart, he placed her hands to his lips and continued kissing them until Lola was burning with desire.

"Alhaji, slow down, my love. We have plenty of time to be together. I want you to come home with me. You need to speak to my mother and make arrangements for us."

"Where are you living, Lola?"

"I have a small flat in Agege."

He turned up his nose in distaste at the thought of the woman he loves and his children living that way.

"It was all I could afford on my salary."

He reached into his pocket and pulled out thousands of *Naira* and thrust it into her hands.

"This is to hire some movers. I have a house in Victoria Island that is vacant. You can move in there until I have time to present you to my uncle, the Emir of Kano. Before we can be married, we have to go through my family. I am sure that there will be no problem. Once they see Taiwo and Khendi, oh—" he stopped, remembering; "I intend to give them one of my names as well. My father's name was Aliyu, and since they are twins they will be called Aliyu and Aliya."

Lola smiled, for things were getting better by the minute. She did not expect Alhaji to be so generous after the way she had lied to him. Kemi was right after all.

"Yes, Alhaji, they are beautiful names, and you are fully within your rights to change their names. Aliyu Taiwo Yaro and Aliya Khendi Yaro. They are beautiful."

"Then it is settled. I will speak to my wives about our marriage and formally introduce you to them. Then you and I will be married. Lola, you and the children will never want for anything again."

It is said, "all's well that end's well." But not completely...

Lola was introduced into the Yaro family, and though Aisha, Alhaji's senior wife, protested that she was living outside the home, the other wives welcomed her. It gave them somewhere to visit when they tired of their mansion. Alhaji was happy. He had his four wives, and took Lola to all the places that his other wives would not go. Lola was the perfect hostess, able to entertain even the highest dignitaries.

Alhaji was promoted within the ministry to director of the Ministry of External Affairs. Lola took her place by his side at his ceremony. She learned to speak Hausa, and decided to convert to her husband's religion, Islam, so that the children would mix with their half siblings.

Titiloye lived with her daughter in a style that rivaled a queen's. She kept Lola company during her husband's absence. He always spent at least three days a week with her, which kept her satisfied and him more than happy.

Lola had everything. Even Segun and Aduke were impressed when they saw how Lola landed on her feet. Alhaji's other children grew to love Lola, too, and she welcomed them into her home and spent lots of time with them and their father.

Eventually Aisha and Lola had a fight and Alhaji intervened. He threatened to send Aisha to her mother in Katsina if she did not accept Omolola. Hanna and Fatima mended the rift between the women, and eventually Aisha found a true friend and ally in Lola, especially since she was not Hausa. So peace reigned supreme in the Yaro house.

As for Janice and Femi, Charles was soon joined by a baby sister. They named her Abike. Janice blossomed with her two children and gave Femi all that he wanted — a woman who loved him and two beautiful children. What more can a man ask?

End

Look for the final book in 'The Other Wife" trilogy,

"Agree to Disagree"

Wanda Arrington Akorede is the author of other quality works of fiction. Some of her upcoming works are: The Diplomats Wife, Jamaica Blue, The Charm Bracelet, and many more....

www.ingramcontent.com/pod-product-compliance
Lightning Source LLC
Chambersburg PA
CBHW032155190626
46808CB00020B/103